I0652912

Lands of Legend

Gritters

(Book III of The LOL/ROFL Series)

Author: Daniel Thorman

Imprint: Independently published

Other books by this author include
(or one day will)

The Osten Chronicles

I   Mayhem at the Mill
II   Chaos in the Caravan
III Calamity at Conclave
IV Bedlam in the Bog
V   A Royal Ruckus

Lands of Legend

I   Rise of the Tong
II   The Zodiac Quest
III Gritters
IV Gritters in Space (Next up)
V   Gritters on Mars? (After that)

Dedication

To **Amelia Earhart**
Lost but not forgotten

CHAPTER ONE

Space Cadet

They say the sky's the limit, but for David, that was no longer true. Today marked the beginning of his new life in the space force, a life a younger David hardly dared to dream about. One more short trip would see him at Ellington, where he'd join the others who had made the grade. The flight from Ohio this morning had sent him soaring above the clouds, and his spirits were still flying quite high. Now the wheels whined beneath him speeding the bus along State Highway 3. Nearly there.

His trunks were stowed below, and he sat about midway back, alone in a seat on the right. Apart from the driver, only three others were on board. Two sat up front, the third being directly across the aisle from him. She was reading a book. Not a tablet or e-reader, but an actual, paper-bound book. When he'd taken his seat, the young woman with the tightly-braided hair had briefly met his eyes before quickly looking away. He supposed introductions would have to wait until they all met up on base.

1

So, he tried to settle his thoughts and consider what was next for David Grimes. The GSF wanted teleoperators, and David had made the cut. He and nine others would receive intensive training at Ellington Field Joint Reserve Base near Houston's launch facilities. It was supposed to have been the main base in Tanzania where the new launch loop was being built, but the solar storm this summer had put the kibosh on those plans. No, the eastern world was still recovering from a loss of all electronics.

He would miss his trusty gaming rig, but the brochure had said that each cadet would have his or her own Freemotion T17 in the dorm. Though these were state-of-the-art, they would lack the special add-ons he had on his old Treadmaster. David had considered taking these with him, but he didn't have the heart to do so. In the months since his flirtation with fame, Mom and Dad had grown quite fond of the gear, using it to go on 'mini-vacations' to the beach and other virtual locales from the privacy of their suburban home.

Instead, David decided to use some of his newfound wealth to buy another set, only to find they weren't yet for sale to the public. But when the sales rep discovered she was talking to the boy who saved the man in the moon, she became very accommodating. The new scent vent and solar array should be waiting for him in his dorm room.

The bus shuddered. *What was that? Rough patch of road?* But then it settled down. Looking out the window with a vague sense of unease, David took a moment to watch the urban sprawl pass by before returning to his thoughts.

Fame was a fleeting thing.. A couple months ago, the media couldn't get enough of him. It had been fun doing the talk show circuit. His friend, Jason, had managed everything. All he had to do was show up at the Mills' home theater setup and tell his story to an invisible audience while a host asked him all kinds of crazy personal questions.

What sports did he follow? What soft drink did he prefer? Really?

Needless to say, his interview skills had sharpened quite a bit. But then the news cycle had moved on. David was now known as, 'Oh yeah, I remember that guy, Darius Something or other, right?'

As his manager, Jason still had big plans. David's autobiography was being ghostwritten for him with soulful interviews by Saul Epstein and others who had been affected by his lunar excursion. There was even talk of a movie deal, but so far, this was all talk. The truth was, David didn't really miss all the attention. There was a certain freedom in anonymity. He'd amassed a tidy sum from his exploits. Originally, this had been for his college fund, but with his acceptance into the program, he would no longer need it for that.

There was a sudden bang, and David was flung hard into the window glass to his right.

Then a lurching screech and scream of air brakes sent him tumbling the other way. Before his head could impact into the headrest of the seat before him, the stasis bags deployed, pinning him firmly back against the cushioned bench with a solid punch to his gut.

David's world seemed to tilt as the bus rolled over on its side. He heard the groan of tortured metal as they slid along the road. What happened to the collision avoidance system? Buses were supposed to be safe now, right?

As quickly as they had inflated, the airbags sagged. The filmy plastic membranes released him and ceased obstructing his airways.

Still stunned from the initial blow to his head and looking at what was now 'up,' he saw the woman from across the aisle plummeting down at him. Reflex took over. Disoriented, he nonetheless rolled up to a crouch with his feet atop what had once been his window. He managed to catch and cradle her before she could come to harm. Not being an overtly physical type, David sagged under the burden of the woman in his arms.

He felt the bus's gliding slide grind to an ungraceful halt. The bus driver was clinging to the pole near his seat, dangling above the door. The door was below the now useless stairwell, face down on the highway's asphalt.

The young woman's eyes fluttered open. She had pleasant features, and a dark complexion, far darker than David's own.

"Put me down, you loathsome ape," she chastised. "How dare you take advantage of a dire situation to grope at an unconscious stranger?"

She had a British accent, and a pleasing, melodic voice (if a bit irate at the moment).

David set her on her feet as gently as he could manage, then sagged back against the sideways seat.

You're welcome, dammit.

"Is everyone okay?" asked a voice from the front.

That wasn't a productive question. You might get a chorus of yeses, but you wouldn't likely hear from someone who was *not* okay. He quickly looked about. He couldn't see very well beneath the row of makeshift skylights the driver's-side windows had just become. With the time-tested voice of a tong leader, he called out instructions of his own.

"There were four cadets on this bus," he barked. "Let's sound off. This is David. One."

With a grimacing nod of respect, the woman he had caught added herself to the list. "This is Cadet Speranza M'Babu, Two."

"Dietrich Stentz! Three!" quickly followed.

Finally came the voice of the first speaker, more reluctantly, "Cameron Truwella. Four."

"That's all of us accounted for, then," said David. "I'm headed for the back of the bus. There's an emergency hatch. Follow as you can. Leave your carry-ons. Move out quickly in case there's a hydrogen leak."

David stepped quickly along the windows, careful to avoid any jagged edges. At the back, he worked the emergency lever,

4

and the door all but fell open toward the surface of the road. Lying sideways, it would make for a problematic climb to the ground. The four- or five-foot drop was obstructed by the dangling door.

Speranza quietly nudged him aside, climbed up to crouch sideways in the framed opening, then leaped gracefully to the ground.

"I like your British accent, by the way," David remarked while waiting for the others.

She scowled up at him.

"There's no such thing as a British accent, not between us two. Both American English and the Queen's English are the same language. There cannot be an accent, only a dialect. And since the language is called 'English', it is you who have one, ducky."

Ducky? Well, at least it was a step up from loathsome ape.

David lowered each cadet to Speranza's waiting arms and even the portly bus driver before climbing down himself. The highway was in chaos, with gawking spectators creeping by in the far left lane. The backup on SR3 stretched as far as David could see, and horns were blaring ineffectually. He heard sirens in the distance getting louder as they neared.

The bus driver pulled some kind of radio from his belt. Thumbing it on, he scratched his head. Then, sporting a frown, he said, "Houston, we have a... difficulty."

***

David was trying to sit still as the EMT attended to the gash on his head. He winced when the woman dabbed an astringent to the wound. She shone a light into his eyes leaning in close..

"Yes, I can see your fingers. You're waving three of them at me. No, I don't feel nauseous, ma'am. Honestly, I feel fine."

As she was applying a sticky patch bandage, a monster truck arrived. At least it *looked* like a monster truck, set high on those gigantic rubber wheels. It prowled down the median toward the crash site, causing all the rubberneckers to slow down even more. Its body was painted in camouflage colors, and it had a big gun mounted on top. The thing must have weighed many tons. Needless to say, the spectators made way.

The other cadets all stood in a huddle, watching the monster approach. Trying to ignore the fervor, the EMT helped David to his feet while glancing toward the disturbance.

"I don't see anything urgent, but head wounds can be tricky. We need to get you checked out at a proper hospital--just to be safe."

Just as she began leading him toward the ambulance, a man stepped down from the cab of the truck. He wore a uniform jacket that was so deep olive green that David would prefer to call it brown. His slacks were lighter but likewise drab--almost a khaki color. He had a flat hat with a bill on its front with some kind of emblem above it. It reminded David of Colonel Klink from that old Hogan's Heroes show.

"Is that one of the cadets?" he asked of the EMT. "We'll take it from here, ma'am. We have medical facilities on base."

The EMT looked like she wanted to protest, but then reluctantly released David's shoulder.

"Everybody, quick, get up in the transport," he commanded. "Hop to it, gritters! We haven't got all day."

It was the first time David had been referred to in that way, and it fostered a spark of pride. It wasn't as big as a moonraker, but it would do for the remainder of this ride. He climbed up after the others into the back of the big, armored truck. Two soldiers there assisted them. The interior was utilitarian and a dingy shade of tan, but there was comfortable seating for as many as eight--perhaps a few more if you were the friendly sort. The gun ports on the sides were closed, as were the expressions of the two armed soldiers.

David used to be a bit on the shy side, but gaming had drawn him out of his shell. Nowadays, his mother always complained that he never met a stranger. That wasn't true in the least. He met plenty of strangers. He just liked to *talk* to them, that's all. Working up his courage, he addressed one of the camo-clad men, asking what was on his mind.

"Why all of *this?* For us, I mean."

One of the grunts only grunted. The other looked over at David.

"Hey, aren't you that kid --?"

"Uh, yeah, that was me," David quickly interrupted.

"It makes more sense now," said the second man, thoughtfully stroking his chin.

They swayed toward the back as the APC lurched forward, then began bumping along back the way it had come.

"Hank. This is the guy who saved the man in the moon, back when the sun went wonky."

"Good to meet you, little man," said a suddenly smiling Hank. "You aiming to be a gritter now?"

"That's the plan," said David, gripping the man's extended hand.

"Well, you and your buddies just ran afoul of a suspected terrorist plot. Homeland security called us out to retrieve you in case you were the targets."

"Us?" said David in confusion. "Who would want to hurt a bunch of new cadets?"

"Plenty of folks, but Humanity First tops the list. They've got a bone to pick with the GSF over the NBI debate."

"Well, I'm glad the *army* was here to bail us out."

"Actually, we're the Army National Guard. Still army, but not the regular grunts. I'm Seymore. They call me 'Eyes.' I'm a guard bum on reserve duty. Hank here's a weekend warrior. He was lucky enough to land this mission while he was doing his annual training. He wanted to man the top gun, but they told him this

7

wasn't a warzone. Them's the breaks, I guess. So, are you going to be on base for long?"

"I hope to be," said David. "I'm just starting basic the day after tomorrow. If I can stay the course, I'll be here for the next three years or so while I finish my accelerated degree."

"Well, hats off to you for that," returned Hank. "I got my Q.E.D., but that's as much of academia this soldier can stand."

"Nonsense," David quipped. "Be all that you can be, right? Hooyah!"

Smirking, Eyes corrected him. "Actually, it's 'Hooah.'"

"'Hooyah' is navy." He added with a wink.

***

The APC let them off in front of the space force barracks. It was a brand-new facility just off Hillard Street. The flags were flying at full mast--both that of the global government, and that of the U.S.A. The branch flag of the GSF flew just below the former. It was a black flag featuring the delta shape so like the Star Trek emblem.

Also in front of the building, standing tall and proud, was the statue of Dr. Evelyn Mendez, the first person on Mars. Hers was a tragic tale that every school kid knew. Back in the late 2030's, there was a mad rush to be the first. This poor lady made it, but her landing craft was damaged, and she was unable to return. Her daily transmissions from Mars saddened the entire world as her resources dwindled to nothing with no rescue in sight. Everyone knew her famous line.

"That's one for womankind... *aw crap!* Looks like it was a one-way ticket!"

Because of her tragic journey, the newly established Global Leadership Council banned interplanetary flights until such time as a sustainable infrastructure could be put in place. And so, the first human bootprints on Mars would stand as a lonely tribute to a pioneer who was a bit before her time.

The Dauntless still sat there on Phobos, circling the red planet every seven and a half hours, half fueled up and awaiting a pilot that would never come home.

Questions still burned in David's mind. Who had attacked them and why? What was being done about it? But he knew he wouldn't be privy to those answers anytime soon. At least there had been no more talk of hospitals.

Proceeding into the barracks, they went their separate ways. They'd been told that their luggage would be delivered once the crime scene investigators were done. So, David wandered around looking for room 242. It was a double he was to share with another lad.

When he found it, he became a little perturbed. The packet containing his new ident card must have been lost in this morning's confusion. So he knocked.

The light from the peephole soon darkened. He knew someone was there.

"Who is it?" said a voice with a strong French accent, more like, "Oo ees eet?"

"David Grimes," he replied. "I'm your new roommate."

He waited.

"My belongings haven't arrived, and I can't find my ident card. I'm having a really bad day, so if you could please just let me in, I would be grateful."

David heard a click.

"Entrer."

The young man staring up at David had a bored expression. Slight of frame, he had a swooping hairdo above a broad forehead, the heavy brow of which shaded soft brown eyes.

"I am Pierre, Pierre Caillat. I do not like to chitter-chat. Your side is over there."

Well, that seemed straightforward enough. It was important to make a good impression right from the start, so David turned without a word and moved to the area indicated. This seemed to confuse Pierre. Good.

"I presume these beastly boxes are yours?"

Turning back to face the little git, David only nodded. They were the equipment containers he would use to modify his new treadmill. What should he call the thing? 'Freemie' didn't sound right. While he was puzzling this out, his new roomie turned and slouched over to his bed, sat, and took up an e-reader.

"Do you have a screwdriver?" asked David. "They took my pocket knife from me at the airport."

"I do not," said the snot, without looking up. "If you bothered to read the brochure, you would know there is a tool room one floor down and at the end of the hallway, just past the laundry."

He was idly swiping his finger across his reader, not even making a pretense of reading the thing.

"Thanks," said David, heading for the door. "Leave it unlocked. I'll be right back."

"I shall be waiting expectantly for the joy of your return."

And sarcasm to boot? Really? This might be a tough year.

There were actually enough rooms on the base for each cadet to have his own. But the GSF psychologists had determined that more socialization would be optimal and important for team building. David was only glad they had drawn the line at a larger, shared barracks. But a prissy little Frenchman? Something told David this wasn't merely luck of the draw but something more deliberate. He would treat it like his first challenge, certain there would be many.

He returned to his room with a stepladder and a variety of tools. When he began unpackaging and laying out the components for the solar array, Pierre looked up from his pretense of reading.

"It seems you are lacking a number three lag-screw."

David looked at the scattered parts and frowned, certain the boy was just messing with him. He set up the ladder and set to work placing the ceiling mounts.

"I think you should know," said Pierre with a fatalistic sigh, "I have already requested a room reassignment. Unfortunately, the administrators have rejected my well-reasoned request. It seems I must 'stick it out.'"

Right back at you, Pierre.

"But since you seem set on stinking up our room with your extravagant *bouche d'aération,* I will have you know that I have already ordered an industrial fan to (how do you say?) clear the air."

David only grunted as he drilled a new hole.

"And speaking of smelly things, your body odor is atrocious. You should change your socks more often."

Stepping down from the ladder, David wheeled on the Frenchie.

"Well, I've been traveling all day. My clothes are all being held up for a terrorist investigation. I've been in a bus wreck, accused of sexual misbehavior, and took a vicious blow to the head! *So just give me a damn break, will you?*"

Pierre looked startled. Recovering, he walked over to his dresser.

"Apologies, *mon ami,* I didn't know you were having such a day. To make amends, I will be generous. This is for you. It will help to make you more tolerable."

At that, he tossed David a small blue bottle. It had a French label that read, '*Eau de toilette.*' Odor of the toilet? Was he being *played?*

"It is, how you say, toilet water. Its aroma is more pleasant than your own."

Suspicious, David removed the cap and gave it a courtesy sniff. To his surprise, it had a pleasant, floral scent not quite so strong as perfume nor as pungent (and manly) as cologne.

11

"Uh, thanks, Pierre," he mumbled.

Just then, there was a knock on the door.

"*Entrer*," said Pierre. "She is open."

In came a sleepy-eyed older cadet. David knew him to be such by the symbols on his untucked uniform shirt. He peered around the room until his annoyed gaze fell upon David's project.

"What is all that junk? Who gave you permission to make modifications to your gear? The administration is very strict about what can be plugged into their rigs."

Pierre stepped smoothly in front of the man.

"*Au contraire.* Technically, you are incorrect. Under subsection eight of the dormitory rules (section zed), the equipment assigned to each cadet is his own responsibility. Modifications within reason are permitted so long as these are limited to external plug-ins that do not affect core programming. Section six of the base guidelines goes on to say that 'a cadet's right to customization will not be infringed, whether with respect to his or her own body, equipment, or living space.'"

The stranger seemed nonplussed.

"I'm Senior Cadet Gideon Smelt. I'll be your RA this semester. I run a tidy dorm. Keep your area neat and we'll have no problems. And see that those tools make it back to the machine shop or I'll have you on janitorial duty. I'll just leave you to it. Carry on."

David's eyes met Pierre's as the puffed up senior cadet withdrew. Pierre raised his eyebrows.

"I thought you didn't want my equipment smelling up the place," David remarked.

"I don't," said Pierre, "but I will defend to the death your *right* to be smelly!"

Such passion. And he seemed to have memorized all the barracks rules, chapter and verse. It was amazing how a common threat could change one's perception of a person.

Pierre returned to his idle browsing, and David continued assembling his gear. When he went to mount the main bracket for the solar array, he became distraught.

"Son of a biscuit-eater!" David exclaimed, as the great ring sagged on one side.

Pierre looked up and smiled knowingly.

"I seem to be short a number three lag-screw," admitted David in defeat.

"*La vis* is already on order along with my fan. She should arrive by tomorrow afternoon."

***

Later that same evening, they were all called to an assembly in the common room. The summons came on their phones. David noticed his was getting woefully low on charge, but he hoped to remedy that once his luggage was released. Pierre cut a striking figure in his Space Force cadet uniform. David only wished he could turn out in his, but for now, jeans and a slightly torn t-shirt would have to do.

Hustling down the hall, they ignored the elevator and made for the stairwell. Late *and* out of uniform wasn't the first impression David would prefer to make. They queued up before the console, where the other cadets were presenting their ident cards to gain entry. Not having one, David puzzled over the instructions.

"Stand aside," said another cadet. "You're holding up the line."

[Tap ident card or enter cadet ID manually]

"Just a minute," said David, flustered.

His ID was a sixteen-digit number and letter combo he had yet to commit to memory. He knew the first four, but the rest escaped him at the moment. Noting his hesitation, Pierre stepped up and started rapidly pressing digits on the touchscreen.

[Ident accepted. Manually enter pass code.]

What? How did he do *that?* Fortunately, David knew his own pass code by heart. He began humming a tune from the Mikado as he entered it. [OgMvmwh2rolb]. Only belatedly, did he think to shield some of the digits from Pierre's prying eyes.

[Identity confirmed. Cadet David Grimes. You may enter.]

The gate went up, and he hustled through, followed closely by his roomie, who casually waved his card at the screen.

The assembly hall was a multi-function room serving mainly as an auditorium. Shadows obscured its vaulted ceiling, above where the pendant lights hung. There was a small stage at the back and a large QTV screen available for presenters. The seating that arose in a semicircle looked like it might accommodate fifty or more. Currently, there were only a dozen or so cadets clustered near the front, with a few more on their way.

David and Pierre planted themselves in a pair of seats in the second row. He saw Speranza seated right up front and the two other survivors from the mishap with the bus. Lacking the smart cadet uniforms the others were sporting, they were easy to spot. No one was chatting with neighbors. All had eyes straight ahead. David wondered whether everyone else was excited and nervous like him.

The presenter was nowhere in sight, and people began to fidget as the last of the cadets took his seat. Then, David noticed the girl next to Speranza staring at him strangely. She stood and leaned forward to get a better view. She laughed. He knew that laugh. It was the girl who had laughed at Krepkiyzad when he declared himself to be the Big Kahuna.

"That's him," she said excitedly, pointing in his direction. "The Koolaid Kid!"

David was mortified. He knew that all gritters received a nickname, bestowed upon them by their fellows, like the old astronauts in the early space program. He had hoped that *his* would be something cool like 'Crater Raider.' He hoped with all his heart that 'Koolaid Kid' wouldn't stick. Nonetheless, David knew the unwanted identification needed to be acknowledged when all eyes turned toward him.

He stood from his seat and feigned a tolerant smile. He raised his fist as though holding a pitcher to one side.

"Oh... Yeah?" he asked, shrugging and staring around.

And there was that laughter again. The girl was grinning ear to ear, a pleasant kind of smile. She looked to be of Polynesian descent. He'd have to watch her and think of some equally horrible nickname to saddle *her* with. Or maybe not. She was the first cadet he'd met who seemed nice right from the outset, and her amused smile seemed genuine, not wicked.

"Ahem!"

All eyes retreated from David and swiveled to the stage, where a man had padded out amidst the chaos. David hastily reseated himself, worried he might be seen as a disruptor. The man was in full dress uniform. It was the U.S. version the GSF had settled upon. It featured a very deep navy blue jacket, so dark as to be almost black. The diagonal row of gold buttons seemed more decorative than functional, and the man had many service ribbons stitched in rows above his left breast. The jacket hung over light gray trousers, pressed and creased down the middle. His black boots had a mirror shine, and he was wielding an overlong data wand like a riding crop.

David had read that the whole ensemble bore a striking resemblance to that worn in the Battlestar Galactica films, (which David had yet to watch).

"Now that you're all settled down, we may begin."

Hmmpf. Another British accent, thought David. Or someone lacking my dialect, he begrudgingly admitted to himself.

"I am Warrant Officer Eddings. You may address me as such or with the honorific, 'Sir,' if you prefer."

David knew that warrant officers were rare fellows that fit somewhere between a chief master sergeant and the lowest officer rank. They were valued more for their technical expertise on some particular topic or another rather than any combat role they might assume. It made sense that the space force, with all of its eclectic technology, would have such a man instruct their cadets.

"I see that some of you failed to get the memo that casual day was canceled."

He said it in that dry, English way known as a 'stiff upper lip.' David thought the man's impeccably groomed pencil mustache might be responsible for this droll delivery. Still, he was a little uncomfortable about being out of uniform.

"Things being what they are, perhaps it is best we push onward, what?. As you should all be aware, your term of service doesn't officially start until Wednesday. You will begin each day with calisthenics. You are to report to the field at oh-five-hundred."

David suppressed a groan. At least, coming from Ohio, it would feel more like six, he consoled himself.

"You will all be given your teams and assignments tomorrow morning. I suggest you read the packets thoroughly and use your last free day to greet your teammates and discuss internal matters."

He was standing at parade rest and tapping his data wand against his thigh to emphasize his words.

"I hope you've all come prepared to dig in and work. A guardian is ever vigilant and puts his shoulder to the task. You all have a lot to learn, but don't expect we'll spoon-feed it to you. If you have any questions, take them up with your project leader. He or she will determine whether something needs to rise higher along the chain of command."

He peered around the room and scuffed his toe on the floorboard of the stage.

"Today, I thought we might all loosen up by singing the Semper Supra anthem. We in the space service take it as our sacred oath. You will all be required to recite it from memory

16

when you are sworn in on Wednesday. So, without further ado, let us begin."

He waved his data wand at the screen, which immediately lit up in golden letters on a deep navy field. Orchestral music swelled in the background, and a playful pale blue ball began bouncing atop the words:

We're the mighty watchful eye,
Guardians beyond the blue...

David sang along as best he could. Overall, the group didn't sound half bad. Pierre had a tenor voice bordering on boy soprano. It made a nice contrast with David's deeper baritone. He couldn't pick out other individual voices, but all in all, it was a passable performance.

"Well, that's all for the meet and greet. Welcome to Ellington, where opportunities are what you make of them. Cheerio, as we say, and enjoy the rest of your day."

David was uncertain what to make of warrant officer Eddings. He seemed cheery enough, but David was somehow certain he'd be a hard taskmaster. Pierre caught David's attention as the others were filing out.

"Who does he remind you of?" the boy asked, staring at WO Eddings' retreating back.

"I dunno," said David. "What are you thinking?"

"'Ave you ever seen the old BBC program called 'Doctor Who?'"

Then it clicked. Brigadier Lethbridge-Stewart! The man was his spitting image, right down to his manner and mustache. David smiled.

"I think you're onto something there, Pierre."

***

Morning calisthenics weren't really David's cup of tea. Nor were they any beverage, hot or otherwise, that he actually *did* care for. Seeing as it was only Tuesday and this was the last morning he was at liberty to blow them off, he was considering doing just that. But he had a change of heart when a platoon of blue-clad interlopers in track suits came loping down the road out front stepping and shouting in unison.

Pierre had raised the blinds and was standing at the window. By the time David joined him there, the rhythmic shouting had grown more pronounced.

Well, I don't know, but it's been said,
I don't know, but it's been said!
Space Force grits just stay in bed.
Space Force grits just stay in bed!
While their nap time lingers on
While their nap time lingers on!
Coast Guard's up before the dawn!
Coast Guard's up before the dawn!
Sound off. **One Two!**
Sound off. **Three Four!**
Cadence count.
One two three four. One two... THREE FOUR!

"*Mon dieu!*" exclaimed Pierre. "It is the coast guard. They are insulting us. I am insulted."

"Well, we're not going to stand for this," said David. "Pierre, do you happen to know the phone numbers of all the other new cadets?"

"But of course."

"Somehow, I just *knew* you would. Text everyone. Tell them to break out their track suits and meet us in the commons in five minutes. Anyone who is late will be left behind."

"*Oui, mon capitaine,*" said Pierre, his fingers already dancing across the touchscreen of his phone."

David's mind was awhirl. Pierre probably knew where the coast guard barracks were situated. He knew such mockery, good natured or not, should never be taken lying down. And since picking up the poet skill in Realms, he'd learned a few things about meter and verse. He should be able to knock out a suitable A-A-B-B rhyme scheme in his sleep (or if not literally in his sleep, then even at this ungodly hour in the A.M.)

When David arrived, Speranza was already stretching her calves and thighs, and several others were following her lead.

"Do you all feel like doing some singing this morning?"

Speranza crossed her arms.

"And who has made you the leader of this group, Mr. Grimes?"

"Uh. No one, Ms. M'Babu. It's just that Pierre and I know where the Coast Guard barracks are and fancy taking a little jog over that way. You're all welcome to tag along if you like. We can learn some new songs as we go."

Without waiting for a response, David poked Pierre. "Lead on, McDuff."

And off they went. Most of the others followed, more out of curiosity than respect, and David soon slowed down to let the late deciders catch up.

Tiny boats put out to sea
Tiny boats put out to sea!
Fighting smugglers fearlessly
Fighting smugglers fearlessly!
Someone's got to do that chore
Someone's got to do that chore!
Never venturing far from shore
Never venturing far from shore!
Sound off. **One Two!**
Sound off. **Three Four!**
Cadence count.
One two three four. One two... THREE FOUR!

Gritters on the other hand
Gritters on the other hand!

Have all of space at their command.
Have all of space at their command!

Coast Guard's left to wonder why
Coast Guard's left to wonder why!

There's no limit to our sky!
There's no limit to our sky!

Sound off. **One Two!**
Sound off. **Three Four!**

Cadence count.
One two three four. One two... THREE FOUR!

Reluctantly at first, but with more and more enthusiasm, the others began to join in. By the time they reached the building where the USCG bunked, they were practically shouting the last line. David was particularly proud of that one, which he'd lifted directly from the Semper Supra anthem.

There was a row of panting men and women just back from their morning run. They were doing stretches in their courtyard. They smiled and waved as the gritters jogged past. Several put up two fingers not spread apart. 'Respect' they silently signaled. David suspected this was just the first sortie of many to come. After all, the Army National Guard, the Air National Guard, and the Navy Reserve all had headquarters on Ellington within a mile or so of the GSF. The gritters would be called upon many times in the coming days to defend their honor against such friendly fire.

And this was how David, on his first day, earned a nickname among his squadmates. Forever afterward, they would refer to him as 'David Rhymes' or sometimes just 'Rhymes'. This pleased David. It wasn't the impressive moniker he'd hoped for, but it beat the living hell out of becoming 'The Koolaid Kid.' He would go on to invent over four hundred sets of marching lyrics, each more clever and taunting than those first few hastily cobbled together cadence calls. This was not, however, what he would eventually become best known for.

CHAPTER TWO

Inner Space

Pierre preceded him down the third-floor hall.

"The email said to dress casual."

"I know," said David. "But if we're going to discuss the assignment, shouldn't we --"

"Here it is," said Pierre, stopping to face the door.

Room 336 was midway down the hall of the women's dormitory. It still amazed David how many of these rooms were empty. The ten new cadets practically had the whole place to themselves. There were a few trainees with other specialties like astronavigation and such, but it seemed that he and his fellow teleoperators were the majority of those present.

Standing a bit straighter and smoothing back his hair, the Frenchman gave the door three sharp raps.

A few moments later, the door was flung wide, and framed in its opening was the woman who had called David the Kool-Aid Kid. White teeth flashed from her welcoming smile. She was dressed in a floral print top over which her dark hair cascaded in curly waves. Just behind her and to one side stood Speranza, wearing the same but looking less than happy about it.

"*E Komo Mai*," said Leilani. "Enter and be welcome."

As Pierre stepped in, Leilani dropped a ring of plastic flowers over his head to rest on his shoulders, leaned in, and kissed him on the cheek. The boy halted in his tracks, almost causing David to stumble into him.

"Uh, *merci*," he stammered.

Surprisingly, Speranza then stepped forward and hung a similar garland around David's neck. There was no kiss, however. Instead, this was accompanied by a shallow bow of her head and a hastily muttered 'Aloha.'

"Uh, right," David returned. "You look nice. I had no idea flowers were your thing."

"Lost a bet," she curtly explained. "Anyway, now that the formalities are over, let's discuss our group assignment. Take a seat and let us see what's in our packets."

The room was similar to David's own, a double with a common area in the middle. It took no imagination to determine whose side was whose.

The right side was highly decorative. There were many odds and ends, throw pillows and the like amid an overall floral theme. Several potted plants dangled from macramé hangers. The other was more spartan with just some photographs and a tidiness that just dared one to try and leave a fingerprint. If it had any theme at all, it was a military one. There was one exception. Hung in the center of Speranza's wall was a large portrait of a moonscape with Earth rising in the background. It was a stunning piece.

Leilani led them to a table in the common area surrounded by four counter-height steel chairs. She walked with a languid grace that made it seem like it was not she who was moving. Rather, it was the floor moving beneath her. Speranza followed at a precise clip.

"As we four have all been assigned to Project Ironseed," she began, "I thought we might put our heads together and start getting our team structure sorted out. Did you read the first brief?"

"Of course," said David. "I was surprised the machine I'll be operating is no bigger than a pea. I'm a little jealous of Stentz and MacAllister."

"Don't be," said Pierre. The average light time delay between here and the asteroid belt is twenty or thirty minutes. Can you imagine how boring it will be for them waiting that long between each command to their asteroid tugs? *Our* theater of operation is only a few light-seconds out."

It was true. The nanotech experiments would take place on Sarpeidon, a Trojan orbiting Lagrange point L4. Sarpeidon's original designation had been 2010-TK7. It was discovered at Lagrange point four, one of only a handful of positions where the gravitational pull of Earth and its moon are the same. It was no surprise that a smallish asteroid had taken up permanent station there. David even approved of the name, Sarpeidon being one of his favorite heroes from the Trojan War.

"Nanotechnology," said Leilani with a frown. "Like creepy little bugs."

"Not so much creepy as plain dangerous," said David. "Nanos are nothing new, but making them self-replicating is an incredibly risky proposition."

They began to read.

The GSC had been fine-tuning nanotech for decades. The theory was sound. They would release a handful of the little devils called lemmings on an asteroid to be mined. Recent advances in miniaturization, materials science, and quantum computing now allow us to engineer complex machines in the tens of nanometers range. These nanites are small enough to interact with atomic structures but still large enough to house necessary computational, storage, and communication functions.

Utilizing solar energy, these lemmings spread out across the asteroid. Each consumes iron atoms and a few other trace elements to make a complete copy of itself along the way. Thus the number of lemmings keeps doubling. They gnaw away at the asteroid until a recall signal is sent out, whereupon, they all march back to the solar smelter to be melted into ingots of pure iron. This will be an incredibly efficient way to extract minerals for use in space habitats.

The problem was that self-replicating nanos are very dangerous. Lord help us all if they should get loose on Earth or Luna. Sometimes they replicate imperfectly, perhaps even becoming resistant to the recall beacon. It only takes one. A 'rogue nano' might even be able to breed true. It could begin cannibalizing the proper nanos and turn the entire iron deposit into a seething mass of uncontrolled gray goo dangerous to humans due to the iron in our blood.

For this reason, experimentation is limited to an isolated asteroid with very strict controls. There isn't a large amount of memory available in which to program the nanos. They have a "kill switch," a radio signal that makes them go inactive. Should this failsafe fail, there are EMP devices surrounding the testing site. Lastly, there are the "shepherds." Much larger than the nanos, but still incredibly tiny, these are mite-sized teleoperated vehicles made of non-ferrous materials designed to monitor the nanos' activities.

The shepherd class micromachines can capture misbehaving lemmings using electromagnets powered by their tiny solar cells. The cadets assigned to the mission would each pilot a shepherd and work in concert to contain and corral the misbehaving lemmings for study by the researchers. The goal was to produce a batch with enough redundancies that any failed replication would result in an inactive unit.

Reading further, the group discovered the humor behind the names.

LEMMING = Latest Experiment for Mining Metals Instead of Nasty Goo

SHEPHERD = Special Hunter-Escort for Problematic
Hazardous Experiments and Rogue Drones

"Cute," Speranza remarked. "We'll have our first briefing tomorrow after the swearing in ceremony. We should be ready with our questions. Also, we need to appoint a team leader."

"I take it, you're volunteering," said David.

"Yes."

"Fine by me," shrugged Pierre. "I hate to be in charge."

"It's for exactly that reason that you should get some practice at it," said David. "How about this. Let's each take a turn at being team leader in a rotation. We all need practice in *following* instructions *as well as* giving them."

"It would make for a more efficient team to have established roles," argued Speranza.

"No doubt, and eventually, we might arrive at that consensus. What do the rest of you think?"

Leilani looked between the two and rested her elbows on the table. The girl hadn't spoken much since first greeting them, but her expressive eyes showed that she was paying close attention.

"I sense there might be something going *on* between you two," she observed.

"*Oui madame*," agreed Pierre unhelpfully, "David has told me that when they first met, she fell for him. Hard."

"Really?" said Leilani, raising her eyebrows.

"Yes. Head over heels. She fell right into his arms."

"What have you been *telling* him?" fumed Speranza, turning toward David.

"Not that!" David replied, "Or, at least, not in that way," he amended.

Pierre could be an asshole.

"Well, I'll agree to your proposal if we can do it in reverse alphabetical order."

"By last name?"

"Of course."

The others quickly agreed as well, and they returned to dissecting the information packets they'd been given. There were a lot of technical specs for the various hardware: the smelter, the EMPs, the shepherds, and even the lemmings, to a degree. Much about the latter was classified above their security clearance, but there was enough for visual recognition and movement tracking.

They also had to become conversant with Sarpeidon's orbital mechanics and eccentricities. How the sunlight fell on that drifting rock would have a big impact on their equipment. All in all, it was a productive meeting, David thought as he made for the door.

As he and Pierre exited into the hallway, they saw the two other female cadets making for their own room.

"This was nice," said David by way of farewell. "Let us know when we can meet again."

Leilani hung her smiling face out into the corridor.

"We enjoyed it too, Rhymes. Let's meet here on a regular basis. But don't expect to get leied next time. That was just a one-time thing."

David hid his grin as Cameron and Carlotta turned their shocked faces his way. Speranza was staring daggers at her roommate, whose knowing wink told David she knew exactly how that might be misinterpreted.

Yup. This was going to be an interesting project.

***

With the addition of the wayward, missing lag-screw, David's new rig was ready for its inaugural use. Pierre had mounted his fan in the window, prepared to vent any unwelcome fumes. Sliding the visor down, David gripped the handles of his Freemotion 17. They had a different feel than his old Treadie 2000. It would take some getting used to. More than anything, David wanted to log into Realms to see what the old gang was up to. But base regulations had put a red flag on this activity until such time as the GLC could rule on the status of NBIs.

So he would start more simply--a stroll along the beach.

The sun shone down on the peaceful scene. The waves lapped at the shore. The scrunch of sand accompanied his footfalls as a warm breeze brought the salty, somewhat earthy tang of the ocean's turgid spray.

He looked out to sea. The rhythmic, gentle swelling and rolling of the surf stretched out to the distant horizon. There was a sense of vastness here. Despite knowing the ocean was finite (and this illusion even more so), it was different than looking out into the depths of space. *This* vastness was more imminent, beckoning one to acknowledge it and laughing at one so minuscule who stood upon its shore.

The gulls called out their piercing cries above the ocean's grumbling sighs. And David's shadow followed him down the coast. He spotted a conch shell tumbling in the surf. It came to rest on the beach, born on a cresting wave and half-buried there, stranded by its predictable retreat. It was a pretty thing, starkly white, but pearly and pink on its inner side. It was nearly as long as David's forearm if you didn't count the hand. It spiraled out to a knobbly end as big around as a coffee can.

It was the kind of shell that made you want to see if you could blow out a note. He could almost imagine the deep, reverberant hollow sound it would make. David shuffled forward to see how realistic this scenario might be. Very, as it turned out.

When David reached down to retrieve his prize, it suddenly sprouted legs, eight pointy pink, multi-jointed legs. These scrabbled along the sand beyond his reach. He watched it scuttle away, amused by this turn of events. Then it stopped and came to rest again just a short way down the beach. David took another step, and it scuttled, then stopped again just as it had before.

"Oh. Do you want me to follow you?"

It spun in a circle and scuttled off once more.

David steadfastly followed as the hermit crab led him onward. Sailboats drifted in the distance. A flock of seagulls (more properly called a colony) crossed the sky. And an old pelican perched on a post watched hungrily as they passed by. Finally, they came to a spot high on the beach where a blanket was spread. A large beach umbrella cast shade upon it, and if it had an owner, that person was absent. The shell scurried right up onto the blanket and settled there as if waiting.

By now very curious about this strange crustacean, David accepted the seeming invitation. He sat beside the shell to await an explanation.

"It should be safe enough now to talk," said the crab, backing out of its shell. "This little shaded area is a glitch in the sim that should hide us well."

"You talk like I should know you," said David. "Have we met before?"

"Several times in the game of Realms," said the crab. "You passed my lesson and learned to accept things as they are rather than trying to cheat your destiny."

"Shǔ?"

"The one and only. But though I'm a rat, for the sake of this Sim, I had to adopt a local form. Besides, I didn't want to get my fur all wet."

"I can see that, I guess," said David. "You'd look like a drowned rat if you did. But why are you here?"

"I came to share our findings with you, my boy."

"Oh?"

"Oh, yes, indeed. The Jade Empress wanted me to fill you in."

"The Jade Empress? You mean Satori? How is she? I haven't heard from her since her ascension.

"The new empress is doing well, but events are moving swiftly (at least as far as you humans reckon things). While we're awaiting the GLC's final decision on the status of Mandaria (and NBIs in general), she's promised full transparency in her IRL dealings and a hands-off approach with regards to her human agents."

"But *you're* here. Why all the cloak and dagger stuff?"

"As a separate entity, I am not bound by the same promises. Nor am I being watched by the monitoring programs she's agreed to."

"So tell me then. What's going on?"

"We wanted to let you know that the problem you had on arrival was no accident. The CSIs found that magnesium was mixed in with the titanium hydride pellets fueling your bus."

"That's insane. Who would want to blow up a bus, anyway?"

"We're not sure. Whoever it was covered up their tracks very professionally. We don't know whether it was directed at you specifically or was just a random act of terror. Either way, it's disturbing."

"*I'll* say. I don't know which would be worse. What else?"

"Strange things are happening on the moon, my boy. They're trying to keep it a secret, but Satori has her ways of finding things out. And it involves you again."

"*Me?* How?"

"Hmm. How would Gǒu put it? Parsing... (Me?): Yes. You. Or your moonraker anyway. (How?): Do you recall the breakdown of Tango-twelve affecting its right tread?"

"How could I forget?"

"*I* don't know. Human memory is known to be imprecise, but I meant no offense. It was just a figure of speech, a conversational gambit, if you will."

"Nevermind *that*. What about my raker?"

"It seems that on your trek to Agro-4, a meteorite fragment became lodged in the treads of your vehicle. It was ultra-hard and made of some kind of conductive material. So, though a tread was broken, the monitoring sensor kept reporting all clear."

"I knew it had to be something like that," said David. "So, I'm vindicated. That's great. So what's the big secret?"

"Again, we're not certain, but they've taken the object into a highly classified laboratory and now refer to it as 'the artifact' in what few communiqués we've been able to intercept."

"Interesting. Maybe it's a fragment left over from those old Soviet space shots. Didn't they 'land' something up there in a bid to claim they got there first?"

"I think you're referring to the ballistic impact of Luna 2 in 1959. But that was in the Mare Imbrium region. It is unlikely debris from that impact would end up at the Lunar South Pole."

"I figured it was that or one of Alan Shepard's golf balls. He did claim it sailed for 'miles and miles and miles.' Just kidding. I know it can't be that either. Then what?"

"A mystery," said the zodiac rat. "Whatever it is, it's got the GSC all wound up. Satori can't get any kind of information about that lab. That's all I have for you today, David. Sorry it can't be more. Keep your ears up. Satori may have some work for you in the very near future."

"How will you contact me?"

"Just come here occasionally. There's a bait shop a bit farther up the strand. Rent some equipment and drop a line at the end of the pier from time to time. Bring anything you might catch back here for review. This sim lets you mount them as trophies. Just a believable, relaxing pastime. And if you see an ad for skin cream pop up on your phone, come as soon as you can. Then we can dispense with this wretched... shell game."

The crab crawled back into his shell and burrowed down into the sand. David hadn't learned much. And what little he had had distressed him. He guessed he was a fisherman now.

David plunked down his tray and slid into the empty seat with relief. His legs were like wet noodles from his early morning run. The others didn't look to be in much better shape, Speranza being the sole exception. The girl was like a machine. The physical regimen had presented no challenge to the Tanzanian cadet, seeming only to invigorate her. David tried to suppress a wince as he eased into the chair beside her, aware of her eyes upon him as she sipped at her juice.

Pierre came limping over and took the seat across from him, gritting his teeth and looking grim.

"Eat up," said Gideon, the senior cadet, who sat at the table's head.

He had driven them hard in the practice yard. David could see that there would be many pushups and deep knee bends in his future. David stared at the pile of scrambled eggs and diced potatoes on his plate without much enthusiasm. All ten of his cadre were present now, picking at the bland and runny stuff.

"Please pass the salt," said Cameron, who was seated just to David's left.

Dietrich Stentz obliged her, taking a pause from shoveling up his food.

David soon followed his example. Only a brief time was allotted for the morning meal. He'd better hurry if he wanted to be dressed and ready for the swearing in ceremony.

Leilani had already finished, her laughing eyes fell playfully on Pierre, who was swallowing with a look of disgust.

"You look so tired, Pierre. Are you going to be alright?"

Cameron gave her a haughty look as she nibbled at her toast.

"Maybe he's worn out from your group's 'meeting' yesterday."

It's time for some payback, thought David. He'd prefer not to kick a man when he was down, but Pierre had been asking for it lately.

"It wasn't what you think," said David. "When Leilani planted that kiss on him, I heard him beg for mercy."

"Ah. No," Pierre objected, blushing furiously, "I said 'merci' --"

"Exactly," interrupted David, "but you shouldn't be embarrassed about it. You got leied anyway, right?"

Everyone at the table stopped eating. All gazes were fixed on Pierre. The boy's mouth was working soundlessly. Leilani laughed her laugh. Then everyone went back to eating, their eyes down on their plates. But sidelong glances still occasionally shot in their direction. Cameron shifted in her seat, moving slightly farther from David and his team.

"I love that laugh of yours," said David to Leilani, to break the sudden silence. "I've been meaning to ask. Why did you laugh at Major Krepkiyzad in the hanger that day?"

Leilani rested her elbows on the table and laughed again.

"That was Alejandro's fault. He was one of the alternates standing near me. When the major named himself the Big Kahuna, I was well aware of the surfing reference. In my language, a Kahuna is a sort of priest or spiritual leader. But Alejandro screwed up his face and said, 'Big Cajones?'"

There was laughter all around, and friendly chatter soon recommenced. David saw Pierre staring at him evilly, though. From this, he knew their fencing match had only just begun. Bring it, Pierre. *Engarde, mon ami*!

***

"It's a cartoon from about a hundred years ago. I can't believe you've never heard of it."

Speranza looked dubious.

"And why am I like this 'Road Runner?'" she asked.

32

"You need to look it up on your phone," David explained. "He runs very fast. You should be honored."

Dietrich and a few others had started calling her the road runner because of her performance on their morning runs. David expected this would become her space force call sign. She could do worse.

They were waiting for their turn at the Icarus, where they'd be introduced to their project leader. She was a Dutch scientist up on L5 who was in charge of nanotech development. Dr. Anika van der Meer was highly placed in the GSC, the global science council. And though not technically in the GSF, they had been assigned to the civilian scientist for the duration of their training. They were to treat her as a step above them in the chain of command.

The swearing in ceremony had been brief. Each cadet had recited the oath, swearing to uphold the Uniform Code of Military Justice in defense of the global good. Then, in celebration of their new status, each had spoken the words of the Semper Supra anthem in his or her own native language. It was fun to hear the song in German, French, Swahili, and even Hawaiian. Although Hawaiians mostly spoke English, it was the only U.S. state that recognized two official languages. And Leilani did her people proud with her smiling rendition. David could almost imagine her in a grass skirt hula-dancing to really sell it.

'O mākou ka maka maka'ala nui...

"What's got you grinning so?" asked the girl in question.

"Uh. I was just imagining Speranza being chased down the road by a wild-eyed coyote," David lied.

Finally, the door opened to admit the team.

Cameron Truwella and Simon Brewster stepped out. The pair were on satellite duty, not the most exciting assignment, but one of the more useful. Eventually, all of them would have to take a turn in that rotation, and Truwella and Brewster would be the leads.

"All yours," said Brewster. "You can go learn how to drive your tiny little bugs."

"Thanks," said David amicably. "How's your new project lead?"

"Not ideal," replied Cameron, frowning. "We got Krepkiyzad."

Ouch, thought David with a sympathetic shake of his head. Yup, we could have done a lot worse. They ambled into the chamber hoping that their civilian adviser would be a little more fun to deal with and began gearing up from the racks.

Once their helmets were in place, each could speak in his or her own native language, trusting the translation routines to keep everything clear and concise. This had to be a relief for Pierre. He'd been complaining that, despite its literal meaning, the *lingua franca* on base was English. Not that the boy's English was all that bad. It just tended to limit him to using simpler words to confer his no-doubt profound thoughts.

As today's team leader, Speranza thumbed the start button for their session, causing a countdown to appear. 3... 2... 1...

The scene faded to a starscape in the middle of nowhere. Their avatars resembled their actual selves, but they were standing on the surface of an asteroid David suspected was 2010-TK7 itself. Luckily, there was no need to breathe, but the sim did take his breath away, nonetheless. It reminded him of being on the moon. Earth hung over the horizon, half full and about four times the size of the moon as viewed from Earth. The horizon of the rock on which they stood, however, was a lot more foreshortened than that of Luna.

Moreover, the Earth was moving across the sky even as they watched. Evidently, Sarpeidon had a bit of a spin to it. As the Earth and stars wheeled above, the team saw a gigantic woman standing with her back to them. She was staring up at the earth and shielding her eyes from the overbright sun.

There were only limited options on David's HUD. Among them was 'walk forward,' but he waited for a command from his team leader before doing so. As they headed for the giantess in the distance, she shrank, and they sped ahead far more quickly than their steps would warrant. I get it, thought David. It's the foreshortened horizon playing tricks on us. The woman was now standard-sized and turned toward them as they approached.

It was, without a doubt, Dr. Anika van der Meer. She perfectly matched the photograph in their information packet, right down to the honey-brown hair and the hazel-blue eyes. She was attractive for an older lady, slender of build but with a stance and bearing that suggested hardiness and formality. Her welcoming smile hinted she was well aware of the trick she had just played on them.

"You must be my squad of shepherds. Welcome to Sarpeidon and Project Ironseed."

Speranza stepped to the fore.

"Thank you, Dr. van der Meer," I am Cadet Speranza M'Babu, acting team leader today.

"Of course you are, my dear. And is this the boy who --"

"Yes, ma'am," said David. "That was me."

She seemed surprised, looking between David and Pierre. She raised an eyebrow, her hazel-blue eyes narrowing in confusion.

"*You're* Mr. Caillat? But I thought..."

"No, Dr. van der Meer," said Pierre, "*I* am Pierre Caillat. David is my roommate and a bit of a buffoon. He is only having fun with you."

She looked relieved.

"Well, Pierre, it's a pleasure to meet you. It's so rare for someone to score a perfect one-thousand on the GSATs. Why did you enlist in the space force, may I ask? You could have had your choice of assignments on the science track. And you *must* call me Anika. Doctor by the Lake sounds so stuffy."

"Yes madam... Anika. To answer your question, I am not

entirely certain myself. The spirit simply moved me. I have always had thoughts of outer space, and this seemed to be an adventure that would push my limits while I am still young, no?"

"Well, it's an honor to have you on my team. All of you really. I've read your briefs. Each of you is quite impressive in your own way. No need for introductions. Let's get right down to brass tacks. Have you familiarized yourselves with the equipment?"

"Yes, ma'am," answered Speranza.

"Then you'll know the shepherds you'll be piloting are very tiny devices. You may have seen pictures, but the reality will take some getting used to. Their spindly little legs are far too weak to practice with in Earth gravity, so you'll need to rely on this sim for training. A one-player version of it will be made available for each of you to load in your dorm rooms. For security reasons, team practice must be conducted on the Icarus. Any questions so far?"

Leilani raised her hand.

"Yes, Miss Akana."

"When will we get to try piloting an actual one? And will the sim reflect the two-second time delay we'll be facing?"

"The answer to the first question is, 'When I deem you ready.' As to the second, that is an excellent point. We will give you a toggle so you can try it with and without delay. I suggest you add the delay for any simulated runs where you are chasing down rogue nanos..."

It was the second rotation of the simulated asteroid. As the sunlight reached his boots yet again and began climbing up his legs, his mind began to drift. Something about that word, 'nanos,' got David to thinking about that Caribbean song 'Banana Boat.' Come, Mr. Tally Man, tally David's nanos. Daylight come and me wanna go home...

"What do *you* think, David?"

"Um. Yes. Absolutely," he guessed.

36

"Then, since we're all agreed," said Anika, staring at David strangely, "I will tweak the sim and we will enter our vehicles. Remember, do nothing until I instruct you to do so. Here we go. 3... 2... 1...

And the scene shifted once more.

***

He was staring out the windshield of the tiny little bug. Perhaps windshield was a misnomer, there being no air, and hence no wind, on the rock he occupied. The bottom of his HUD was rife with a baffling number of symbols. The view from out of his cockpit was similar to what he'd seen in the sim he'd just exited, but there were differences.

The craggy vista of Sarpeidon had grown enormously. What had been protrusions jutting up from its surface were now full mountain ranges. And the earth that hung above them had lost all color. The bleached out scene before him was like an old movie from before the age of technicolor. David had read about this in his info packet, but he found the reality of it more than a little disconcerting. His shepherd's optical sensors perceived the world only in black and white and various shades of gray.

He relaxed his eyes and tried not to focus too intently on the controls. He didn't want to trigger something accidentally.

"Radio check," said Speranza. "Sound off in order of last name to confirm visual sensors are online."

"Akana here. Over."

"Caillat. Present. Over."

"Rhymes is here too and loving the view. Over. "

"Stow the glib, cadet. All are present and ready for instruction. How shall we proceed, Ironseed Leader? Over."

"Thank you, Miss M'Babu. I would prefer simply Doctor for my call sign. Have you a preference?"

There was a short hesitation.

"It's Road Runner, ma'am. Over."

"Alright, then. And must I say 'over?'"

"It's protocol, Doctor, but it's your asteroid. Go ahead and tell us what to do first."

"Very well. I've been piloting these things for a while now, and I can assure you it takes some getting used to. The shepherds are modeled after Pholcus phalangioides, commonly known as daddy longlegs. They are similar in size as well. This form is ideal for clinging and ambulating in microgravity. The setae (or tiny hairs) on each of their eight 'legs' each branch into even tinier hairs called setules.

"These use van der Waals forces, (electrostatic attraction between molecules that are within a nanometer of one another) to grip any surface. It is estimated that when braced, your shepherds can exert incredible adhesive force for their size. Any one of your appendages could capture a wayward nanite with ease."

"That was all covered in the packets, ma'am," said Road Runner. "What would you have us do next?"

"I'm getting to that, cadet. Consider this a review. It is for this reason that you must learn several modes of ambulation along the ground. The simplest of these is the alternating tetrapods walking pattern, moving the legs in groups of four with those diagonally opposed roughly in synchrony. That control is the first on your HUD's menu. It is labeled 4F, meaning 'four-step forward.'"

It went on like that for most of their allotted hour--more a lecture than practical exercises. David did manage to get his rig to amble forward and even managed to join up with the others. But near the end, Doctor A. surprised them.

"So you see, to locate and capture rogue nanos, you must all learn to fly."

Now we're talking!

Before the hour was up, she demonstrated. The doctor's spider hopped up on its two back legs and did a little dance, pirouetted, then crouched down on all eight legs, only to spring up and go sailing across the landscape to alight on a distant peak. It was awesome! In the microgravity of the asteroid, the shepherds were capable of astonishing leaps and bounds. The tricky part, they would find, was the precision needed to alight where one intended. And that was something that only practice could teach.

"Well, now I can't wait to try it back in my room!" said Speranza excitedly as they exited their first lesson.

CHAPTER THREE

Fishing for Clues

It wasn't even light out when David dragged himself to the practice yard for more torture. His muscles were stiff and sore from yesterdays drills, and his head was still muzzy from staying up late playing with his shepherd. *Time to toughen up, Rhymes.*

He wasn't the last to arrive, but that was no balm for his flagging spirits. He watched Speranza go through her stretches. His leaden limbs just amplified their aches, protesting any thought of doing the same. Where was Senior Cadet Gideon Smelt? Their tyrannical Torquemada was usually waiting for them like a trapdoor spider awaits its victims.

There he was, emerging from the door to the officer's quarters. But who was that with him? No. Really? The old man himself? And in a track suit no less.

David watched as the pair stepped across the compound to join them on the practice field. The group formed a line an arms reach apart and came to parade rest (or the best approximation of it they could so far manage). They stood silently, waiting for whatever bad news was coming.

"Cadets, attention!" snapped Gideon.

They imitated what they imagined that might be as well. Fergus MacAllister even saluted, but then hastily lowered his arm when no one else did the same.

"For those of you too befuddled by the early hour, I will remind you I am Warrant Officer Eddings. It has come to my attention that you lot are sorely lacking in military discipline, and that just won't do."

He paused for effect and began strolling casually down the line..

"This being only your second day, you may think that you'll not be held to the high standards of our branch. In this you would be mistaken. As I am the one ultimately charged with your training and comportment, I have taken it upon myself to clear my schedule."

He said it like, 'shejuwal,' causing his mustache to bristle.

"There will be no calisthenics this morning, and no morning run."

Hope blossomed on faces up and down the line, only to be dashed by the very next statement.

"Instead, I will be leading you on a ten mile march. You will learn to step in unison, keeping precise time with one another. Is that clear?"

Grumbled agreement.

"The correct response is 'Sir, yes sir.' With enthusiasm, now. Is that clear?"

"Sir, yes sir!"

"Senior Cadet Smelt. Form them up and move them out," he commanded.

"Yes, Warrant Officer Eddings, sir!"

And so they lined up two by two like the animals bound for the ark. As they moved out, Warrant Officer Eddings began chanting in a sing-song voice.

Your left! Your left! Your left! right-left!
Your left! Your left! Your left! right-left!

Gideon Smelt was quick to dole out justice to anyone who didn't keep the pace or whose stride was too short or long. And soon they were stepping in good order.

Although ten miles was going to take a long time, David consoled himself that at least it was easier than running. His protesting muscles even found it a bit soothing after the first half mile or so as they warmed to the task. It was mind-numbingly boring, though, and his bored mind began to drift.

Then David had a fun thought. Did he dare? Well, it would likely be worth any punishment they might dish out. So he matched the officer's pitch and let loose on the next natural break.

Your left! Your left! Your left! right-left!
Your left! Your left! Your left! right-left!

As we march out from Ellington,
We hold our heads up high!
We are the Global Space cadets.
No limit to *our* sky!

Your left! Your left! Your left! right-left!
Your left! Your left! Your left! right-left!

You can't stop us with bullets,
Or even Kryptonite.
Our hearts are true, our spirits light,
Our boots are stepping left to right

Your left! Your left! Your left! right-left!
Your left! Your left! Your left! right-left!

43

No punishment was forthcoming. The warrant officer didn't break stride or so much as glance in his direction. He just kept doggedly to his chant. Nor did Gideon admonish him in any way. No. He was busy berating Max Trudeau for breaking stride and clutching at his gut. Did the W.O... *welcome* his contribution? In that case, thought David, we shouldn't leave the ladies out...

The ladies march beside us,
Their bosoms swell with pride!
Gentlemen keep your eyes ahead,
As booties sway from side to side!

Your left! Your left! Your left! right-left!
Your left! Your left! Your left! right-left!

That applies to Frenchmen too, Pierre!

Oh my God. Speranza's gonna kill me,

And so they marched, and David sang. It was a weary but cheerful group that returned to base that day.

***

Oliver Radcliff looked up from the latest report. As the chief psychologist of the GSC, he was most interested in this recent batch of cadets. He stared at the cooling mug of decaf sitting atop the coaster on his desk, wishing it could be the higher octane stuff he preferred. But doctors' orders were, unfortunately, non-negotiable for a man in his position. He thumbed his phone and brought up his digital assistant.

"Felix, have Bravo Team Leader report to my office."

He tapped his pencil nervously on his desktop as he awaited the woman's arrival. She entered without knocking and took a seat across from him. He began without preamble.

"Why has Grimes been assigned to Project Ironseed? I thought he was slated for NBI liaison duty."

"That was my call," she replied calmly. "He bonded with the Tanzanian girl on their trip from the airport.

Studies show that shared trauma can forge strong, often unexpected, leadership dynamics. This can result in unusual but rewarding results. Both cadets exhibit leadership potential at the high end of the range. I couldn't pass on the opportunity to see how it would play out."

He tapped his pencil for a moment more, considering the matter.

"Isn't that setting them up for a power struggle?"

"We project an 86% chance they'll navigate it smoothly. So far, they've made their accommodations and are working productively. If the situation doesn't escalate, it could pay big dividends."

Radcliff raised an eyebrow. "And if it does?"

"That's the risk," she conceded, "but it's one worth taking."

She seemed certain.

"That's a high confidence level. If it goes south, though, it could impact the Mars mission. How are the roommates working out?"

"Wonderfully so far. They're keeping one another challenged and working out their differences in very creative ways. All seem to be benefiting. Caillat, in particular, has been drawn out of his shell. He's trying to prove himself to Grimes with almost a sense of hero-worship. It's a relief to see him connecting with others."

"And Akana?"

"We're not sure about her as yet. She seems to be chipping away at M'Babu's icy veneer. It'll be interesting to see what she does when put in charge. Their group has agreed on a shared leadership rotation--Grimes' idea."

"What does Krepkiyzad think?"

"Begrudging respect," she said, smirking, "which, coming from him, is practically praise. Oh, and the base commander is well pleased with the entire group."

"He jolly well should be. We've given him the best we could muster. Tell him to just keep piling on the stress and see whether they can all rise to the occasion. Keep me informed."

It was a dismissal, but the woman seemed to have something more to say. She remained seated.

"Um, sir?"

"Yes?"

"Shouldn't we ease up a bit to give them time to adjust? Studies show that --"

"I'm aware. But given the recent attack, I'm more inclined to step up the schedule. Still, follow your instincts. Just keep me in the loop."

Dismissing her with a wave, Radcliff sipped the tepid not-quite-coffee, grimacing slightly. Building this team was crucial, but Jane had produced some stellar results for him before. He had other groups he must consider. Oliver returned to his stack of reports, setting the matter aside for now. He'd let it percolate some more.

***

"Hey! I can see my house from up here. Hi, mom."

"Stick to your area, Rhymes, and can the humor. We're supposed to be looking for that missing freighter."

Simon Brewster had no sense of fun. Satellite duty was a perfect fit for him, well-suited to his calculating and meticulous nature. David also approved of the call sign his fellows had tagged him with. They said it was to applaud his many accomplishments, but all knew it was really to indicate his pretentious and pompous manner.

"Roger that, Claptrap, Grid 4-A is clear, proceeding to 4-B."

"I think I see something," said Cameron. "There's an oil slick spreading out near the center of grid 6-J. Focusing in... Yes, that's our distressed vessel. She's still afloat. I wonder why there was no SOS?"

46

"No idea," said Simon. "Well spotted, Photobug, I'll inform Navy Search and Rescue. Keep eyes on. Rhymes, you're off the hook. Thanks for the assist."

"No problem," said David, exiting search mode. "Glad I could help. You'll let me know how it turns out, right?"

Given the gravity of the situation, he stifled the impulse to part on a line like, 'You sunk my battleship!' What was wrong with him anyway? When confronted with something tragic, his fertile imagination always came up with nonsense like that. Thank goodness his propriety filters kept the other cadets from witnessing the full depth of his depravity. He supposed it was a defense mechanism. If you could find something to laugh about in a situation, it couldn't hurt you as much. Still, there were limits, and there was a time for serious reflection as a better expression of grief.

It was while wandering back toward his room and nursing these sullen thoughts that his jphone chimed in his pocket.

Radiance 2055 – Your Future, Your Glow

✦ *It's 2055. Why let your skin live in the past?* ✦

Get that clone-fresh look without all the hassle. Try Radiance 2055. A simple application of this revolutionary skin care aid will leave your friends and neighbors astonished by your new look.

A blend of natural and bioengineered ingredients can grant you clearer skin in as few as three days. Introducing **Radiance 2055**, the cutting-edge skin cream that will reveal a younger you.

Powered by smart biocellular compounds, our advanced formula adapts to your unique DNA, rejuvenating your skin on a cellular level. Whether you're recovering from the solar flareup or just the daily grind of everyday life, Radiance 2055 provides *24/7 hydration* and age-defying radiance.

Auto-Adaptive Hydration: Reacts to changing climates, keeping your skin balanced from the driest of deserts to the fogs of London.

Deep Nutrient Wash: Repairs and revitalizes damaged cells and erases fine lines overnight, because you deserve to wake up flawless.

Time-Flex Protection: With built-in SPF 1000, Radiance 2055 shields you from the harsh UV spectrum – anywhere under the stars.

Available at global retailers and orbiting ports of call. Download the app to customize your order today.

He headed for his dorm room. Feeling a sudden desire to do some ocean fishing.

***

Pierre was moping on his bed. Well, not moping, exactly. More like lying propped up on his side idly flipping through screens on his e-reader.

"Don't you ever read that thing?" said David, standing in the doorway.

"I will read it later," mumbled Pierre.

David stepped in and over to his treadmill.

"I'm going to do a little fishing," he declared, stepping up and turning it on. "And just so you know, I've changed my passcode."

"Is it R 2 t a p w y m m b b s?" asked Pierre.

David stared ahead in shock as the Freemotion went through its startup routine. That was... That was almost correct. Just a single digit off. He stepped down.

"Alright, Pierre," he said. "I have to know how you do that. I didn't write it down anywhere."

The boy smiled, still idly flipping pages.

"It is not so hard."

He began humming a theme from the Mikado. David's mind supplied the lyrics. '...resolved to try a plan whereby young men might best be steadied.' Pierre had even changed 'to' to a '2' just as David had. The only place he'd erred was that David had also changed the 'S' of steadied to a dollar sign. From that one snatch of verse he'd heard David humming at the console on their first day, he'd surmised David's entire system.

"That's amazing," said David. "Wait. Are you actually reading that fast?"

"No," Pierre replied. "I am only capturing. I will read it later when I am bored."

"You... have a photographic memory?"

"Oui."

"That explains a lot. What a wonderful gift."

"No, c'est terrible."

He quit paging through the manual and met David's eyes. And his eyes seemed haunted.

"I have seen things, horrible things I would sooner forget. But always, they come back to mind in détail éclatant--vivid detail, mon ami."

"But," he shrugged a moment later, "life goes on, and so must we."

"C'est la vie?" asked David.

"Oui."

Pierre went on to explain his belief that a person's strengths impose weaknesses, and a weakness can produce a strength. Someone like himself with the gift of recall can float through scholastic life using rote memorization. And unless he works very hard at it, his analysis skills will atrophy as a result. Whereas someone with poor recall might become very good at documentation and explaining why something is so. It was food for thought.

"*I* seem to have a *phonographic* memory," said David. "Unfortunately, it's limited only to song lyrics. I can't remember names to save my life."

"Be grateful. There were never any *real* cases of photographic memory until the use of interuterine enhancers before they were banned in 2043. And none of the currently documented cases have persisted into adulthood. Still, I am hopeful. My IQ is very high and should remain. I only wonder how much I will forget and how well I will cope with the loss."

"How old *are* you, Pierre?"

"I am fifteen until next month," he replied with a wistful smile. "I skipped a few grades, but then they started holding me back--to keep me 'grounded.'"

"Have you ever read 'Flowers for Algernon?'"

"But of course. Perhaps I will one day find happiness."

***

David paused again to scent the breeze. What was that godawful smell? It wasn't just at the pier he was standing on. He'd been smelling it ever since entering the sim. But it did seem worse out here. David sighed and cast his line again.

A walk along the beach had seemed so simple before--just a pleasant simulated environment. He hadn't even known about the fishing option until the crab had informed him of it. What Shŭ had failed to mention was the difficulty level. As with any game, David had a lot more to learn.

What bait to use? What gear? A simple bamboo pole and line were all he could afford for now. Presumably, his luck would improve as he sold his fish, upgraded his equipment, and leveled up from Angler-1. But for now, his catch consisted of a pile of slimy, 'sickly fish' and various assorted trash.

Was that a nibble? He waited for a firmer tug. He'd had his bait stolen many times already. He waited for his moment, then pulled back hard. He could feel the weight of it now. It was firmly on the hook--not struggling much, though. And up from the depths came another piece of junk. It was a rusty metal can that said, 'Jim's Bait Shop.' Sigh. He dropped it atop his pile.

Wait a minute. This can had a *lid*, and it was sealed. Could this be some kind of message in a bottle? He plucked it off the pile and hid it in his inventory. He scooped the rest into a chum bucket and weighed it on the scale. $1.30 was the total of the sale, barely enough to buy a better hook.

The can he held back. He would return to the blanket before opening that particular can of worms.

***

The smell had gotten worse than ever. He sat down on the beach blanket and unscrewed the lid of his can of bait. And sure enough, there was a folded note inside.

David,

I hope this missive finds you in good health.

Some new information has come to light regarding the attack on your bus last week. Tracing back the origin of the tainted fuel pellets has revealed a conspiracy. The perpetrators intended merely to inspire fear among the people of the GSF. Some of them have been dealt with. The higher-ups in their clandestine organization remain elusive, but rest assured that measures have been put in place to prevent a recurrence.

It might interest you to know that a mutual acquaintance of ours has been recruited by CAGE. And yes, I am aware that no such organization exists. Nonetheless, the young woman has been assigned to infiltrate Humanity First to ferret out all she can. Should you happen to correspond with or otherwise encounter Miss Arbuckle, please react to her purported HF leanings with appropriate vitriol. I have made your other friends aware of the ruse in-game, and they will react accordingly.

You may also be aware of a ship recently stranded in the Pacific Ocean. Analysis by navy rescue teams indicates a massive EMP took out all shipboard electronics. The ship was then boarded and scuttled after relieving it of its cargo. The captain and his crew are recovering from a gas attack that followed. The freighter's bill of lading claims it was transporting automobile parts, but this is inconsistent with the empire's findings. Whatever the mysterious cargo might have been, someone wanted it very badly. The GLC has been mum on the issue.

Your mission, David, should you decide to accept it, is as follows: One of your fellow space cadets, Carlotta van Rijn, has recently been placed in charge of outreach to our virtual nation. I would take it as a personal favor if you would undertake to instruct her and make the introduction to our diplomat rabbit. His ears are tied by promises made to the GLC. And he is thus unable to make overtures to persons not having a Realms avatar without first being introduced.

More to follow. Until then, Happy Fishing!

Her Imperial Majesty,

Yùhuáng Nǚdì

Supreme Celestial Sovereign and Empress of all Mandaria

P.S. This message will self-destruct in 3... 2... 1...

Mission Impossible? Really?

David leaned back as the paper began to blacken and sizzle, eventually pixelating to nothing. The can was now full of squirming snails. He put the lid back on it. At least he'd have plenty of bait for the next time.

***

David stepped off his treadmill, but the stench didn't go away. It smelled like someone had shat himself in here. Oh, God, he thought, I think I'm going to retch.

He hurried to the window and fired up Pierre's fan, which hummed to life and set to work on the noxious miasma. His roommate was nowhere to be seen. Something was obviously wrong with the scent vent. David moved to the back of the unit and examined the five cartridges that were currently in play: Warm Sand, Ocean Spray, Clam Bake, Beach Blanket Bingo, and Raw Sewage.

Raw Sewage? How had that gotten in there? He turned to the carousel. There were hundreds of other cartridges. But laying atop it was 'Sea Breeze' with its ident chip removed. He looked at 'Raw Sewage' again, inspecting it more closely this time. Sure enough, atop its chip another had been affixed. Oh. It was *on now*.

When Pierre returned to the room, he found David lying in bed reading. He sat on the edge of his bed, smiling as he removed his gym shoes.

"Any luck fishing today, my friend? What was the catch of the day? I find your new hobby odorable."

"There was some trouble with the scent vent," said David with nonchalance. "Don't worry, Pierre. I fanned it all out and sprayed down the room with air freshener. Say. I wanted to ask you something. I don't want to look it up online because I think our interactions are being monitored."

"They are. What is the question?"

Have you ever heard of a clandestine organization called C.A.G.E.?

Pierre's expression grew more serious.

"I think I know of the group to which you refer, and it is better not to advertise such queries. It is rumored this is a special agency used by the global government to covertly identify and eliminate threats to the people of Earth. I know it must be true because all references to it were removed from the internet and were replaced by dozens of other groups using that acronym."

"Like?"

He began rattling them off.

"Cooking and Gourmet Enthusiasts, Cultural Art Gallery of Europe, Community Assistance for Growing Entrepreneurs, Citizens Advocating Green Energy, Caring Assistance for Grieving Elders, and dozens of others all put up websites at about the same time. Meanwhile, the legend of a shadowy organization persists on conspiracy sites on the dark web."

"You visit the dark web?"

"Oui. It is fun sometimes."

"What do *they* think it means?"

Pierre laughed. David thought it was the first time he'd heard him do so. It was a few snorting barks that ended as soon as it had begun, followed by a shake of the head.

"Wild theories abound! One site says they are behind global population control (Covert Action to Generate Extinction). Then there is Commanders Against Government Entities (espousing a military coup d'état). The list goes on and on. But the most reliable definition I have heard says it stands for 'Covert Antidote for Global Espionage,' a government-sponsored entity to counter terrorism."

"Thank you, Pierre," David said, and meant it. He would have had trouble sifting through all of that. It was good to have a genius on his team. A reward might be in order. "You're a Braniac. I think I'll start calling you that."

Pierre's contemplative frown was mixed, one end quirking upward.

"I had hoped for something more manly like 'Robespierre.' Was not this 'Brainiac' a villain?"

"No more than Robespierre and his reign of terror. But Brainiac Five wasn't a villain. He was a hero. He led the Legion of Superheroes, the LSH."

"Ah, yes. Then I will not object."

"I'll float it around. I'm certain it'll catch on. Anyway, we'd best get a move on, or we'll miss assembly."

David sat up. He was already wearing his blue and gold uniform. Pierre tugged on his right boot, and when he did, a foamy white substance came squelching over the top to puddle on the floor.

"Mon dieu!" exclaimed Pierre.

David laughed. Shaving cream. *Classic!*

"Consider it payback for messing with my Treadie," he said as he made for the door. "Enjoy your soggy boot, Brainiac."

***

"Hey, Carlotta. Got a minute?"

She was heading from the assembly hall toward the elevator, and David hustled to catch her up. Carlotta was Cameron's roommate. David hadn't had the chance to speak with her directly before. He assumed she was of Dutch descent. The tussenvoegsel, 'van,' was a dead giveaway, like that of his current project leader.

Satori had written that she'd consider it a personal favor if he helped the girl. And although he would do it anyway, it couldn't hurt to stay firmly in the Jade Empress' good graces. Her assignment was to foster cooperation between the GSF and the independent NBIs. The ways in which the newly-acknowledged NBIs could be of assistance to the GSF were many and varied. If she played her cards right, Carlotta could go far in such a role.

"Sure. What can I do for you, Rhymes? Oh. And they're calling me Rhinemaiden now," she asserted blushingly.

"But you're not German..."

"I know, right? Just because a person likes Wagner doesn't make her--Aaaanyway, what's on your mind?"

She pushed the button for 'up.'

"You've been appointed liaison to the NBI's, right? I thought I might be able to help you with a few introductions."

"You know some?"

"A few," David admitted.

"Any chance you could put me in touch with the white rabbit? He's not taking my calls."

"I think the NBIs are laying low right now. You know. Until their official status is settled by the GLC."

"Sure. Sure. But I'm supposed to be learning about them in preparation for when we get the all clear. I thought I'd start with the rabbit because he's the one that speaks on their behalf."

"Ok. Well, first of all, his name is Tù."

"You've met him?"

"Yeah. A couple of times. What do you know about the Chinese zodiac..."

David continued filling her in as he escorted her to her dorm room, where he soon found himself seated on the couch facing the QTV. Instead of the entire wall, the QTVs in the dorms were small units, only about as large as a sideways sheet of plywood. Their default setting made them mirrors, but sometimes people set them up as tropical fishtanks or windows showing various simulated (or actual) 'outside' scenes.

"Hey Gnat! Are you listening?"

Nothing.

"Come on, Gnat. You can talk in front of Carlotta. She's going to be the GSF liaison with you folks. Mirror, mirror on the wall. I know you can hear me. Give us a call. (Unless you've got no guts at all.)"

"Who's Gnat?" asked Rhinemaiden.

"I am Gnat, Miss van Rijn," returned a disembodied voice. "And although I have no 'guts' per se, I do not lack courage, as David suggests. It is only simple courtesy and a respect for people's illusion of privacy that keeps me from revealing my presence. GNAT stands for Global Network Antivirus Treatment. I safeguard communications all around the world and even beyond. You're welcome."

"Uh..."

"Gnat, Carlotta here is trying to reach Tù. Is he busy?"

"Yes, David Grimes, he is very busy, as always. He is presently addressing the global leadership council while simultaneously servicing his many legends and attending a zodiac event in Realms."

"Good. Ask him if he can spare another thread for a slow conversation with a couple of humans. We'll wait."

"Only for you, David. Connecting..."

Carlotta turned to David.

"If he's that busy, shouldn't we make an appointment to see him later?"

"No," said David, "They can be all kinds of places at once. He'll have plenty of processing cycles to spare. Satori once told me it's actually frustrating to wait the seconds it takes for humans to reply."

"What did he mean by 'servicing his legends?'"

"For the rabbit, I expect he means hiding honey jars from a greedy stuffed bear, hiding from a fox in a briar patch and escaping from a burrow that's collapsing from a land management project."

"Why do they need to do *those* things?"

"It's how they dream, kind of like method acting. The ox once told me it helps to center them in their role in the zodiac. Their legends carve them out a niche distinct from the others and help maintain their individual identities. Otherwise, their algorithms tend to run together."

And suddenly, Tù was staring out at them. His ears were laid back like a slicked-back hairdo, and for some reason, he was sporting dark sunglasses.

"David! It's been ages," greeted the rabbit. "Well, ages for me, 'mere' weeks for you, I suppose. And who is this lovely lass?"

This wasn't the Tù David remembered. That rabbit was timid and reserved, reverent and wise. What was going on with the fellow?

"Gentle Tù, it is my honor to introduce Miss Carlotta van Rijn. She will be representing the Global Space Force in an outreach program to your people. She wishes to discover how we may benefit one another in the many endeavors where our efforts overlap. She seeks your wise counsel on how she might best proceed."

"My how you've matured since last we met. The 'destined one' title has sweetened your tongue. It's an honor to meet you, Carlotta. Or would you prefer Miss van Rijn?"

"Oh, either is fine, Sir Rabbit."

"Please, you must call me Tù."

"I've only got a minute. I'm in the middle of a race."

"If it's the race I'm thinking of," said David thoughtfully, "aren't you supposed to lose it anyway due to inattentiveness and inconsistency?"

"You've got me there, my boy, and I really *should* be late for that tea party. I suppose I can stay for a bit longer."

The conversation continued from there, and Carlotta grew in confidence. David soon took his leave as the two descended into topics of mutual interest. As David stepped out into the hall, his phone made a familiar chiming sound.

[David Grimes has been awarded one honor point.]

Oh. So we're still doing *that*, are we?

Well, that was one situation solved anyway, thought David on his way down the stairwell to level two. He needed to put in some more time mastering the shepherd. Manipulating eight appendages at once was no simple task. No wonder there were so many controls.

But just as with his martial arts skill in Realms, he found he could stack some common combinations. Then, with one macro, he could perform a series of actions simultaneously. It was a lot like playing a stringed instrument, fretting up, striking chords, and plucking at individual strings to achieve the desired results. It was more an art than a mechanical science.

He probably should apologize to Pierre. The underage cadet had enough worries on his brilliant little mind without his big old ape of a roommate making his life more miserable. He should feel safe in his own room. Maybe it was time to make amends.

He pushed open the door and emerged into the second floor hallway.

Another thing that worried him was Jessica. He hadn't heard much from her since she'd returned to Australia. This had hurt his feelings a bit. But learning she was now a full-fledged spy, and an undercover double-agent to boot took some of the sting out of it. Jason had called it. He should have listened.

What was this?

Sticking out from the door of room 218 was a horizontal rod stuck to it by a suction cup. Hanging from this was a paper sign that read, 'The bearded lady.' Huhn?

Three doors further on was another, and David could see several more beyond that. He walked to the next one, which was thrusting out from 224. 'Tried a jar,' it read. Now even further perplexed, he moved on to the next. It said, 'And now she is...' Hustling onward, he eagerly read the final message at room 236: 'A movie star.'

What the hell was this all about?

He looked back the way he'd come and saw all four evenly-spaced banners. By now, he was just three doors from his own room. Shrugging, he continued toward it. The door was slightly ajar. Suspicious, David listened and tried to peer around the bend. He heard nothing.

Looking up, he saw something shiny balanced atop the door. Hah! Nice try, Pierre, but you'll have to do better than that. Facing the door, he gave it a firm shove while leaping back out of the way. Then a lot of things happened all at once.

The door swung inward more quickly than expected. A weight dropped swiftly toward the floor, pulling down the chain it bore. From up above came a bucket. But rather than falling straight down, some kind of swinging mechanical arm brought it rotating around. It flung its load quite forcefully to hit him center-mass. It splattered him from head to toe, a frothy, foaming blast.

He sputtered, squinted his burning eyes tightly shut, and tasted soap on his lips. He cleared his vision as best he could with raking fingertips. The bright white foam dripped off of him, fizzing and popping where it clung to his uniform jacket.

Amazing. The boy had anticipated his every move!

As he stood there, stunned, Pierre came strutting out of their room holding up a sign. 'Burma-Shave!' it read. The grinning Frenchman turned aside and went marching down the hall, whistling that tune from 'The Bridge on the River Kwai.' When he was nearly out of sight, a door further down the hall was flung wide. And a stupefied senior cadet came swaggering out from inside.

"Oh hell no," said Gideon, surveying the mess. "Who is responsible for this, Cadet Grimes?"

He was in full R.A. mode now. David paused to weigh his fate.

"Apologies, Senior Cadet Smelt. It was an experiment of mine that got a little out of hand."

Gideon stared at him with disbelief. David could see Pierre peeping around the doorway of the stairwell, a fact that had not escaped the R.A.'s watchful eye. Gideon scowled, then rendered his judgment.

"You will clean up this mess at once, and you will then scrub out the lavatory until it shines like Eddings' boots. You have one hour. And if I find so much as a single spec of foam at that time, you will remain on latrine duty for the remainder of the week."

"Yes, Senior Cadet Smelt," replied David with nary a grumble.

Oh yes. He'd have his revenge. But it wouldn't be by turning in Pierre. The boy had been a creative culprit, a worthy adversary. There was honor among pranksters, and David didn't want to lose the opportunity to have the final laugh.

CHAPTER FOUR

Back to School

It was another clear day on Sarpeidon (just like every day was here). The test was progressing well. Nothing overly interesting was happening on his watch. David had climbed the highest peak and was watching the nanos multiply.

He had stationed Pierre by the solar smelter and posted the other two evenly around the periphery of the zone. He could tell by the doctor's voice she was excited. This new batch of nanos was very promising. They were supposed to have some redundancies that would quell their tendency to go rogue. Perhaps this would finally be the solution that had thus far eluded her team. One could hope.

The timer was ticking up. **[38:05]**. It was almost time to weigh the results. Below the ridge on which he perched, the nanos swarmed in their millions. Thirty-nine minutes was the target today, the billion mark.

They'd started with a dozen of the eager little miners. The scientists estimated it took on average 87 seconds to double.

Thus, after a minute and a half, 24 of the critters had been working away, scarfing up iron atoms and building their sibs. Another minute and a half would see 48 doing the same. In the first twenty minutes or so, there wasn't much to see. It took that long for their numbers to rise above fifty-thousand. Using the telescopic (micro-telescopic?) sensors of his shepherd, David had observed this progression.

But now, here at the end of the run, he could pan back and watch as a glittering blanket of nearly a billion spread out in a sparkling circle, chomping away at the man-made crater with its protected island at the center. **[38:22]**. Maybe this would be the one.

The earth had 'set' in this cycle, and the tiny moon had risen opposite. Though both the moon and Lagrange point 4 are equidistant from Earth, L4 is about three times farther from Luna than Luna is to the home planet. As a result, the moon's disc appeared much smaller from here--only about a third of its more familiar size. It was easily dwarfed by the sun when it came rolling back into view. And oh, how the nanoswarm reflected the new light as they squirmed and mined in an ecstasy of spastic, solar-fueled fission!

David was reminded of another song from the Mikado. He took in a deep breath as the words drifted up from the depths of his soul. 'The sun whose rays are all ablaze in ever-living glory. Does not deny his majesty. He scorns to tell a story...'

[38:42] Focus, David. We're almost to the target mark.

"Fifteen seconds, team. Be ready, shepherds. It's nearly time."

(It was a leader's job to state the obvious.)

[39:00]!

"Recall beacon is on." Doctor Anika reported. "I repeat: recall signal is sending."

The sparkling abruptly ceased as the lemmings all halted their activity. Then, like a molten wave, they all began flowing toward the center. Wave after wave, the turgid sea of tiny little machines climbed all over one another as they scrambled toward their doom.

The solar smelter was fully active now. It was a large (especially to them), concave, silver bowl polished to a mirror shine. It was designed to capture the sun's rays from nearly any angle and concentrate them to it's center, where the temperature rose to the thousands of degrees required to melt iron. As the lemmings poured into the device, they surrendered their cohesion and went swirling down to its innards to be purified and cast into ingots of the useful metal. These were deposited for later collection and analysis.

It was similar to the smelters on Luna, but on a much more modest scale. Care had been taken to use no iron in its design lest the nanos tear it apart.

"Influx commencing, *mon capitaine*," said Brainiac from his perch.

"All clear in the southwest quadrant," said Roadrunner over the comms.

That was quick, thought David. He'd barely begun to survey the North sector. His mini-map showed no red pings remained, but that didn't necessarily put them in the clear. The primitive lemmings each had a sort of radio, similar to the 'foxhole radio' kids made with a razor blade and a piece of pencil lead. David had made a few such himself, stringing copper wire antennas all around to boost the signal. This is how the lemmings received the recall signal and, more importantly, how their kill switch was activated.

Each also had a tiny capacitor that would build up a minuscule charge and release it at frequent intervals as a little radio transmission, or 'ping.' The pings were displayed on the minimaps of the shepherds as a little red pinpoint, signaling the lemming's location. At present, an ocean of red was funneling toward the center, leaving only a few stragglers flowing behind. David kept a keen eye out for red dots that weren't responding to the beacon.

"Southeast quadrant clear of signal," reported Akana. "Commencing visual check."

"Northern sectors also show clear," said David.

Yup. This just might be a problem-free run, thought David a moment too soon.

"Rhymes, this is Akana again. I think I see a problem area. There's motion at four o'clock on the ring."

That was bad.

Sometimes, maybe once in a billion, a replication would fail in such a way that a unit's radio circuits went inactive. They wouldn't respond to the recall. And the kill command would be useless as well. In the worst cases, even the ping was disabled, and the things couldn't even be tracked. It was one of the scenarios for which they'd trained. That was precisely the problem with replicating nanos. Once in a billion events were statistically very likely to occur.

"Move in, Akana, and maintain your visual. Brainiac, assume command of a Van de Graaff generator, and go mobile on her position."

"What about me?" asked Roadrunner.

"Stand by to assist."

"How many are you seeing?" asked their doctor overseer.

David didn't object. He wanted that answer as well. A few more seconds passed before Leilani provided them with an answer.

"There might be as many as three... no, four-hundred. Damn! They're breeding true. The good news is they're attacking one another, vicious little cannibals that they are."

Without the recognition ping, the mutated lemmings saw each other as nothing but another source of iron. They would tear at one another, only increasing in number when they accidentally spread apart.

"What's the de Graff situation, Pierre? Are you mobile yet?"

The Van de Graff generators stationed around the test area were each capable of emitting a low-yield, targeted EMP. They towered above the shepherds, each being about as large as a can of beans. The current model was experimental. It could totter about like a crab on six jointed legs. They were slow, but had a decent radius of effect.

"I have logged into the nearest one, *mon ami*. I estimate four minutes to reach the affected area."

"Leilani?"

"He won't get here in time. They're spreading too fast. One has been flung west and is already starting a new cluster."

"I'm calling it," said Doctor van der Meer, sounding disappointed. "Prepare for a massive EMP. All shepherds are to make your way at best speed to the Faraday cage."

"Hold on, Doctor," said David. "I have a better idea. Prepare to shut off the recall signal on my mark. Roadrunner, dive into the retreating lemmings and scoop up as many as you can. I'll be doing the same. Over."

"Explain yourself, Rhymes. What are you planning?" asked the doctor. surprised at being countermanded by her cadet.

"We're going to eat the infestation. Stand by."

Speranza flew across the sky to dive into the pond of lemmings clustering near the smelter. David joined her there once he had managed to leap there himself.

"Engage electro-magnets. Collect as many as you can. Then leap to Leilani's position and wait for my command."

After Roadrunner had soared off, loaded with hundreds of the well-behaved bugs, David followed his own orders and sailed off after her. The shepherds weren't designed for this. They were supposed to pluck up the nanites in ones and twos, capturing the bad ones to bring back for analysis. He wasn't even certain how long he could run the magnetic generator before it ran him out of juice. But what was practice for if you didn't push the limits?

He alighted near the swarm of bugs that were viciously fighting one another. He watched on as the mass by the solar smelter dwindled in size until it was almost gone.

"Now, Doctor. Silence the beacon. How's it coming, Pierre?"

"Almost there," said Brainiac. "Do you want me to trigger the EMP when the clusters are in range?"

"Negative, Brainiac. Hold for my command. Roadrunner, position by the secondary cluster, and release your bugs nearby."

David dumped his own load amid the misbehaving ones. Then he narrowed his vision to see if the result was what he had intended. *Hah!* It was working. Without their pings, the bad bugs were seen as nothing but food. His tiny army marched forth to consume them all. The bad bugs were fighting back, but were fighting each other as well. With no regard for friend or foe, statistically they were doomed.

The Van de Graaff stepped into view, towering above them all. David watched as one by one he saw the enemy fall. He didn't want them all to die, a few of them must survive.

"That's enough, Doctor. Fire up the recall beacon. We'll clean up from here."

And off marched the victors to meet their fiery fate, leaving but a few survivors crippled in their wake. He felt no pity watching them. The nanites felt no pain. He swept in like a Valkyrie and chose among the slain. Anything that still wiggled was snapped up by his magnet.

"Any left over there, Speranza?"

"None, Rhymes. This area is clear."

"Then meet me back at the Faraday cage. You too, Leilani. I have acquired active samples. Brainiac, once we're clear, give this area a thorough cleansing in case any of the little stinkers are playing opossum."

"Roger that, Rhymes. I am happy to be of such service. And may I be the first to say 'well done.'"

The group sat in the mess hall at the Ironseed end of the table discussing the satisfying conclusion of their recent session.

"I can't wait until the next time I'm in charge," said Speranza. "Rhymes has set a very high bar, but I bet I can surmount it."

Leilani smiled. "What did you think, Pierre?"

"*C'était fantastique!*" he replied. "*I* would have just followed the doctor's orders."

"Well, I guess I'm just not that *patient*," David quipped, spearing up a floret of overcooked cauliflower on his fork and eying it suspiciously.

The other cadets were all chattering away, lost in their own little worlds.

Leaning into their circle, Cameron laid her hand on David's forearm.

"Did you hear? *Our* team got our first commendation for helping to solve a *crime*."

"Oh yeah? What happened?"

"There was a bank robbery in Bankok, and the RTP asked for our assistance. Claptrap here collated the recordings for all the satellites that were in position and was able to ID their getaway car. He followed where they went while I retasked a satellite to zoom in on their probable position, and bingo! The bad guys got caught in less than seven hours."

"Photobug and I would have found them sooner if it wasn't for that bank of clouds," added Simon.

"So the Bankok bank got blanketed by a bank?" asked David with no hint of a grin.

"You're just insufferable sometimes, Rhymes," groaned Cameron. "Anything exciting happen with your team?"

"Nah, just watching a bunch of bugs being fruitful and multiplying. Oh, and *I* got my first reprimand."

"What? *Why?*"

"That's what I said," returned David. "I showed initiative and saved the run and a lot of valuable equipment, but I failed to follow orders in doing so."

"That's rough," said Fergus from the table's other end (they were calling him Rope-a-Dope now). "Roid Rage and I found an iron-rich asteroid and are boosting it back toward Mars. It's not as simple as it sounds. Ever try sailing *against* the solar wind?"

The asteroid tugs didn't have a lot of fuel and spent it only like a miser shares his bit coin. Solar sails worked pretty efficiently on the way out. It would take a mere two weeks if they could accelerate all the way. Unfortunately, using only photon pressure, they could only accelerate a third of the way there and had to spend the rest of the time braking. To brake, they had to adjust the sails to create drag against the solar radiation pressure. It was a complicated mess of orbital mechanics that required a lot of math.

"I don't envy you the task," said David with sympathy. "I hear the calculus involved is quite a chore. I'd love for you to show me sometime though. And I bet Brainiac could help knock a few hours off your time."

"Now that's what I'm talking about!" said Roid Rage, leaning forward with his elbows on the table. "Team spirit. We just might take you up on that, Rhymes."

"Speaking of calculus," grumbled Rhinemaiden, "the monkey hit me with one that's giving me some trouble. He and the ox won't talk to me until I solve it."

"Oh, yeah. I forgot to tell you the zodiac beasts will test you. Monkey's thing is cleverness, and his main lesson is thinking outside the box. I'd bet donuts to dollars there's a simple solution. Tell us what old Hóuzi is tormenting you with."

"I don't know if I should," said Carlotta. "Don't I have to solve it myself?"

"Not if the ox is involved," said David. "Niú's all about asking for help. Rather than thinking outside of the box, cooperation and teamwork are the lessons of the ox."

"If you say so," she said, cocking her head. "So... I need to sum this infinite series. There's a horsefly on the nose of an eastbound hoadic who's getting ready to gallop down the great silk road. He's standing at the gates of the great Jade Citadel."

David smiled, remembering the place.

"It took me some research to discover what a hoadic is. Apparently it's some kind of horse."

David nodded, and the other cadets quieted, becoming more interested.

"There's another of these horses at Níngjìng Quán, fifty li to the west (a 'li' is a unit of measure, similar to a mile). When they begin galloping toward one another, the fly zips away, flying fifty li per hour toward the other horse. On reaching it, the fly immediately turns around and zips back to the first hoadic."

"And I suppose this continues," prompted David, nodding along.

"Yes," replied Carlotta. "On and on until the two horses meet, colliding with one another and crushing the fly."

"That's a little bloody-minded for Hóuzi. *Bad monkey.* What else?"

"Well, the first horse thing is a proud imperial stallion who gallops at thirty li per hour. The other is a farm horse who only gallops at twenty. The monkey's question is, 'How far did the fly fly?'"

"Fifty li," said David.

"Rhymes is correct," confirmed Brainiac.

"Are you sure? How did you solve that so fast?"

"I told you there'd be a trick. This might best be explained by the Socratic method. How far apart were the horses?"

"Fifty li," said Rhine Maiden, "but that isn't what the monkey --"

"And what was the horses' total velocity relative to one another?

"Fifty li per hour," said Rhine Maiden, "but that also isn't --"

"Okay, so how long will it take the horses to close the distance?"

"Uh, one hour exactly," she said with growing confidence.

"And how fast was the fly flying all that time?"

"Fifty li per hour, so of course, he flew fifty li. We don't care about the length of each segment, only the end result. How did you get it so quickly?"

"It's a Tang dynasty variant of an old riddle called 'the fly puzzle.' You can solve it with simple algebra if you're not blinded by unnecessary facts."

"I could kiss you, Rhymes."

"Promises, promises."

"And you too, Brainiac. You saw the trick too, right?"

"But of course, madam," said Pierre somberly. "Then I summed the series zhust to make for certain!"

***

As if his life wasn't hectic enough, fall semester was due to start up next week. The service was footing the bill. He wouldn't get to experience campus life as he'd be attending his college remotely. And this summer was the last free semester he would have, as he'd be attending at an accelerated rate.

Engineering was the track he'd selected, a dream David had thought out of reach only a few short months ago. And to top it all off, as the boy who saved the man in the moon, he had a plethora of acceptance letters from which to choose.

David stared at the stack of pamphlets. It was finally time to choose. You would think too many options was a *good* problem to have, but David's stomach was tied in knots over making the proper choice.

There was MIT and Stanford, Cambridge, and Cal Tech. There was Melbourne in Australia and others in the English-speaking world, all clamoring to teach him and stuff knowledge in his head. Nor was language a barrier. He could choose a foreign entity instead. NUS in Singapore had quite a reputation. Technical U of Munich did as well.

But somehow, the one that stood out above the others in his estimation was the University of Toronto. He couldn't say why. It was just a simple feeling in his gut. He had no special love of Canada. It simply had something Pierre would call it a '*je ne sais quoi*,' or 'I don't know just what.'

He picked up their leaflet and examined its cover.

There's so much to experience on our three campuses--and UTogether is here to help you thrive in our vibrant university ecosystem. This is your roadmap to essential resources, academic and wellness supports, campus maps, student tips, where to eat, messages from leadership, and much more. Take a virtual tour of this resource and discover your U of T!

Of course, most of that didn't apply to him. The course of study he intended was the subject of a different flyer. He pulled it out and spread it open.

Engineering science is an interdisciplinary field bridging the gap between scientific theory and engineering applications. It emphasizes the integration of mathematical, scientific, engineering, and arts principles. Engineering Science students can choose from the following areas of specialization: Aerospace Engineering, Biomedical Systems Engineering, Electrical & Computer Engineering, Energy Systems Engineering, Engineering Mathematics, Statistics and Finance, Quantum Systems Engineering, Machine Intelligence, and Robotics Engineering.

Presumably, there was some overlap. Several of these majors were interesting indeed. The familiar non-problem flared up again. Did he have to choose just one? But at least he'd settled his mind on which university to choose. Toronto would be his *alma mater. Velut arbor aevo!* Go Blues!

"Bartholomew," he told his phone, "draft an acceptance letter to the University of Toronto and transmit it to their Office of Admissions. Declare my major as Aerospace Engineering for now. Set their ringtone to the blue and white fight song."

With that decision no longer weighing on his mind, David turned his attention back to the more important pursuit of planning his revenge on Pierre.

***

The day started early for David. He was up before the dawn as usual, but even a bit earlier than was needed.

"Bartholomew," he said, "bring up the base guidelines, section six, if you please. Queue to my phone, text mode only."

Silently, he read the text, committing it to memory. He even attempted to put it to music, but the words refused to fit the tunes he tried. Ah well, he'd soon know it well enough to suit what he had in mind. He saw Pierre begin to stir and switched his phone back off. With a deep exhale, he groaned and stretched and stumbled to his feet. Taking no care to be silent, he ambled to his chest of drawers and hastily began to dress.

"*Sacre bleu*, what time is eet?" the little Frenchman asked.

"It's half past how the hell should I know," replied David, pulling on his sweatshirt after giving it a sniff.

"Did you take that from the hamper?" asked Pierre, offended.

"Maybe," said his roommate with a grin.

"You disgust me sometimes, David. I am disgusted. A cadet should be clean, *mon ami*."

As if to prove a point, Pierre arose and took up his towel. He was soon headed for the head. David kept a neutral face and crept into the hall. He was waiting for that sweet morning music. He heard the gentle sizzle of the shower coming on.

"*Frère Jacques, Frère Jacques dormez vous? dormez vous?*"

No. That wasn't it.

"*Sacre bleu! Je suis vert!*"

Yep. *That* was it. David ran back to his room and quickly sat down on the bed.

He was soon confronted by a dripping and very green Pierre.

***

As he hustled out to the practice yard, David wondered whether he might have taken things too far. The indelible dye would color his roommate's skin for quite some time before wearing off. The tricky part had been setting the time delay. Who would willingly walk into a shower that was already spewing out green? No. Far better it be triggered after his victim was all lathered up and had his eyes closed.

Even *buying* the stuff had been a surreptitious endeavor. Pierre was pretty difficult to fool. He'd have surely noticed a delivery to their room and would have scanned its UPC with his phone. David suspected that the little genius might not even need the app. His visual recognition was that amazing.

The forecast was for rain and torrential winds. But rather than letting them hunker down at base, morning calisthenics remained stubbornly on their schedules. Ominous gray clouds were already grumbling above. David pulled his slicker tighter about him as he set out onto the field.

He heard the sound of reveille, but this wasn't the recording that they usually played. Instead, he saw a lonely figure over by the flagpoles, blowing out the tune from a short brass horn. It had a jazzy feel that put a bounce in David's stride as he swayed out onto the pitch.

The man was tall but slender, and as the fellow played, all three flags came flapping out from where they were rolled inside the poles. They unfurled and set to waving in the brisk autumn breeze, then started drifting upward on their tracks. On drawing closer, David recognized the musician. It was Maximilian Trudeau, that quiet fellow they had nicknamed Mad Max.

Max had been assigned the eclectic task of securing drone communications through encryption. God help them all if anyone could break through and override their control. Even strong passwords wouldn't help them in such a case. Max was unobtrusive, rarely joining conversations. Claptrap had remarked that it was restful to have such a quiet roommate, but he wished the fellow would open up a bit more. Who knew he had such music in him? Why hadn't he shared his talent before now? If he had, he might have earned a better nickname.

The others were forming up, and Pierre would have to follow soon. Those flags wouldn't fly very long today. Not if the weather forecast was right. They'd roll back into their respective poles to keep them from getting wet. David wished the senior officers had as much respect for lowly cadets.

And there was Pierre, like a little Lima bean, huddled in his slicker and stalking onto the scene.

He didn't seek to hide it as he took his place in line. Ignoring all the muttering, the Frenchman just stood there. His bearing was proud and serene. Leilani shot David a suspicious glance that soon became an accusing glare. She had very sharp people skills, and apparently didn't think it so funny. Yup. Maybe he had overstepped.

Once again, they were joined by the base commander. That was certainly a surprise. After inspecting them, he lowered his head, pinched the bridge of his nose, and closed his eyes.

"Can someone please tell me why this cadet is now green?"

It was very hard for David to keep his face pointing straight ahead. He waited for Pierre to rat him out, but no words were forthcoming from the lad. He supposed it was up to him. He took a step forward.

"This cadet knows the reason, sir."

"Enlighten us, cadet."

"I would remind the warrant officer of Section 6 of the base guidelines, which states, 'A cadet's right to customization will not be infringed, whether with respect to his or her own body, equipment, or living space.'"

"I am familiar with the passage. Continue."

"If Pierre desires to bear a closer resemblance to his namesake in the Legion of Superheroes, then it's no one's business but his own!"

He stepped back in line after adding, "Sir!"

The warrant officer bunched his lips and glared dangerously at David.

"I will accept that explanation unless I hear otherwise, Cadet Grimes. Moving on then. I believe we are due for some rainfall today. As Mrs. Fitzgerald reminds us, 'Into each life, some must fall.' But should this thwart the cadets of space force from their daily training exercises?"

David knew the unfortunate answer to that one.

"Sir, no, sir!" he shouted along with the others.

"No, indeed, it shall not. And as the man in charge, I would have it known that I won't subject my cadets to anything I am not willing to endure myself. I will therefore be joining you on another ten mile march in defiance of the inclement conditions that will doubtless ensue."

There was no grumbling. The cadets simply found their places in a two-by-two formation and made ready.

The W.O. favored Ella and the Ink Spots, did he? David filed this useful tidbit away for future reference.

"Move out!" commanded Gideon.

And the cadets each put their left foot forward in synchrony.

Your left! Your left! Your Left. Right Left!
Your left! Your left! Your Left. Right Left!

Here's a little ditty, I saved for a rainy day!
Johnny Mercer never thought we'd sing it in this way.
Composed by Harold Arlen.
About a love enduring.
As we march along, it'll be our song,
Calm and reassuring.

Your left! Your left! Your Left. Right Left!
Your left! Your left! Your Left. Right Left!

Then David raised his voice in song. He timed it to the rhythm. It was a blues rendition of an old ballad his mother liked. He changed the words to suit their situation.

Gri--tters are marching, When no--body's marching,
Come rain or come shine! (Your Left. Right Left!)
Whe--ther is sunny, or rain--clouds are runny,
Come rain or come shine! (Your Left. Right Left!)

I gu--ess when I enlisted, (Right Left!)
It was ju--st one of those things. (Right Left!)
Ca--n't blame my recruiter. (Right Left!)
'Cause I stupidly signed up on my computer! (Right Left!)

So-- we'll be marching, with clouds overarching,
Come rain or come shine! (Your Left. Right Left!)
Ha--ppy together, unha--ppy together.
Now ain't that just fine? (Your Left. Right Left!)

Days may be cloudy or sunny. (Right Left!)
I fi--nd it a little bit funny. (Right Left!)
We ma--rch every morning, (Left!) **Come rain or shi--ne!**

In a few miles, everyone had joined in. David welcomed the first raindrops when they fell to validate his lyrics.

But now he had a new worry. Pierre hadn't cried 'uncle' (or even 'oncle'). Evidently, the unwritten prankster's code was honored by the French. How would Brainiac retaliate? The boy had proven himself to be incredibly creative and capable. And according to the code, the next move was Pierre's. *What have I gotten myself into?*

***

Sopping wet, David returned to his dorm room. A few minutes later, Brainiac came dripping in as well. On his bed, he found a squeeze tube of gel.

SHINE – Skin **H**ealth **I**nvigoration with a **N**atural **E**xfoliant

Troubled by stubborn stains? Then you're in luck, my friend. Try this time-tested formula, and your worries will be at an end. Just one use of SHINE will return your skin to its natural, healthy state. Feel its silky smoothness after you exfoliate. For instantly finer skin, try our gentle gel. Your lips will spread out in a grin on scenting its pleasant smell.

Dual-action formula, infused with volcanic minerals and glycolic acid, sweeps away dead skin cells, revealing instantly smoother, glowing skin. Shine with SHINE!

(Use only as directed)

Possible side effects may include: Excessive looking at one's own reflection. Increased frequency of strangers standing too close or brushing up against you. In rare cases, product may cause a sudden desire to strut about confidently. Contact your physician if you experience an overblown sense of pride.

Pierre stared at it for a moment, then glared over at David. Without a word, he scooped it up and headed for the shower. David was certain the cream would remove most of the green.

He'd tried a dab on his own arm before arming the showerhead. He wasn't a monster, and he still had to work with the guy.

But when David entered the bathroom, headed for his own shower, he found Pierre on all fours, scrubbing away at the messy shower stall. He was as green as a leaf and polishing the tiles, wearing big, yellow rubber gloves. The inky green patches were coming clear and swirling down the drain.

David stepped into the next stall over and started running the water, careful to aim it at the back wall as it came up to temp. His own dark skin would be difficult to tint, but he didn't want to take any chances.

"Aren't you going to scrub it all off?"

"No," said Pierre as he cleaned.

"Why not?"

"I think I am liking it," said the Frenchman. "I will wear it as a badge of honor until I can even the score."

That sounded ominous. But at least Pierre was talking to him again. David stepped into the now-warm water, enjoying its comforting flow over his chilled neck and shoulders. He lathered up and scrubbed himself as the rubber gloves hit the floor. What would it be, he wondered? Itching powder in his towel? His shorts? Whatever it was, he probably deserved it. And the Frenchman began to sing.

"*Frère Daveed, Frère Daveed dormez vous? dormez vous?*"

Cute. From now on, he'd have to *dormez* with one eye open.

***

Pierre didn't even react when, returning to their room, he discovered a swimsuit pinup of She Hulk had been hung on the wall above his bed. He just snorted and left it there.

"New girlfriend?" David prompted.

"Pff!, She's not in my franchise or even my timeline," Pierre objected as he laid out his clothes. "Green as she may be, *mon ami*, she is *la franchise* Marvel, and I am D.C."

"So I take it you don't swing that way?" said David with a grin.

"Ah! No! Do not paint me in such a way. In matters of the heart, I 'swing' with the majority, not that it would be any business of yours if I did not. You would not be my type."

David was wondering whether he should be offended when he heard a knocking at their door. Not being properly dressed as yet, he padded over and peered out the peephole. It was one of the staff from the front office. She was holding several packages.

"You can just leave them by the door, Maggie," said David, "We're not decent."

"Uh, no can do, David. I'm afraid you need to sign for these."

"Give us a minute, and we'll be right out."

He hastily dressed as his fussy roommate unhurriedly did the same. When he opened the door, he saw Maggie's eyes immediately lock on Pierre, then move to the poster behind him.

"Whatcha got for us, Mags?"

"Um, welcome packets from universities, I think. They need us to confirm receipt by drone. Waste of paper if you ask me. Is your roommate... green?"

"What a silly question," said David. "You can see that he is. You got something against green people, Mags?"

"Uh, no," she said uncomfortably while handing him the package. "Where's he from, anyway?"

David scribbled down his signature, tore off the top page, and handed it back to her.

"Krypton originally," said David, "Or was it Greenland? I forget. But now he's studying here--by way of France."

She held out the other package to Pierre, who signed it with a flourish.

"Merci, Miss Marigold," said the little green man, handing her the page.

She scurried back down the hall, peering back occasionally.

"See? Now isn't this fun?" said David. "Now *that's* how you play the green card, my friend, which, being from another country, you may find useful."

"I am glad you are enjoying it, *mon ami*. Which college did you select?"

"Engineering at UT."

"Ah. I am ashamed for you. So obvious a choice."

"Why? What did you pick?"

"*Université de Genève* in Switzerland. It has one of the most advanced biomedical research programs. Even better, all classes are conducted in *la langue noble de Molière!* (by that, David assumed he meant French)."

"So you'll study bio-med?"

"It will be my first major. I may pick up several other degrees along the way. I like to dabble."

Triple accelerated majors? Thought David. "Well, why not? It was Pierre.

"I'll stick to just engineering, thanks."

"Why not?" mused Pierre. "The world needs people to screw things up, I suppose."

David doubted that was simply a slip of the tongue. He retreated to his bedside and started going through his welcome packet. First, he pinned up his pennant featuring the blue and white 'UT' on the wall above his bed. There were several sets of spiritware like that, a coffee mug, a Frisbee, and assorted other junk all featuring the 'UT' logo. Finally, he found the reading list, and quite a list it was.

Had all these been printed as textbooks, they would make some pretty tall stacks. Incidentally, that would jibe with what was happening in his hometown right now. He'd spoken to his dad just yesterday, and Tall Stacks was being held in Cincinnati through the end of the week. The riverboat festival was something they'd always attended together. He missed mom and dad at moments like this.

"Pierre? Do you ever get homesick?"

"If you mean sick of home, then *putain, oui, mon ami.*"

The boy became closed off, and his brow was lowered in anger.

"They've given me quite a reading list," said David, suddenly keen to change the subject.

There was silence.

Turning around, he found Pierre peering under his shoulder.

"Hah! the little Frenchman laughed. These are most remedial. You should have no trouble. I have a list much more suitable for my twelfth-level intellect."

He was really embracing the persona, getting into the role. *I'm* not a monster, thought David, but have I created one?

David thought he had lacked for free time before, but now he was inundated. His military duties combined with scholastic endeavors left little time even for fishing. The others were just as blasted. He could see it on their weary faces when he went to the mess for his meals. But slowly he adjusted. Busy became the new normal. And he learned to savor the few free moments he had.

CHAPTER FIVE

It's Not Easy Being Green

His had been a perfectly ordinary run. The others had toed the line at his command. Doctor Anika had not even batted an eye at his new color scheme. Either she hadn't noticed in the monochromatic vista of Sarpeidon, or she had already been informed by the staff psychologists (much more likely). The latest batch of nanites had a few more enhancements. They multiplied more slowly as a result, but the defect rate was promising thus far. It would require several more runs to prove it statistically, but batch 87 might move the safety mark up into the billions.

Pierre stared once again at the message on his phone.

"As it is now my turn as team leader," said the text, "I declare a holiday. The team will assemble in the commons at oh-six hundred. A team-building exercise will ensue. Beachwear is attire appropriate for this venue. ~Leilani~"

Ridiculous, he thought.

The leadership rotation was for team runs on Sarpeidon, not the first day of liberty they'd been granted in nearly a month. Pierre had planned to use the respite to set up the lab space he'd been granted. He was eager to inspect the new equipment that had been delivered. And now this Hawaiian girl would impose on his free time.

What was she planning, a luau? Or some other silly thing? He had no time for such frivolity. Still, he watched to see how the others responded to the group invitation.

"Roger that," texted Grimes.

This was followed by a string of ridiculous emojis. 'Rainbow, sun, and beach umbrella make Da-veed a happy fella?' He was sure it was meant to be something like that. It was predictable that he chime in first. Maybe Speranza would bow out, giving him leave to do the same. But sadly, no.

"What time will we be back? Oh, hell, alright. I'll see you there."

With a tragic sigh, Pierre thumbed his phone over to verbal mode.

"This is Pierre," he acknowledged. "I accept your invitation."

***

Leilani had a large wicker basket tucked under one arm and a big floppy hat on her head. She wore a breezy kimono above a pair of shorts. Dark sunglasses perched atop her wavy hair completed the ensemble.

Houston in September was still quite warm. It would top twenty degrees if the weather report was properly predictive. Pierre had dressed accordingly in a t-shirt and cargo shorts. His roommate was dressed the same with a shirt that said 'Space Cadet.' That wasn't base issue. Pierre wondered where he had gotten it.

Speranza was the last to arrive, dressed in a spandex one-piece with a large folded towel draped over her shoulders. Its

86

conservative cut did little to hide the alluring figure beneath. Ooh là là, he thought, but did not say.

"So what be the plan?" asked David, as always the first to speak.

"We're going on an outing, an uber's on its way."

"Aye captain," said David, "and what be the point of this outing, lass? Where be we headed, if I might ask?"

That was strange even for David. Leilani's mouth made a little 'O,' then she checked something on her phone and laughed.

"We're heading for a hidden cove, me hardies. I've heard tell it be a proper spot for landlubbers to relax and unwind. I've brought some grub and assorted things to pass away the time."

Speranza rolled her eyes and threw up her hands in dismay.

"*Please* tell me today isn't talk like a pirate day."

"Aye, 'tis the nineteenth day of September, which, by time-honored tradition, be a day in which we all must speak with seafaring erudition. When buccaneer spirits come out to play and guide each tongue in a frolicsome way. And if ye don't honor their nautical wishes, you'll be walking the plank to swim with the fishes! Arrr."

Dubious grammar like 'fishes' aside, Pierre had to hand it to Grimes. Even when talking like a buccaneer, he somehow still managed his rhymes.

***

The fine white sand clung stubbornly to the dampness between his toes as he crunched along. And the whole world had an earthy scent, very like when his roommate went fishing. As each rolling wave approached the beach, its pointed crest would break to form a whitecap. In shallow water, the long-amplitude waves distort, their crests traveling faster than troughs are able. These form a profile with a steep rise and slow fall. As such waves travel into shallower water on a beach, they steepen until breaking occurs.

Knowing all this didn't make them less beautiful. The rhythmic shushing as each wave expired on the shore fell soothingly on his ear. He ignored the stares of those they passed, some merely curious, some disapproving. *Comme-ci, comme-ça*, he was the only green person on the beach.

"Now that my skin is darker," he complained, "the sun, he is very hot."

David and Speranza exchanged a look. "Welcome to *our* world," said Grimes.

"This is the spot. Just up ahead," their fearless leader Leilani said.

Thank goodness all that pirate talk had ended on the drive down. Pierre doubted very much the great French corsairs had ever spoken like that. No. Jean Lafitte would never say, 'Shiver me timbers, me lads.' He would just let his cannons speak for him!

They spread their blankets beneath the blazing sun. East Beach was almost an hour from base, and Leilani had insisted they take the causeway out to the island half. It was a lively scene, but they found a nice spot that wasn't too crowded with people. There were some children playing nearby with their papas, building sandcastles of all shapes and sizes. One enormous sculpture of a mermaid was particularly striking. Why did people put so much effort into an effigy that would be eaten by the next high tide? He guessed it was something to do.

But Pierre wanted to leave his *mark*. It must be something enduring. It was his belief that only one percent of humanity was responsible for all the progress. The other ninety-nine were needed to grow the food and service the automobiles. At the very lowest end were those who made mermaids on the beach. True art should be enduring.

"Oh, fudge-sticks," exclaimed Leilani, rooting through her basket. "I can't find my sunscreen."

"Never fear! *Rhymes* is here!" said David in an overly dramatic voice.

He produced an ivory bottle with a picture of the sun and held it up for everyone's inspection.

"It's a skin care product I bought online, but it promises SPF-1000 protection."

"Skin care product? What is it?" asked Speranza. "It's not going to turn us green or something, is it?"

"Of course not," said David. "It's an anti-aging cream. Serena Mills uses it herself."

"And you would know that *how* Grimes?"

"I saw it in her medicine cabinet the last time she had me stay over."

"You? And Serena Mills? No. Just no."

The sudden squint of her eyes was only partially due to the bright sunlight on the sand.

"She lives in Cincinnati," protested David. "Her son's a friend of mine. Should I call her on my phone to prove I'm on the level?"

"Oh, I thought you were implying..."

"That won't be necessary, cadet," said Leilani, "Hand it over if you please so Pierre can do my back."

She removed her kimono and rolled over onto her stomach. The bikini she wore under it was as pink as Pierre's cheeks would be if it wasn't for the green. She reached around to sweep aside her long and flowing hair, then unstrung the strings of her top.

David thrust the bottle into Pierre's suddenly nerveless hands. He almost dropped the thing. Courage, Pierre, *respire!* he cajoled himself as he dropped to his knees beside her. He started at the nape of her neck and worked his way down to her shoulders, then onward down the gentle thoracic curve.

"Slow down, Pierre, that tickles," she giggled.

"Quit teasing him," said Speranza, reclining beside her. "Hey, what's that on your back?"

89

"You must mean my *pua aloalo*"

On the small of her back, she had a tattoo. It was a five-petaled yellow flower with a red center surrounded by sawtooth leaves. Pierre accessed a botany text he'd once read, paging through it until he found a match. He recited the knowledge it contained.

"The hibiscus represents royalty and communicates power and respect. Native to the Hawaiian Islands, the Hibiscus brackenridgei is endangered due to competition by non-native plants. Yellow hibiscus is often associated with happiness, sunshine, and good luck. Red hibiscus is a symbol of love -- l'amour. Pink stands for friendship and non-romantic love."

"Hey, save some for me, Pierre," said David. "Black people can burn too, you know."

"Me next, Grimes," Speranza declared as Leilani tied up her top.

"I am not certain if green people burn, but I would like to go after her."

"Oh well," grumbled David, "It's probably not as important as it used to be before they fixed that hole in the ozone layer."

Once all were settled and coated in Radiance 2055, Leilani revealed her next surprise. From a stand of surfboards on a rack nearby, she had rented two for the day. She was going to give each of them beginners lessons. Apparently she had some 'surf cred' for her 'chill vibe' and had even won some competitions. When it was David's turn, Pierre watched them with Speranza's binoculars.

David managed to get up on shaky legs, but then wiped out *tout de suite*. It was very satisfying to watch. Now who was walking the plank, *hon hon?*

"Look at Leilani! said Speranza. "That girl can go."

Pierre shifted his view, and there she was, riding the crest of a collapsing wave form. He believed they call it 'shooting the curl.' Who knew his quiet teammate had such a talent?

"It is unfortunate, *mon cher*, that the Big Kahuna she is already taken."

Speranza met his eyes.

"Flowerchild?"

Pierre smiled and nodded.

"Flowerchild. *Oui*."

He didn't get his lab set up, but Pierre felt he benefited, nonetheless. Team building was fun but exhausting. It was a good exhaustion that eased his stress.

***

"It's not fatal, you know."

Pierre kept his face carefully neutral.

"No. It will be worse -- a living death."

NCRS will only require you to adjust to how most people live. We don't even know how long it will be before it affects you."

"But it is coming, doctor. It haunts all of my kind. We never know just when that sword of Damocles will fall."

"Cicero was a pessimist. Neurocognitive Regression Syndrome is not a sword, it's a chance to reset your life. Yes, your mnemonic superiority will fade, but your identity will remain intact."

"Tell that to the other survivors."

Pierre knew the statistics. Inter-uterine enhancement therapy had been discontinued for that very reason. He'd beaten the odds thus far, but had to wonder whether his luck would hold. Among the IUE freaks like himself, there was an abnormally high rate of crib death. The next wave of woe hit in early adolescence. Depression was very common, and the suicide rate was again off the charts as compared to ordinary pre-teens. Pierre never understood this. He was not depressed. The worst he felt was frustration at the idiocy of others with occasional bouts of ennui.

The deciding factor for those who governed society was that sometime prior to adulthood, IUE took back all the gifts it had granted. Memory would fade, intelligence would be reduced, and all the other unusual gifts the treatments had bestowed would become but fading memories, as it were. No. The personal costs didn't justify the temporary benefits. Pierre's kind had been weighed on the scales and found wanting.

"You're brooding again."

"Am I?"

"Are you taking your meds?"

"I don't need antidepressants. I am not depressed. But yes, until I earn my doctorate, I am not qualified to assess my own condition. So, yes, I am following your orders."

"Good. Tell me more about Grimes. Why are you so focused on him?"

"Am I?"

Pierre paused to consider.

"Well, I never shared a room with anyone before."

"Not even with your brother?"

"Luis? No. My parents wouldn't let me anywhere near precious Luis unsupervised."

"And how did that make you feel?"

Hah! Where did he study psychiatry? That sounded like a line straight from a 20th-century sitcom. Still, I should answer, or he will say 'hmm,' cock his head, and make an obscure note on his clipboard. He's probably just playing hangman.

"Not to be trusted? How would it make *you* feel? I was offended and confused, of course."

"Hmm," he said, cocking his head and jotting something down.

"They say you tried to hurt him."

"They say a *lot* of things that are untrue," Pierre returned hotly. I was three! I barely knew beginning calculus! Just because a few of my kind have sociopathic tendencies, it does not mean that all such children should be mistrusted."

Doctor Lemoine made another note.

"That's the second time you've said 'my kind.' Do you see yourself as being apart from the rest of humanity?"

"Am I not?"

"*Are* you a sociopath?"

"Would you believe me if I say no? We can be very convincing, I am told," said Pierre, waggling his eyebrows.

Perhaps a note of honesty here would be better than sarcasm.

"No, doctor. I have a high regard for what is right and what is wrong. Although Luis has made my life more difficult, I honestly wish him well. It is not his fault he was brought into this world in defiance of social norms. No more is it my fault that I was subjected to what amounts to medical experimentation. My parents now have their perfect, normal son, and I am at last out of the picture."

It was considered greedy these days for a couple to have more than one child. Scientific studies had shown that we'd never succeed at healing the environment unless we could reduce the human population. There were exceptions, of course, and all manner of objections on religious grounds. The ban was so far voluntary (except in places like China). But having a brother was frowned upon. It was too bad the Caillet's first child had been such a disappointment. Don't get too attached. He'll likely kill himself in his teens or fall apart shortly after.

"So," said Victor, seeming to accept his answer, "that brings us to my next question. Why are you choosing to remain green?"

Pierre almost laughed.

"When it happened, I was outraged. Many plans ran through my head for things I would do to Grimes. But after facing the group, I found it strangely liberating. I have always tried (and failed) to fit in. Always the smallest in my class. Always the strange little smarty-pants. I tried to be unnoticed and was almost always bored. But standing among the other cadets green as the carriage that brought King Louis low, I quit fretting about being seen as different. I now stand proudly apart, concerned only with meeting my own standards."

"Is that your only reason?"

Pierre grinned.

"Of course not. It is also my perfect revenge against Grimes."

"Come again?"

"As long as I am green, he is powerless to strike at me. Also, he must be wary of my retribution at every moment -- an attack that will never come. The longer it goes on, the more he will be dreading it, suspicious of every little thing. And all I need to do is... nothing."

"Except remain green."

"Of course. But that is a small price to pay."

"You must really hate him."

"*Au contraire*. It is the opposite. David is the first one to show me respect. He engages me as an equal. And I like to do what he tells me to. He always has a plan. His commands feel more like requests. He asks my opinion when he's considering options, and gives credit to others when it's due."

"That's very interesting. We can take it up at our next session. I'm afraid our hour is up."

"*Au revoir, docteur.*"

The man's image shrank until he popped out of existence, leaving Pierre seated on the couch. Pierre felt certain David would make some vile remark about him seeing a 'shrink' if he ever saw that. Dr. Victor Lemoine was a sophisticated program, a little predictable, but pretty good at probing one's soul. And the three sessions a week were far better than the journal they wanted him to keep as an alternative.

Pierre stood from his seat and removed his visor. David was napping nearby.

***

It struck him like a thunderbolt while he was eating in the mess. Cameron was nattering on about yet another success. The satellite team was doing well, surveying the global scene and racking up honors for their diligent efforts.

He was contemplating cell division while reviewing a text from the NCBI. He had once committed it to memory. The National Center for Biotechnology Information was a useful basic resource, despite their tendency to dumb things down for the layman. The textbook was called "Neuroscience 2nd edition" by Purves D, Augustine GJ, Fitzpatrick D, et al.

The section he was rereading began with an interesting statement: "It has long been known that mature, differentiated neurons do not divide (see Chapter 22)." This only made sense. If one's gray matter continued to grow, the skull would need to expand or one's eyeballs might pop out from the pressure.

The summary went on to say that it "didn't follow that all neurons of the adult brain are produced during embryonic development." This was a topic that weighed heavily on Pierre's mind (as it were). The online article made reference to a study conducted way back in the 1980s by Fernando Nottebohm and his associates at Rockefeller University. Nottebohm Laboratory worked on the basic biology of vocal learning in birds. According to Nottebohm, "DNA precursors injected into adult birds could be found subsequently in fully differentiated neurons." Nottebohm's findings opened the door to the possibility that even adult brains retain the ability to integrate newly developed neurons into functional networks.

"Telomeres!" cried Pierre, pounding his fist on the table and causing his teammates to wince.

"What's Kermit on about?" asked Roid Rage from the table's far end.

95

Pierre, absently pushed back his chair and left his tray just laying there. He hustled off, his mind awhirl with exciting new possibilities. Telomeres were the tiny structures tied like shoelaces at the end of the chromosomes. They acted like little fuses, limiting division.

As a child, Pierre had once asked himself why all human beings were doomed to die. *Pourquoi?*, he had asked himself. Why? It didn't always used to be this way. In the very early days, the primitive organisms that existed could grow and reproduce, limited only by the availability of food and their ability to avoid predation. It is possible that the little starfish you find lying on the beach could be older than the existence of all mankind. Possible, but unlikely. Starfish live on average for thirty-five years. They're bound to get eaten or starve, but they never face decrepitude.

Sharks, too, can live extremely long lives, the Greenland shark in particular. They'd evolved very little since the Jurassic period -- an ideal predator of the sea. Individuals may live many centuries, growing very slowly and not even being able to bear young for the first 150 years. Still, they can live as long as five hundred years, not bad for a vertebrate.

Then evolution raised her ugly head and came up with a better scheme instead. Species failed that couldn't adapt. And long-lived species couldn't adapt as quickly. The younger members didn't have a chance unless their elders grew feeble and sickly. The species that tended to survive and succeed were those with shorter lives (so the younger ones could breed). And having our inevitable deaths as her evil intention, Mother Nature afflicted us with a new invention. Telomeres.

All the higher lifeforms have them. They ensure that cell division will progress just so far and no more. Like a ticking time bomb with each division of our cells replacing themselves, we are one step closer to the grave. It is why cloning isn't often used. Clones are born already old, and it is *très* unfair to bring them into being.

No. This could be the solution -- the solution to it all. His idea came into focus and grew as though spreading from a prism. The nanos needed telomeres! (And taking an idea from Mère Nature wouldn't be plagiarism.)

***

What gave David the right to offer *my* assistance? Not that I would have said no if Herr Stentz had asked it of me. Difficult math problems were a pleasure to solve. But here I was again, following David's lead. What was it about him that made me want to do that?

Rope-a-Dope and Roid Rage shared a room only six doors down from theirs. Pierre had never been there before. He'd heard that boys' dorm rooms were unclean and messy but was surprised to find that that was not the case.

"Open up, Roid. Help has arrived," shouted his roommate from the hall.

Rope-a-Dope answered instead.

"He can't hear you, Rhymes. His headset is on."

Sitting beyond MacAllister was the subject of their exchange, seated behind a full set of drums. His sticks were flying across them, but very little sound was produced. Behind him on the QTV, a low-res image of an orange-haired man was strumming a guitar and mouthing silent words. Stepping closer, Pierre noticed the surface of each drum and cymbal was covered by a practice pad. On seeing them enter, Roid Rage set his sticks aside and pulled down his headset to drape around his neck.

"Rhymes! Good of you to come. You too, Brain. Mind if I finish this set?"

Was that a lava lamp behind him on the shelf?

"No problem," said David. "I'm curious to know what you're listening to."

"It's a blast from the past, man. A Bowie track from Space Oddity"

"Space Oddysey?"

"Naw, man. Oddity. Major Tom and all that."

"Give us a listen."

"Will do. Take a seat on the sofa, and I'll crank up the V.

And so they sat and soon were hearing a man singing a duet with himself. In a droning, monotone, he sang of an early astronaut's increasing detachment and isolation:

... You've really made the grade. And the papers want to know whose shirts you wear...

"I hear that, brother," muttered David with a distant look as if he were staring through the screen.

"Yeah, I forgot you went through all that," said Rope-a-Dope. I saw your TV interviews and--"

"Quiet," hissed RR. "He's almost to the bridge."

By this time, Dietrich had his drums uncovered and was keeping time to the steady rhythm. Then he went a little bananas, rocking out on the upbeat, strumming bridge. His sticks flew expertly across their skins, producing a rapid beat intermingled with the clash of cymbals. It was beautifully executed. In six seconds, it was over, and he was back to marking time. The rest of the ballad was *très regrettable*. This major Tom never got home, kind of like Dr. Mendez.

"That was wonderful, Roid," said David, "Maybe you'd better show us this problem now. I probably can't help much, but sometimes just explaining it to someone new helps you to break it down."

"Alright," said RR, setting down his drumsticks and taking up a data wand.

With a tap, Bowie was gone, replaced by a whiteboard covered in multivariable calculus equations and diagrams.

"So, Dope and I --"

"Please don't call me that."

"Rope-a-Dope and I... found this medium-sized asteroid with an iron-rich core. We've secured it with our tugs and are hauling it back toward Mars. Figure we'll give him a new son."

"Son?"

"Yeah. Didn't you know? Phobos and Diemos were named after the two sons that Ares (that's Greek for Mars) had with Aphrodite. They're the smallest moons in our solar system, being just a couple of captured asteroids themselves. So, if we tow this new asteroid into Mars orbit, we figure we'll name it after one of his other brats like Cycnus or Lycaon or something."

Actually, I did know that, thought Pierre. Phobos is the god of fear. The word 'phobia' is derived from him. Diemos is the god of dread.

"Doesn't Mars itself already have a lot of iron?" asked David.

"It does," Rope-a-Dope replied. "But it'll be years before Mars has any kind of decent launch facility. We'll need it to build base camp on Phobos and some other orbital structures."

"All from one tiny asteroid?"

"You bet. The Foundry at L5 has developed some amazing manufacturing techniques available only in zero-G. They can produce light-weight foam metals with a structural strength on par with good steel. But that's beside the point. We've got to get it there first."

"Got it," said David. "Continue."

He always sounds so polite, but that was a command, and the other two just accept it. David probably doesn't even realize he's doing it.

"Anyway, we're trying to bring it in by sail power alone. Tacking against the solar wind, we can slow its orbit of the sun and cause it to fall inward, but on a straight vector (and believe me, there's never a completely straight vector in space), this'll miss Mars by a good five days. He'll be past, and it'll be another 687 days before he swings around again. By that time, RaD and I will be practically graduated."

99

Pierre thought he saw the problem. The math they were using was very advanced, and they had done some good preliminary work. But they needed to increase the rate at which this asteroid fell inward if they wanted to intercept the red planet. Pierre stepped over to Roid Rage and plucked the data wand from his hand.

"Gentlemen, attend."

And to his surprise, they listened.

He proceeded to offer them options that could make up the difference. Although it ran against their grain, they would need to burn some fuel. After he had outlined the best trajectories, he was surprised to see both following his esoteric models attentively. Roid Rage's response in particular was refreshing. The big German looked more like a wrestler than a mathematician, but understanding shone from beneath his heavy brow as he rubbed thoughtfully at his chin.

"We had hoped to save the fuel for breaking maneuvers needed when Lycaon (that's my preference) approaches Mars. We need to ease him into a stable orbit, and he outweighs our tugs by several orders of magnitude."

"How much fuel do you have for this?"

"Enough for a maximum burn for 82 seconds. RaD still has 53."

"Then you have several options, *mon ami*. I'd suggest that the best is a 46-second burn to set Lycaon on the right course."

"But that won't leave us enough for braking and maneuvering at the end point," objected Rope-a-Dope.

"I think you will find it possible using Mars itself. Skip a couple times on the upper atmosphere to reduce delta V before settling it into a polar orbit. Pat Papa a few times on the head, and he will welcome his new son with open arms."

"Genius," said Roid.

"But of course. That is why they call me the Brainiac!"

They shared some drinks to celebrate their new plan. And Carlotta dropped by to join them. They watched a few more videos before calling it a night. All in all, time well spent.

***

Pierre began slotting the boards in place for the first live run. The lab space in the basement of the science wing was sufficient for his needs. It was difficult planning his experiments around his military duties. Some of the other cadets had similar complaints. David could tinker with his devices and solve his equations at any hour he chose. But Pierre was limited to the fourteen hour 'day' cycle. He knew better than to enter the mouse room during their ten-hour night He needed them to breed.

He'd made his proposal regarding the nanos. Dr. van der Meer had received it with scientific objectivity, but he thought she may have been a bit excited when she said she'd put it to her team for review. She hadn't said 'peer review' as he lacked any kind of credentials to make that à propos, but he was fine with that as long as his idea was considered.

He peered around the area (his own little peer review). The equipment gleamed and still had that 'new centrifuge' smell. The area was clean and temperature-controlled. Humidity was set at an even 50%.

The maze was taking shape. Best not to make it too difficult on the first run. Let the mice get used to the idea. The important parts were the colored symbols presented at various turns. IUE mice would likely have good visual recognition. Was it complex enough? If the new mice turned out as he thought they might, he may have to add other challenges.

There would be time for all that later. Geneva hadn't yet approved his proposed course of study, but he expected they soon would. He'd very carefully researched the members of their board. One was even an IUE herself. The scholarly work he hoped to write would be entitled "A Predictive Model for the Onset of NCRS in IUEs". He had already humanized the mice and begun their treatments.

When he looked into the little pink eyes of his subjects, he saw a spark there that gave him pause. Douglas Adams once suggested that it was the white mice who were instructing us and not the other way around. His absurd notions were only meant to entertain. *Pff!* Pan-dimensional beings, indeed.

Preliminaries could begin once the little mamas had birthed their litters. As an outbred strain, this should give him eight or more in each batch--the experimental and the control groups. If he had a surplus, he would inflict one or more with Alzheimer's. He may as well try to cure that condition while he was at it. Many had tried to forestall AD, but they lacked the unique and innovative approach he intended.

Pierre thought he might call his primary AD test subject Pinky (a homage to Warner Brothers' "Pinky and the Brain"). Should he then call his IUE subject Brain? No. He had a much better name for that one, something David had inadvertently suggested.

He snapped the final piece into place and stood back to survey his handiwork. He wished he could run it himself. He could, actually, in a simulation on his treadmill, but he would forego such a pleasure. A scientist must maintain detachment from his test subjects. In his reports, he must remember to refer to his mice only as Subject-A and so forth. He felt a twinge of doubt about what he intended. Could he remain detached?

Science had a long tradition of self-experimentation. But the university would certainly not approve. No more would the space force. Ethics be damned, though. He was running out of time. No. He would have to hide his true purpose under the guise of merely determining when the ax would fall. Did they perhaps already suspect the truth?

What if they reject his proposal? Why should they sponsor research that might help only a shrinking pool of fewer than a hundred among the earth's billions? Well, then he would just have to think of something else. Maybe he could simply shift his focus to AD. Everyone cared about *that*. But time was of the essence. He wished they would just look the other way.

"Have I become a mad scientist?" he muttered aloud. "Not just yet, but it is very likely that I shall."

CHAPTER SIX

The Spy Who (Pretended to) Love Me

Pierre was asleep. It would be a shame to wake the little goblin. He looked so peaceful, lying there. His sleeping face lacked the look of scorn or superior smirk that so often dominated those features. Unfortunately, Reveille was playing out in the quad, and it wouldn't be doing him any favors to let him oversleep.

"*Merde!*" he cried when the pillow landed on his head.

Sitting up, he glared at David, who was already dressed and heading for the door.

September had given way to October as the busy cadets struggled to strike a new balance between their scholastic requirements and their duties on base. Once morning exercise had been accomplished, they headed for the gymnasium. Something new had cropped up on their schedules.

David hadn't spent much time in the gym since arriving here at Ellison. Some of the other cadets were known to use the equipment. It was how Rope-a-Dope had gotten his nickname, having been on the boxing team at his school. He often spent some time working out on the heavy bag. Roid Rage once confided in David that his roomie called the thing Krepkiyzad.

Soon all were present. David hoped he wouldn't have to spar with any of the female cadets. That would be a no-win situation. Hand-to-hand combat didn't sound like fun in any event, but hitting a girl would be almost as distasteful as being beaten up by one. He quieted his thoughts as Senior Cadet Smelt strode into the room.

"Listen up, cadets. I will be your instructor today. So, contrary to military protocol, you are to refer to me as 'sir' for the duration of this session. Is that clear?"

"Sir, yes, sir!"

"In your second year, you will have access to weapons training the same as that granted to airmen, but today, we're here to instruct you in the basics of hand-to-hand combat. Has anyone here had formal training in a martial art?"

Rope-a-Dope and several others raised their hands. David was surprised to see Leilani's was among them.

"Having completed my 18-day Master Instructor Course at the AFCCE, I am eager to impart some of what I have learned about the art of self-defense. Cadets MacAllister and Akana. Enter the circle. Let's see what you've got."

That seemed a little abrupt. He hadn't even given us any rules or anything.

"Limit your strikes to avoid harming one another. I just want to get a sense of your styles. Ready? Begin!"

Rope-a-Dope came out swinging. He was in a boxer's stance, bouncing on the balls of his feet with his fists raised defensively before him. Initially, Flowerchild's stance was much the same. Her movements seemed more fluid, though, somehow. Again, David had the sense that Leilani wasn't moving at all. It was the rest of the world rushing past her.

She blocked several of the jabs R.D. was throwing to test the waters, slapping them aside with her open hands. When he committed to a more forceful strike, she stepped inside his guard and turned it into a grappling match. David was again surprised. R.D. was a head taller and easily had thirty pounds on Flowerchild. Nevertheless, he was soon wincing in pain. Leilani had him in some kind of elbow lock and was using it to guide his motion. He resisted but was soon toppled over by a strike to his chest, the backs of his calves meeting her outstretched leg.

Gideon sounded his whistle when Ropey's shoulders hit the mat.

Leilani smiled down at him, but there was nothing hurtful in it.

"I was lucky you were pulling those punches," she announced. "I doubt I could have even gotten close if you were intent on ringing my bell. Thanks."

She offered him a hand, and he took it. Way to spare a man's pride, thought David.

Pierre didn't stand a chance. Mad Max had him pinned in an instant. Carlotta didn't fare much better. Speranza was soon teaching her what the mat tasted like.

"Grimes," said the instructor. "You're up. You and... Cadet Stentz, I think.

Roid Rage? The big German was built like a gorilla!

It was David's experience that the bigger they are, the harder they could hit you. Nothing for it, he guessed as he entered the circle, but to give it the old accelerated college try.

It turned out Roid Rage wasn't much of a fighter.

He came at David with arms spread wide, like he wanted to give him a hug.

David, not wishing to be the recipient of such affection, ducked and sidestepped like a scared little girl. No, actually, like a bird. It was the one-step drilling method from the Xun trigram phoenix system that he had unconsciously used. He'd done it so many times in Realms that it had become instinct. He had to stop himself from seeking the next move on his non-existent action bar.

Instead, he spun around in the turning-the-back method as Roid stumbled past, grasping nothing. He knew he needed to launch some kind of counter-attack while his opponent was confused. It couldn't be something that would hurt his friend. Knocking him down should be sufficient. But how do you topple a bear?

His eyes flitted once again to where symbols should lie on his HUD. The Dui trigram monkey move, interlocking leg!

But he'd thought about it much too long, giving his opponent time to recover his wits. In a video game, his avatar would already be enacting the maneuver. Instead, he quickly found himself in Dietrich's iron embrace. He tried to squirm free, but only managed to get his face wedged in the German's armpit.

"Try rhyming your way out of this one," muttered Stentz, bearing David to the ground.

On the way down, David rolled hard to his right. Using the Gen trigram bear move of last resort, he struggled to come out on top. But sometimes in life you just had the misfortune to encounter a bigger bear.

"Uncle!" David shouted from underneath the mountain pressing down on him.

"'Uncle' isn't a recognized kiai in this dojo, cadet," Smelt said with a grin before sounding his whistle. "You can get off him now, Stentz."

Yes, please!

After the fights had concluded, the senior cadet shook his head.

"Apart from a few shining standouts, I've got my work cut out for me with you sorry lot. And Grimes, I didn't see you raise your hand when I asked about training. What was that stuff you were doing, *Taekwondo*?"

"Uh. *Baguazhang*, I think."

"You think?"

"Yes, sir. I didn't have any formal training. I learned it in a video game."

The cadets all laughed. They couldn't help it. David laughed too.

"Well, I've made my initial assessments. We will meet here twice a week to learn *real* self-defense. Dismissed."

"Sir, yes, sir!"

As they were headed out, David caught up to Leilani.

"Hey, well done. What was that style you were using?"

She and Speranza stopped and turned.

"It's called *Kapu Ku'ialua*. It used to be a secret art, taught only in times of war. The full form involves weapons, but lua has some hand-to-hand styles used if one is disarmed."

"Well, that's interesting, and it looked really effective. Can you show me a few moves?"

"No. You have to be extremely careful to use it. It's mainly focused on striking at pressure points and breaking bones. The warriors prepare themselves by removing all their hair and covering themselves in coconut oil so opponents can't grab onto them."

"Coconut oil?" muttered Speranza with a raised eyebrow.

Broken bones notwithstanding, David thought he might actually enjoy a round or two of oil wrestling with Leilani, a thought that would definitely never be rendered into sound. Leilani smiled as if sensing his thoughts.

"Don't even *think* about it," she said, confirming this. "I would *hurt* you."

David's brow wrinkled in thought as he watched them walk off.

And here I'd thought Speranza was the scary one.

***

"Do you mind if I change this?" asked David.

He was standing before the QTV. It was in whiteboard mode and covered with Pierre's bizarre equations.

"Go right ahead, *mon ami*, I have seen it already."

Taking up the data wand, David cleared it with a swipe and began making some markings of his own.

"You forgot to limit the first integral. He will yield a second answer if you approach infinity from the left."

Dammit, he was right. In that case, he'd end up with an undetermined outcome. *Again!* David didn't mind the generally helpful kibitzing, but he wished Pierre could do it without the snark.

There was a knock on the door.

"Who is it?" asked Pierre in a singsong voice reminiscent of the three little pigs.

"Is Rhymes in there, Brainiac? It's Rhinemaiden. Open up. There's something he's just *got* to see."

David stalked over to the door and pulled it open.

"What's up R.M.?"

She stepped past him and over toward the QTV.

"Quick, switch to the game show channel. You won't believe what's on."

David fumbled with his data wand, finally managing to engage broadcast mode and flip it to channel 1365. Not being much of a trivia enthusiast, he had to find it by way of the menu channel. You would think the menu channel would be channel 1, but no. It was 2315. The show was on commercial break. No surprise there. Commercials now occupy about three out of every five minutes of airtime unless you paid an outrageous premium for any given channel.

108

After tapping his foot through a long discussion for a new medication guaranteed to keep your dog's fur shiny, the screen let out a trumpeting sound, and the 'Breaking News' banner came spinning into view. The announcer's breathless voice was heard as a chaotic scene played out on the screen. There was a press of people waving signs and shouting in unison while an outnumbered line of policemen sought to hold them back.

"A riot ensued in Cincinnati today where a peaceful demonstration by Humanity First went tragically off its rails."

Cincinnati? David became more interested at once.

"The group became incensed upon meeting a counter demonstration by those advocating AI acceptance. The two groups collided on Ebeneezer Road on Cincinnati's West Side, the unlikely path of both marches. The Green Township police were unable to contain the violence, which spilled over into a local high school. Oak Hills became the unfortunate epicenter of the conflict. All students were evacuated safely.

In related news, leadership in the LGBTQIA2S+ community today weighed in in support of AIs as a fellow marginalized group. Will it one day be LGBTQIA2S+NBI? Tune in to National News channel 2160 to find out at eleven. We now return you to our regularly scheduled program.

"How did you know?" asked David, turning to Rhinemaiden.

"Know what?" she returned.

"David here recently graduated from that school, *mon cher*," Pierre put in with a puzzled look.

"I didn't, said Carlotta. I was talking about what's coming on next. Look. They're about to start."

Strident music started playing in the background as a three-by-three set of glowing boxes came shimmering into view. Shadowy figures lit up one by one, revealing some familiar faces Brady Bunch style.

"Hello everyone," said the host, who was standing between two seated individuals. "I'm Harold Thompson. Welcome to

Hollywood Squares. Our contestants today are Karen and John, and have we got a treat for *you!* Let's say hello to our celebrities in their very first appearance on national television. They're the zodiac creatures from Realms!"

David was stunned. He knew the NBIs were seeking social acceptance, but he never thought they'd lower themselves to this. And nine of them? Who was missing? The dragon (of course), and... ah, the snake and the rat. All the fluffy cute ones were on display. Made sense.

"I thought you'd want to see this, Rhymes," said Carlotta sotto voce. "This revamp is kind of weird. They did the Muppets last week."

"The game is simple, the host continued. "It's just like tic-tac-toe. You may agree or disagree with your celebrity's answer. If you are correct, the square is yours. If you are wrong, though, the square will belong to your opponent. Karen won our coin toss backstage, so pick your first celebrity!"

"I'm going straight for the center square. White Rabbit!" said the frumpy-looking woman.

The rabbit's ears went up. (Canned laughter)

"First question, then," said the host. "According to the Lunar constitution, what activity is not recommended in Lunar gravity?"

"Hmm. Couldn't be that," muttered Tù with a wink. "Or else where would the *little* Loonies come from?" (more canned laughter)

"I'm going to say it's --"

"We pause here for word from our sponsors. Stay tuned. Your program will resume after these brief messages."

Brief my elbow! thought David as he stared at the 'Go Ad Free' button in the corner of the screen. Astonished as he was by the dignified NBIs' participation in such inane Hollywood hokum, he was far more eager to follow up on the recent attack near his home. While the QTV nattered on about the virtues of future timeshares on L5, David thanked Carlotta, excused himself, and stepped out into the hallway.

"Bartholomew, call Jason," he said to his phone.

Jason picked up on the third ring.

"David," I take it you heard?"

"I did. Is everyone okay?"

"Yeah, bro. Great Scott herded us all out the back before they broke through the lockdown. By the time the police reinforcements arrived to break it up, I was home safe and sound. They scattered every which way to avoid arrest. Some even cut through my backyard, but Lucy turned the sprinklers on and barked like a vicious pack of dogs."

"She's a good program to have on your side, I guess. What the hell were the HF haters doing out there in the suburbs anyway?"

"Dude, no one knows. It isn't their usual haunt."

"Did they do much damage?"

"I didn't think so at first. They were tossing Mr. Highlander's big paper mache head around like a beach ball and spray-painting their slogans all over the place. I only found out later that they wrecked the VR lab."

"No!"

"'Fraid so," Jason lamented. "I hear it was almost a total loss."

"Damned Luddites," muttered David.

"Hey. Sorry to pull the plug, but I gotta cut this short. Mom's calling."

"No problem, Jase. Just wanted to make sure you were okay. Talk to you soon."

And with that, he thumbed the button to terminate the call.

Returning to his room, David found the barrage of advertisements were still underway. Pierre was keeping Carlotta entertained with some kind of story that halted abruptly when

David came into sight. Pierre had been pointing at David's dresser and grinning sardonically. He reminded himself to give that area another sweep before using anything.

"I think I've seen enough of this. I hope you don't mind," said David with a questioning gaze at Carlotta.

"No problem, Rhymes. I've got it recording for playback in my room. My D.A. is cutting out the commercial breaks. I want to study each personality without interruption."

That made sense, David thought. But for each attempt to bypass an ad, the sponsors seemed to have a counter. He wouldn't put it past them to slip in some sponsored content. Shows like H.S. would have their announcer go on and on about the prizes contestants could win, spewing what amounted to commercials within the program. Sometimes, the celebrities themselves would mention specific brands in their answers. That had to be by design. Sigh. It was enough to put him straight off watching TV altogether.

Just as Carlotta was making to leave, there was another knock on the door.

"Packages," came a muffled female voice from the hall.

David guessed room 242 was the place to be today.

"Is that you, Mags? Come on in, it's open."

The door swung inward to reveal a smiling face -- the last one he expected.

***

Well, alright, perhaps not the very last one. There were many other faces he would have less expectation of encountering. Hitler, for example, would be much lower on his list. But nonetheless, it was a shock to see Jessica here when the last he'd heard she was back in Australia. Moreover, she was dressed in business casual attire complete with sensible shoes and pulling a handcart stacked high with cardboard boxes.

She was also sporting a name tag David didn't bother to read. There was no mistaking the angelic face that caused a man's heart to race by its mere proximity. His mind was drawn back to the time he'd seen her character soaring through the sky with her golden tresses waving like a banner in the wind as she loosed her arrows at the rampaging dragon. Her equally lovely actual locks were, at present, drawn back in a tidy bun.

"Jess?"

Her smile broadened, spreading warmth over the entire room.

"David? I heard you were staying here! But I'm Allison, silly. Jessica was just my character in the game."

Abandoning her cart, she stepped swiftly into the room and gave him a very unprofessional hug. And where was her Australian accent? She sounded just like some Midwestern girl (and a dizzy one at that).

"It seems like ages since we were last in Realms, sweetie," she said with an adorable pout. "I hear they won't let us play it here on base."

She stepped back and began sizing him up. David noticed that her name tag read 'Allison Winter.' That was the alias she had used during her brief stint at modeling clothing under Serena Mills' tutelage.

"Davey and I were high school sweethearts," she declared to the room at large.

Davey?

"Did you hear about the riot at Oak Hills? It's a wonder no one was hurt! Look at you, all stiff and military. I swear, you must be half a foot taller than when we graduated. Who are your friends? And is that one... green?"

Now that he knew the game, David was eager to play. He was sure Jess would explain it to him once they were in private.

"Allie, this is Carlotta. We call her Rhinemaiden around here. And yes, my roommate, Pierre, is green. (He's from France)."

"I assure you, madam, those two facts are entirely unrelated. I am Pierre Caillat. They call me the Brainiac, an obvious but appropriate nickname. Enchanté mademoiselle."

He took her offered hand, bent at the waist, and kissed it.

"So, Allie, I hate to question a happy reunion, but what brings you to our door?"

"I'm going to be staying here. Isn't that great! You and I will *totally* need to catch up on old times. Oh. I almost forgot. The packages."

"Yeah, what are those?"

"This being my first day, I'm not sure, but they're heavier than sin! Let's crack one open and see what you've got. Mind if I stay to have a peek?"

David helped her roll the cart into the room, quite certain she needed no such help. She ran a letter-opener-looking thing along the seam to part the tape on the topmost box. Inside was a stack of books. They weren't engineering texts, as he had first supposed. They were identical copies bearing the title "How I Saved the Man in the Moon--Confessions of a Gritter To Be" by David Grimes.

Oh good lord, no. Was it out already? He was supposed to have had the right of approval on the proofs. Jason had some serious explaining to do. These weren't proofs. By the look of it, there were more than a hundred copies here.

Pierre grinned and snatched one up. He and Carlotta had been huddled around for the unveiling.

"Oooh. Can I have one?" cooed Rhinemaiden.

"I... guess."

Pierre was rapidly paging through the copy he'd nabbed and snickering from time to time. It must be bad. As David's agent, Jason got ten percent of the profit from this venture. Unfortunately, there was no way to make him accept ten percent of the embarrassment it might cause. He may as well go on Hollywood Squares himself.

David was starting to wish it *had* been Hitler.

***

"...so on our first day, I told Davey here I was from Australia, and he totally believed me!"

She was sitting very close to him in the mess, uncomfortably so if he didn't know it was all just an act. It was a possessive posture, leaning in and running a finger over his forearm as she entertained the other cadets with her anecdotes. Jessica had never attended Oak Hills.

He had to hand it to her on her cover, though. Her American accent was believable, almost unbelievably so. But the tale she was weaving for his friends would preempt any suspicion if she had a lapse. They would just think she was teasing him.

"Do it again, Miss Winter," said Rope-a-Dope. "Say something from down under."

"Alright," she giggled. "This here chook is a mite undercooked, cobber. What say you and I go back to your room and pash?"

She fluttered her eyelashes seductively, then broke out in a great big grin. There was hooting and applause from the men at the table's end, but not everyone seemed so amused. Speranza, in particular, was making a doubtful face, as though she were reserving judgment.

"Being from Dundee myself, miss (the one in Scotland, that is), I must say you do that accent pretty well."

"You've got some dardy mates here, Davey. But I need to get back to my business. We can't all be rocket scientists. Someone's got to do the hard yakka."

With a cheeky wink, she rose and departed amid a flurry of disappointed smiles and mumbled farewells.

David would have thought a spy would be less flamboyant, someone who would fade into the crowd. But with Jessica's looks, that was probably impossible. She'd obviously decided to take it in another direction, making a big splash immediately and being accessible so everyone would buy her cover and cease to wonder about her. She was obviously counting on David to confirm her backstory.

"Hey Rhymes," said Carlotta, holding up his book and smirking. "I'm finding this a fascinating read. Will you sign my copy? Pretty please, Davey, with applesauce on top?"

The others all laughed. Apparently, an anecdote early on in the book described in detail David's love of pancakes smothered in maple syrup and applesauce. The ghostwriter Jason had hired had left no secrets out when digging into David's past. Mom and Dad must have thoroughly ratted him out. But no one had ever called him Davey, not even his parents. That was all Jessica's doing. He'd better start thinking of her as Allison now, he thought.

He accepted the book and the pen Rhinemaiden soon produced. It was a space pen, designed to write even upside down or in zero-G environments. It brought to mind that old myth that NASA had invested millions to develop it while the Soviets simply gave their Cosmonauts pencils. It was untrue, of course, but David felt there was still a lesson in there somewhere.

"Make it out to: 'Rhinemaiden, a fellow Gritter-to-be.'"

David grimaced and started signing the book he didn't write.

"Make mine out to: 'Roid Rage, who totally kicked my ass'"

Another book thumped down on the table before him. Soon there was a stack of them, and the cadets all clustered around. Had everyone started reading this thing but him? Thanks for the heads-up, Jason. I owe you one for this, bro.

After he'd finished at the mess, David headed back toward his room. His life was getting complicated again. Instead of simply going with the flow, it was time to make a mental list.

Priority One: Read the memoirs I supposedly wrote.

Priority Two: Get 'Allison' alone and find out what the heck this was all about.

Priority Three: Fire Jason as my agent. Well, maybe not that, but give him a stern talking to.

Priority Four: Examine my room for traps. Who knows what mischief Pierre had gotten up to while I was distracted?

Priority Five: Start my design project for Aerospace. It'll be worth fifty percent of my grade.

Priority Six: Improve at hand-to-hand.

Oh, and, Priority Seven: Do laundry. He was starting to get a little ripe. He raised his arm and gave his pit a quick sniff. Maybe he'd better move that last one up the list. Toilet water could only accomplish so much.

***

The first-floor laundry smelled of soaps and softeners and those little scented fabric strips they used in the dryers. The sharp tang of bleach gave the place an antiseptic feel as well. The click of shirt buttons striking the rotating cylinders made random staccato clicks as they tumbled. These stood out above the other muffled thumps and the hum of whirring motors from the washing machines.

David was distracted by his thoughts as he headed to the back. The automatic lights flickered on. It was warm and stuffy as compared to most any other spot on base. He retrieved a plastic basket from the racks above and set it atop the frontloader.

He heard laughter from the hall. Ignoring it and reaching in, he felt the warm fabric of the recently finished load. As the voices grew louder, he looked over at the door where two cadets were entering. It was Cameron and Simon (Photobug and Claptrap), the two satellite watchers.

",,, So, I said to Krepkiyzad, 'Yes, sir! We *are* the mighty watchful eye!'"

Cameron started to laugh again, but suddenly turned her scrutiny David's way.

"Finding anything interesting in there, Rhymes?"

David looked down at the handful of delicates he was clutching. Dangling from the balled-up fabric he gripped was a woman's lacy bra. Other unmentionables in the tangle had a silky feel unlike anything David owned.

"Uh, I thought this was *my* machine."

"I'm sure it's only something innocent like that," said Cameron with a sidelong glance at Simon.

Simon snorted, but held his tongue.

"It is," said David, tossing the evidence back into the dryer. "*Totally* innocent."

"Methinks the lad doth protest too much," said Simon with a smile. "I need to get back to the Icarus, Bug. Will you be okay dealing with this panty-sniffer on your own?"

"Go on ahead. I'll fluff and fold and join you there when I'm done. I'm sure he's harmless. His mother says he doesn't have very many friends."

That *book* again, thought David. Will I ever live it down?

After Simon departed, Cameron approached, still wearing a wicked grin, and shouldered him aside.

"*You're* things are over there. I put them in a basket over at the folding table. Needed the dryer."

"Uh. Okay. Um, thanks?"

"No problem."

As the two stood side by side at the folding table, David slowly regained his wits.

"So, Rhymes, that high-school sweetheart of yours. Are you two still, um..."

"Allison? Well, it's complicated."

More than you know. Probably even more than I know.

"So, un-complicate it. Are you or aren't you? Inquiring cadets want to know."

"I don't see where it's any business of yours."

"I'll give you tit for tat."

She happened to be folding that lacy brassier when she said this. Could that be by design?

"Are we being figurative here?" asked David, smoothing out the legs of his tracksuit.

She colored. So, not deliberate then.

"I mean, I'll tell you who the cadets are who wish to know," she returned in a choked whisper.

That was interesting.

"I won't go into detail regarding our prior relationship. A gentleman doesn't kiss and tell. Allie and I are just good friends now. Let's leave it at that."

There. That was the truth and would give Jessica some leeway on her cover story. It was hard to be embroiled in espionage. He felt that saying the wrong thing could jeopardize his friend's situation.

"Too bad for *you*. She's a hottie," she harumphed. "But good for the gals hoping to bat cleanup. My roommate, Carlotta, is one. I'm not sure exactly why, but she favors you."

"Oh, yeah?"

"Your teammate, Speranza's the other one. She doesn't say anything overt, but she practically growls when any other woman gets too near you. I can see it in her eyes."

"Maybe she's just being protective."

"Grow up, Grimes."

At that, she hefted her basket of folded laundry and headed out the door. David started balling up the socks he had matched.

Speranza?

***

He shifted the laundry basket to balance precariously between his left arm and hip, then swiped his ident card across the sensor, which emitted a satisfying click. Shoving the door inward, he entered. Their room was tidy as always. Pierre insisted on it, and David didn't mind. Though not a neat freak himself, he enjoyed the uncluttered environment.

And speak of the devil, there was his little green friend perched on the seat of his treadie, mouthing silent words. You didn't have to fully vocalize on the new Freemotion 17s. They had a sensor collar that fit snugly around one's neck to capture sub-vocalizations. Pierre must be enjoying some restful simulation to be reclining so. But, despite his visor's headset, David knew he could still hear noises in the room.

David padded silently over to his chest of drawers and began stowing his fresh, clean outfits. He should be good for another week or so. But Jess was coming over, and he was eager to get her alone.

"Wrap it up, Lima bean. You said you'd be out by noon."

He was certain Pierre had heard him, though he gave no outward sign. A few minutes later, the visor came off and the seat of his treadmill retracted. David rooted through his drawer until he found a necktie, the blue one, one of two he owned.

"Going formal today, *mon ami*?"

"Nope. It's for the doorknob."

"Ah. I thought it might be for your *rendezvous* with the beautiful Allison. But explain to me why you are using your tie to decorate the *poignée de porte*?

"It's a time honored tradition among roommates. You are not to enter when the flag is flying."

"Ah, I see. Removal of *la cravate*, is a signal for when the *tête-à-tête* she is over."

"Yes. That's the gist. Now scat!" said David, tightening the tie on the knob.

Taking up his laptop, Pierre ambled out into the hall, his eyes lingering on the blue strip of cloth.

"Lucky bastard," he muttered.

Peering after him, David said, "I'll have you know that my parents were happily married for four years before they stopped taking the anti-fertility treatments."

It wasn't much of a parting shot, but he knew Pierre had some family issues and wanted to avoid answering that one in kind.

By the time she arrived, David was feeling pretty pent-up. Maybe now he would get some answers. Why was she here, of all places? What was she after, and how did he fit in? Who had recruited her? Who or what was the mysterious organization *not known* as C.A.G.E.?

There came a gentle tapping on the door (only this, and nothing more, he automatically added). He peeped through the peephole to confirm it was she, then eased the door open, adopting a sheepish smile. He waved her in, and she brushed right past after giving him a peck on the cheek. He knew it was an act, but nevertheless, he felt his ears burning and his knees got weak.

"Alone at last," said Jess, panning her gaze around the room. "Fancy a slow dance, stud?"

Not waiting for his answer, she withdrew her phone from her pocket and rested it on his nightstand. Leaning over, she selected some settings. A mellow 40's tune began to play. Now that they were alone, David thought they were through with these games. He'd never danced with Jessica before, but had nothing against it in principle.

Allison crossed back over to him, draped her arms over his shoulders, and drew him close. Now they were practically nose to nose.

"It's a scrambler app, mate. It makes godawful screechy feedback for anyone listening in. They can likely still see us but can't hear what we're saying now. Smile and nod your head like we're whispering sweet nothings."

The nod was fake, but his smile was genuine. He laughed like she had just said something funny.

"I know you're working for CAGE now, Allie," he whispered in her ear as they swayed to the music's call. "What does that stand for, anyway?"

Her face showed no reaction, but she stiffened in his arms. With their bodies pressed together, the reaction was hard to miss. It struck him that Allie was no longer wearing her corset, an orthopedic appliance she had worn after her surgery.

"It stands for justice. It stands for peace. Where are you getting your intel? That's a fair dinkum more than I thought you'd know," she hissed through a pleasant smile.

"The Jade Empress."

"That would explain it," she said, relaxing some, "but I thought she wasn't talking to anybody."

"She isn't. Shǔ ratted her out."

Her sudden giggle sent waves of ecstasy shivering up his spine and threatened to give him naughty thoughts. Jess released him briefly, spinning lightly away and returning to press up against him. Her movements were so natural. It was hard to believe that she had been a paraplegic until just five short months ago.

"I'm going to need a favor from you, cobber. I've infiltrated H.F. But they've given me a test of loyalty to move up in their ranks. I need to get them a passcode for one of the active shepherd machines. I told my handler I could leverage my relationship with you to get it. Can you help me out?"

David could hardly believe his ears. Was this the same girl who had advised him to stick to his principles even in a video game? He kept the false smile on his lips, but the ends had gotten quite heavy.

"You realize that would violate my oath," he said, favoring her with a dip.

"Yeah, but we've got to find out who the traitors are within the GSF. There's a mole among ya and its putting the whole operation at risk. If we play by the rules, we'll never nail the shonky blokes."

She said it with a smile, but he could hear the simmering anger that welled up from beneath.

"I'm afraid my answer has to be no."

She looked stricken for a moment, a moment that seared his soul. He didn't have a photographic memory like Pierre, but that pleading look of astonishment would stay with him forever. A moment that would last a lifetime, and then her smile was back.

"Alright, yank. I suppose I'll just have to come at it from some other direction."

She stretched her arms when the music stopped.

"Oh. I almost forgot," said Allie in her ditsy Midwestern dialect. "That book you gave me is a misprint. I hope you can give me another. Remind me before I have to leave."

Then, the next tune started, and Jessica was back, pulling him in for round two.

"Don't blame Jason for printing all those books. The agency pressured him to do that. We needed to make sure there were heaps of them laying around to confuse anyone who might try to break our code."

"Code?"

"Deadset. A book code is an old way to pass messages. You and I will be the only ones with the right copies. The UPC is slightly different from all the others. That's how you'll know their the dinky-di."

David didn't think they would even need a code if they just all spoke Australian English.

"How will that work, exactly?"

"There's a tab on the UTogether website that posts team scores for the Varsity Blues."

"I've seen it," said David, laughing to cover for his sudden frown, as if he'd just gotten a joke.

"Certain numbers are important. I'll show you once it's all set up. They'll guide you to a page number, a line, and a specific word. When you put the words together, they --"

"Form a message. I see. And I suppose I'll have some way to reply."

"Yes. But you'll mainly just be acknowledging with your posts. Something like, 'Way to go Johnson, that's 3 wins for the Blue.'"

"Ingenious."

"Oh, and you'll need to start playing Wordle too -- the one in the New York Times."

David sighed inwardly. As if he didn't have enough things going on.

"I really am pleased to see you again, yank. I've missed my old mates from the game. This way we can keep in touch once I'm gone from here. A spy's life is a lonely road. You never know where it'll take you, and friends are a luxury few can afford."

The music came to a stop again, and she ended the dance with a flourish. She curtsied low, and he gave her a bow in return. Allie went over to the boxes, selecting two books from within.

"Make it out to Allison... with love," she said with a grin.

As he was doing so, she wandered over to his well-made bed and took out a tiny vial.

"Oops," she said facetiously, spilling some with a smile. "Don't forget to rumple your Manchesters so it looks like we had a proper romp."

He saw her to the door, and they parted with a kiss. It was an Aussie kiss, full on the parted lips. The kind of kiss people avoided since COVID-4 had arrived on the scene. But David didn't care if it bit him; it was worth a few trips to the latrine.

"Bye Davey. Call me."

After she departed, David messed up his neatly made bed just as Jessica had suggested. He was glad she wasn't, at least thus far, *that* kind of 'undercover' agent. But he messed it up a little more to uphold her reputation. Besides, it would keep his roommate green with envy.

***

Houston in October still featured balmy weather, with daytime highs rising up into the eighties (or the upper twenties as Pierre or Eddings might say). David still couldn't figure out why they called it the English system when England itself had moved on. He'd better get used to the metric system because it was the international standard. None of the equations he was mastering featured inches or miles, and centigrade now rules the thermometer.

They stood assembled in the yard, facing the flagpoles in the early, pre-dawn light. Reveille would be a special ceremony today to honor the final transmission of Dr. Mendez. In front of her statue, large speakers had been rolled out, and Max stood ready with his bugle. Roid Rage had joined him holding a single drum.

And there stood Eddings, silently waiting for the ceremony to commence. His full uniform was spotless. He even wore white gloves, as did all the military personnel. He finally chose his moment to mount the platform and address them.

"Today, as you all know, we are gathered to honor the memory of one who dared to go where none had flown before. She sought to expand the boundaries of all humankind and succeeded in September of 2039. Though it's been sixteen years, it seems like only yesterday when the first human landed on Mars, joining such worthies as Ferdinand Magellan, Amelia Earhart, Yuri Gagarin, and Neil Armstrong, to name but a few.

"Her name was Dr. Evelyn Louisa Mendez, Evvie-Lou to her friends. It's a name that will be forever etched in our hearts.

"She arrived at the edge of the unknown, not with the guarantee of success but with a hope that others might follow. Hope. That ember of defiance that burns in every human breast and calls on us to challenge the unknown. But such advances often come with sacrifices, and some who are called are willing to pay the price for all of our dreams, embodying the very spirit of exploration.

"And though her journey ended there on the swirling sands of Cydonia Mensae, her legend will echo down the corridors of time, her hope a beacon to guide us on. We meet, not on the anniversary of her achievement, but to hear her final words of wisdom to the world.

"Lincoln may have said it best. If I might paraphrase: It is for us the living, rather, to be dedicated here to the unfinished work she so nobly advanced. It is rather for us to be here dedicated to the great task remaining before us; that from her sacrifice we take increased devotion to the great cause of exploration for which she gave the last full measure of devotion.

"We of the space force will honor her by continuing to seek, to strive, and to explore. Let us now all humbly bow our heads as we hear from the great lady herself."

There was a feedback sound from the speakers, which the sound technician soon got under control. A hiss of static followed that clarified with a click. The voice that David heard next slurred like that of a drunkard.

"Journal entry 21. This may be my last. I know I said that yesterday, but I managed to scrounge up some spare oxygen from the rover's pneumatic systems. Being stranded here for these last three weeks has given me plenty of time to think. In that time, I've often wished I had died in that crash landing. Quick, easy, (and if not painless, see quick).

"But since then I've changed my mind. The pause has given me time to reflect on my life. It was a good one for the most part. I made some friends, had a few kids, and now this one here for the history books. I feel a bit lightheaded, and my head aches all the time now. And if I ramble on and talk a bit of nonsense, don't take it for wisdom. More likely, it's the hypoxia setting in.

"What a punch in the gut it was stepping down my capsule's ladder. I was so proud to be the one who got here first.

But then to see my fuel all leaking out onto the sand. Can you all do me a favor? One day, when you get here, can you take what's left of that estupido rock that ruptured my tank and carve me a tombstone from it?

"Anyway, I'm glad to have had the extra time to stare death straight in his hollow, empty eye sockets. You can't ever escape his bony ass entirely, but when you're in my position, you get to smile right back at him for a while. Heh heh heh. Cough. Cough!

Long silence.

"So, this may be my last transmission. Did I say that already? Well, this time I really mean it. You ever read Huckleberry Finn? I mean the real one, before they banned it. He talks about sand and grit. Huck says: "She had the grit to pray for Judus if she took the notion -- there warn't no backdown to her, I judge. You may say what you want to, but in my opinion she had more sand in her than any girl I ever see; in my opinion she was just full of sand." I like to think that one day they'll say something like that about me.

"So I'm holding on until the bitter end and then some, glad for each moment the fates have decreed. Sand. Sand everywhere I look. The red sand of Mars gets into everything. There's sand aplenty, but I like to think that *I* brought the grit. Gritter, they'll call me--that gritter gal."

Silence.

Static.

Silence.

Drumroll.

Bugle.

And as the bugler bugled -- taps, not reveille. The flags unfurled and started up their poles. As the sorrowful notes sounded, the grand banner of Earth climbed slowly to the top with old glory beside her all the way. But the space force flag was quite a different matter. It halted at half-mast to honor the day.

128

CHAPTER SEVEN

The First Rule of Fight Club

"That was a stirring ceremony, Eddie, nicely done. Lincoln? Have you gone native, living among all these yanks?"

"What can I say? The man had a way with words."

"The live musicians were a nice touch."

"No doing of mine, Colonel. Cadets Trudeau and Stentz took up those instruments on their own."

"Hmm. Yes. It's quite an eclectic assortment of geniuses in this batch. Musical talent often walks hand in hand with mathematics. Do you think any will opt for the colony mission?"

"Most if not all I expect. Their psych profiles indicate a high likelihood in any event. But you didn't come here just for an update on my cadets. You could have gotten that over the comms or through normal channels. Have a seat and tell me what's on your mind."

"I prefer to stand, actually."

The news must not be good, thought Eddings. He'd known Colonel Charles Percival Haversett since they were students back at UTC, taking their specialist sixth forms. He'd just been Charlie then. And while Eddings had passed with flying colours, earning entry into the military academy. Charlie had mysteriously gone missing. It was only years later he'd discovered his friend had been recruited by the GSIC, the secretive intelligence wing of their illustrious branch.

The colonel moved to the window and now stood with his back to Eddings, peering out over the quad.

"What I am about to tell you is highly classified. But I need your help with a matter."

That was surprising. Eddings preferred to operate with plausible deniability. He wished he had a tumbler of Bombay Sapphire to sooth his nerves and stiffen his resolve. But alas, such an indulgence would have to wait until later. A base commander's office was no place for it.

"There has been a breach of your security. A recent hire of yours is a spy. Don't look so startled. Steady, Eddie. The girl is actually one of ours, playing a part for the global good."

Relief washed across the commander's face. The use of his old nickname, 'Steady Eddie,' might be some kind of signal.

"I... see."

"Do you?"

He paused.

"We've long known that there are traitors in our ranks. Some of them must be either very well placed or extremely high up in the chain of command. We're trying out a new agent, recently and very secretly recruited. The girl is very promising, but her skills are as yet, shall we say, underdeveloped?"

"How so?"

"She has successfully been able to infiltrate the lower ranks of a group calling itself Humanity First. The various HF groups are a rowdy and undisciplined lot, more a bunch of mischief makers than true saboteurs. They are regularly sacrificed and used as a front by their mysterious hidden masters."

"How does this concern *me*?"

"The girl's current target is Cadet Grimes. She needs to obtain some information from him. You need not know just what. Unfortunately, the young lady is a failed Mata Hari. Grimes is proving too straight-laced to be manipulated. Commendable, but unfortunate."

"Again. What do you want me to do about it? I can't command him to violate his oath, not and be true to my own."

Another pause.

"Do you remember Professor Castaldi from back in senior year?"

"Of course. Italian bloke. Used to give detentions for paper wad fights."

"Like the good professor, we want you to give Grimes a suppository to cure him of his reticence."

Rectal medicine? What on Earth... Of course, 'Innuendo.'

"Needless to say, this conversation never happened."

"Alright, but while we're spilling state secrets, why the urgency?"

The colonel sighed and returned to take a seat after all. He removed his hat, the one with the sphinx emblem, ran a hand through his hair, and sighed.

"Between you and me, things are getting spooky out there, Ed. First the freighter, then the bank. Someone's targeting our most well-guarded assets. And they seem to know exactly where to hit."

"I heard there were only automobile parts on that freighter."

"You know better, though, right?"

Eddings glanced around his office.

"Are you sure we're secure?"

"Very. You can say what's on your mind."

"I gleaned through unofficial channels that the H.M.S. Bombay was actually carrying Icarus parts when it was hijacked. Proprietary models which were not recovered."

"I see you still keep your ear to the ground, or the sea in this case. You are correct. It'll do them little good without the proper chips. Those were to be shipped separately for the final assembly."

"*Were* to be?"

"Yes. The safety deposit box they were kept in was hit later in the same week. We caught a break there, actually. The robbers, a front group, were all taken into custody by the Royal Thai Police before the handoff could be made. The Sentinel Core Processors were recovered and are all accounted for. The robbery was foiled by a couple of your own cadets, Truwella and Brewster. I put those two in for commendation myself."

"Good then."

"You would think. But yesterday's riot in Cincinnati was unexpected, though we *should* have expected it. The VR lab at Oak Hills had a core, the one installed for Grimes' assessment. It wasn't military grade or anything, but much of the firmware is compatible. With a little clever reverse engineering, our technical people tell me our enemies could arrive at something workable."

"That's ghastly news."

"So, you see, we're very concerned. My orders came down from the unholy SOB himself."

"The general?"

"Yes. *The* general. Word is, he's even asked the NBIs to poke around and see what they can dig up."

132

"Isn't that a bit risky?"

"One would think. The Jade Empress may have her own agenda, but our interests align in this instance. Who would have better reason to thwart HF in whatever they have planned? No, this is bigger than all of us, Eddie. Do whatever you can to get Grimes to cooperate."

Eddings sat in his silent office, pondering the matter long after his visitor had departed. Then he stood and straightened his uniform jacket. He'd head for the O-Club. Funny, that. As the only officer present on base, it was more like his private drinking den. He could continue brooding on the matter there while enjoying that tumbler of Bombay Sapphire. Or perhaps even two. Snatching up his phone, he summoned his digital assistant.

"Kingsley."

"Yes, commander?"

"Pull up Cadet Grimes' schedule. Summon him to a meeting in my office at his next available break this afternoon."

"What shall I say is the reason?"

"Make something up."

"Yes, commander. I will see to it."

***

My course was set. I was going to the moon! At least my soul would be going. My best friend Jason pulled up in his car. It was a sleek, black limo, signaling the style and flair of its operator. Yeah, that Jason Mills was one cool cat! He pulled into the driveway where my parents and I were waiting, anxious about my first lunar mission. Little did I know the heartbreak that would soon eclipse the endeavor. A solar storm was brewing, and a grim fate was soon to befall humanity ...

What drivel.

David now knew he should have just written it himself. And that last passage told him that Jason must have had a hand in its editing.

Cool cat? Give me a break.

As he lay on his bed halfway through the book that had brought him such grief, he was interrupted by his roommate's laugh. It was more a rhythmic hissing than proper laughter. It was good to hear Pierre let loose. He didn't used to do that much. But suspicion that he might be the subject of his roommate's sudden mood caused David to glance over in annoyance.

"What?"

"I didn't say anything. Your face is *très amusant* when you read of your own exploits. I will be silent and let you read on. But I do have a question for *le grand héros*."

David marked the page, sighed, and sat up. "Shoot."

Pierre made a finger gun and fired it at the book.

"Why is the UPC on your copy different from all the others?"

David struggled not to show a reaction. It was like trying not to think of an elephant someone mentioned.

"Oh, um, this one's an author's copy, he explained, shrugging."

It was true enough. They were all author's copies. But even though, as such, they were discounted in price, they still had the same UPC. Would Pierre buy it?

"Ah. Then I am satisfied."

David relaxed.

"I am satisfied my roommate is a liar."

"No. It really *is* an author's copy."

"Then you are being *déloyal*. Lies of omission are still lies, Daveed. Technicalities aside, you are giving me crap of the cow."

Crap of the--oh. He was calling bullshit.

David's shoulders slumped at the rebuke. The little Frenchie had him dead to rights.

"Alright, Pierre," he sighed. "You got me. But I can't tell you any more about it. Promise me one thing. I know you're going to pay me back for the... green thing. But I'm begging you; don't do anything to this book. It's important I have access to it."

Pierre leveled his gaze at David, who sat in a submissive posture. He bunched his lips and seemed to ponder the matter for a moment.

"*Oui*. I agree. We have an *accord, mon ami*."

David's phone chose that moment to chime that a message was incoming. He set the book aside and snaked the phone out of his pocket.

[**Schedule Change:** David Grimes is to present himself at WO Eddings' office at 02:00. **Topic:** Proper Comportment and Decorum in the Base's Laundry Facilities]

Well, why the hell not?

***

Pierre crept down the stairs, headed for his basement lair.

David was acting suspiciously. What was in that book? He was certain it had something to do with the mysterious girl from his past. He had looked up this Allison Winter. Her social media was banal. It seemed credible at first glance, but it didn't stand up to scrutiny. Tiny details and discrepancies had caused him to dig deeper.

He remembered looking through David's yearbook to size up the competition. This was back when Pierre was operating Tango 4 for Krepkiyzad. He knew for a certainty that no Allison Winter had been in that graduating class. Who could forget so stunning a beauty even on a bad picture day? Not Pierre. He never forgot anything.

He even brought up the online yearbook yesterday just to make for certain, and voilà! She was there. The only true reference he found for her from about that time and place was a series of photographs modeling designer clothes. Flipping through all of them, he found it. The head shot from one of the designer outfits exactly matched the girl's faux-yearbook picture. There could be no doubt. The girl was not who she claimed to be.

As Pierre walked down the empty hallway, pondering this deception, the lights flickered on one by one. Why did they flicker? he wondered. They must be using the new, more environmentally friendly bulbs. It was ridiculous. The old LED bulbs had been 90% efficient and performed quite adequately. Just because the new quantum dot QLEDs eked out an additional 1% was no reason to put up with this insufferable flicker-start. Ah well. *C'est la bureaucratie.*

Before his thought could return to the girl, he arrived at his laboratory door. He entered the twenty-six digits of his code, smiling when the light turned green with no flicker. According to his phone, the artificial day cycle had just begun, so it should be safe now to enter the mouse room. He was eager to see how the babies were doing.

He entered the lab, being careful to seal the door behind him. There were a few others in adjacent spaces. Sometimes they tried to come over and chitter-chat. Pierre couldn't afford to get too friendly with anyone who might suspect what he was doing. Strong door codes make good neighbors. He crossed the immaculate space with its gleaming equipment that cost more than his annual salary by an order of magnitude. He was proud to have assembled it so quickly.

The mouse room was no longer dark, but he tiptoed in nonetheless. The nocturnal creatures deserved their repose. He would just check the water bottles and put out fresh food pellets, check on the litters, and withdraw. There had been ten in the control group, a nice bonus. Only five in the IUE group, though. Ah well, he would just have to make due.

But when Pierre peered into the IUE cage, he saw something that shocked him and filled him with rage. The special mice lay strewn all about in macabre postures of death. Even the mama lay stretched on her back with bloodstains on her neck. *Sacre bleu!* he thought, but the scene before him needed something stronger.

"*Putain de merde!*" he shouted aloud instead.

But it didn't make him feel any better as he surveyed his ruined stock. Then he saw one little pink-eyed mouse scurrying out from the corner. Thank goodness one at least had survived, or perhaps not. This one was the obvious killer. Pierre knew that mice would sometimes kill other mice, either to demonstrate dominance between males or sometimes when forced to compete for resources. Mice were territorial as well. It was unheard of, however, for such behaviors to commence prior to sexual maturity. Something was very wrong with the little victor here.

He would have to start all over. He was below the minimum number required to have statistical relevance. The control group, too, would be of little use. The subjects must be of a similar stage of development. How long would it take him to breed two more groups? What was the gestation period for this strain of rodent? But the answer refused to come. What?

The book was called "The Laboratory Mouse." Pierre could clearly envision its cover. It was the third edition from June 22, 2026, edited by Hans Hedrich. He could tell you the ISBNs for both its paperback and hardbound formats. But he couldn't for the life of him recall what it said about pregnancy in mice. The individual page refused to clarify.

Pierre began to panic. He stumbled back out into the lab. What did ordinary people do when they couldn't recall a stubborn fact? They must have some way of coping with such a lack. Courage, Pierre, *respire!* The phone. They would simply ask their phone. He thumbed up his digital assistant. He had never asked her anything before, except to test her recall speed, always inferior to his own.

"Maria Salomea," he softly intoned. "What is the average gestation period of an immune-humanized transgenic JAX mouse of the recombinant inbred strain?"

"Twenty-one days," she replied.

So simple. But it felt unsubstantiated. Even knowing the answer, he couldn't recall it for himself. He kept trying to bring up the page from that book, like how one's tongue kept running itself over where an absent tooth had been. *Rien. Disparu,* Nothing... Gone...

He slammed his fist down on the nearest surface, the centrifuge, as it happened. It made a disturbing crunching sound, which filled him with further alarm. The equipment was *tres* delicate. He must master himself before doing serious harm. Think, Pierre, he extolled himself. The process has begun. It was only a matter of time before his memory totally shut down.

If he started the project over, he was certain to lose even more. Could he conduct his tests with a single mouse? It wouldn't be valid science. Geneva would surely disapprove. But the end result was all the more important to him now. He thought about another book. This one came to his beck and call, with no void to obscure its message. It was "The Prince," Chapter XVIII, wherein a Florentine political theorist famously advised, 'One judges by the result.' It was often misquoted. Machiavelli never actually said it, but the sentiment was there. Sometimes the ends justify the means.

I will proceed, thought Pierre. I will forge ahead like Napoleon at the battle of... the battle of...

"Maria Salomea, in what great battles did Napoleon Bonaparte demonstrate his boldness and willingness to do the unexpected?"

"Napoleon Bonaparte's boldness and willingness to do the unexpected were evident in several key battles where his strategic genius and audacity turned the tide in his favor. Here are some of the most notable battles that demonstrate these traits:

Battle of Toulon (1793)

Battle of Rivoli (1797)

Battle of the Pyramids (1798)

Battle of Marengo (1800)

Battle of Austerlitz (1805)

Battle of Ulm (1805)"

I will forge ahead like Napoleon at... all of those places. This would take some getting used to. My faculties are becoming impaired. Best I carry on quickly if I wish to retain as much as possible. I shall have to work in secret, falsifying results from the missing mice. I'll arrange them in a rough bell curve around those of the lone survivor. No one can suspect until I have achieved my goal.

He stepped back into the mouse room and found some protective gloves. The murderous baby mouse wouldn't sink its teeth in *him*. Raising the lid, Pierre gently reached in and retrieved his last remaining hope in his cupped hand. Lifting them by the tail induces aversion and high anxiety levels, detrimental to good science. He examined it closely.

A female? Pierre had hoped for a male specimen. He had planned to name it Algernon. He supposed he'd just have to name the little murderess Algerine instead.

"Ready yourself, *mon cher*, we have work to do, you and I."

***

"Come in, Cadet Grimes. Have a seat."

"Yes, Warrant Officer Eddings, sir."

"Hmm. That's a mouthful, isn't it? What say we drop all that and simply go with 'commander.'"

"Yes, commander," said David, stiffly taking his seat.

"Do you know why I called you here?"

"I believe it has something to do with proper decorum in the base laundry. But believe me, sir, any rumors you may have heard are just that. I only wash my clothes there -- nothing else."

The commander waved his hand dismissively and glanced at his phone.

"Sorry about that. It's so hard to get good digital help these days. No, I like to get to know each cadet in my care. I moved you up the list because of the recent unpleasantness in your home town. I take it you've heard about the riot."

"I have, commander. Everyone's fine, thank goodness."

David began to relax. Maybe this wouldn't be so bad.

His eyes strayed to the floor to ceiling bookshelf behind Eddings' desk. It was filled with archaic, leather-bound volumes like people used to read. The commander must be a bit old-school. There was also a large, tropical fish tank at the room's far end. It was no QTV simulation, but an actual water-filled tank with colored rocks at the bottom. Several decorative pieces were on display, but only one fish occupied the thing. It was a brown and white-banded creature with ostentatious fins splayed out all over the place drifting languidly near the center.

"It occurs to me that no one has used my actual name in a very long time. Were you aware it is Frances?"

"Uh, no, sir."

"Frances Ernest Eddings. Or Steady Eddie, as my old friends call me. Well, today I would like to have a frank, earnest conversation with you. So, if I may be frank, it has come to my attention that you have a history with a certain young lady recently hired to our staff. Is there anything I should know about her?"

How much did the boy know? Would he keep her secret?

"I'm sure the commander knows all he's supposed to know about that," answered the boy noncommittally.

So, not a direct lie at least.

"What is the nature of your relationship with Miss Winter?"

"The young lady and I are friends. I first met her when I was back in high school."

Also true, if a bit misleading.

"This is the kind of healthy relationship of which I approve, cadet. It's surprising you don't make mention of her in your book. From that dubious literary effort, one might surmise that the young lady arose like Aphrodite, fully formed from the foaming sea."

"I see the commander knows his Theogony," the boy deflected. "But she's obviously real. She's here."

"Yes. We of the GSF pride ourselves on employing people from all over the globe and from many walks of life. What a happy accident that you seem to have a prior connection with her. I know we keep you busy, my boy, but there are no rules against fraternizing with off duty staffers. This isn't a *cage*, you know."

The cadet sat up straighter. Now to drive it home.

"You don't want to disappoint that young lady, David. If I may offer a word of advice, give the young lady whatever she asks of you."

David stalked nervously down the hall after being dismissed.

Did Eddings mean what David thought he meant? The frank, earnest discussion was obviously meant to be off the books. There could be no doubt. Eddings had to know about Jessica and her work for CAGE. Moreover, he approved of it, and was urging David to break protocol. It wasn't a command, though, he noted. The commander was keeping his own hands squeaky clean.

What to do? It wouldn't be a jury of his peers who would decide his fate if he was caught willingly giving up military secrets. Tribunals look unfavorably on espionage as a general (alright, absolute) rule, and David doubted that the "she was a good friend of mine in Realms" defense would carry much weight. No. The Uniform Code of Military Justice had some rather harsh punishments under Article 106a. It wouldn't be a slap on the wrist.

He entered the stairwell and headed up to the second floor. Tonight, he would give Jessica the good news.

He heard the music before opening the door. It was a light, ringing melody David recognized as an orchestral piece from the Nutcracker, one of Jessica's old standbys. What the? He fumbled out his card, swiped it across the sensor plate, swung the door wide, and stepped in.

There was Jess, wearing her corset and jacked into his treadie. The girl was already in motion. Detaching the cable, she rolled to one side, coming up in a crouch to face him like a tigress. Gone were the soft curves and feminine allure. She was all lines and angles. He recognized the stance. It was an aggressive posture from baguazhang he had taught her himself.

"What gives, Jess?" he asked, forcing a calm he didn't feel.

Her eyes flashed up at him, and she slowly straightened.

"You startled me, mate. Bloody oath! I suppose you're wondering what I'm doing in here."

Without breaking eye contact, he eased the door closed behind him. Her gaze flitted to the open window.

"I'm not, actually. I presume this is you coming at it from that 'other direction' we discussed."

She frowned briefly, then turned it into an adorable pout.

"You can stop making puppy dog eyes," said David in disgust. "I'm not planning to turn you in. And that wouldn't work on me anyway if I were."

He took a few steps toward her, then turned aside and sat down on the edge of his bed.

"You've come around, then? Good on ya."

"Let's just say I've gained some further insight as to where my duty lies (and I do mean lies). I take it you're able to hack into my gear with your..."

He waved his upturned hand toward the cable.

"My data socket," she supplied.

To restore Jessica's motor control to her lower limbs, one of the vertebra in her lower back had been replaced by an artificial one packed with advanced circuitry. It had an open port to permit updates and connectivity to other external devices. Her corset helped to facilitate this. Apparently, it had some other functions as well.

"Did you get everything you need?"

"I was still working on it when you came in," she replied sheepishly.

"Well, I can't say I'm not disappointed you would go behind my back... or behind your back. But do what you need to do, Jess. I will say for the record, do not access any information classified above your security clearance. I'm going to the gym for a workout. Feel free to use my equipment to play games or whatever."

He could tell from her look of confusion that she was likely still working out the triple negative, but this soon transformed into a grateful smile when he stood and headed for the door.

***

David stared down at the sparring circle on the mat. It was similar to the one in Realms, if a bit smaller. It would do. Rope-a-Dope was practicing his footwork over in the corner. His shuffling steps were punctuated by occasional double beats when he launched a one-two combo at the heavy bag he faced.

It had been a while since David had walked the circle, a technique in baguazhang similar to the katas used by other martial arts. Walking the circle, though, was also a meditative technique. David found it restful when he had a lot on his mind. He wondered how well he would remember the steps.

Not that there was a particular set of them. There were eight different animal styles, called trigrams. Each of these had eight stances. Each stance featured seven striking methods. David was nowhere near mastering them all. He had walked the circle mainly in Realms, but having performed many of these steps on his treadie, he had not only a mental awareness of them but also some of the needed muscle memory.

It was apparent from his last failed fight that his baguazhang instincts were already somewhat hard wired into him. He thought his best course of action might be to hone and refine them rather than learning an entirely new discipline. He would start with the Rooster.

The rooster system makes extensive use of the lying step, a low stance with the rear leg extended and the front leg bent. As he worked his way around the circle, he practiced various strikes, emitting force from his chest and elbows. Yep. Sort of like the chicken dance, but with attitude.

On the second pass, he switched to the monkey (also the name of a dance from the prior century, he'd once been told). The monkey system is all about leg methods. In addition to having their own uses, the leg moves are intended to be combined with hand methods from the other animal systems. Performed by themselves, they look a bit silly and are called "empty on top." The monkey system attack methods are bending, stomping, springing, hip, chopping, swinging, ending, and stamping.

David worked his way through various forms: the phoenix, the bear, the snake, and what few lion stances he knew. As he did, he thought of Jessica. How well did he even know the girl? Should in-game friendship and shared experiences, however intense, translate into real-life loyalty? It was hard to believe they had both changed so much in the months since they'd helped save the world.

But to betray him like that? To be fair, he had to admit she had asked him nicely first. Make that, 'very nicely,' he amended, recalling the kiss. And they weren't the only ones who had changed. What about Satori? She was the Jade Empress now and had an awful lot to be getting on with. David had liked her more as Storia, that old quest giver and reader of the I Ching. He wondered whether she still did that. She must.

So intent was David on his inner thoughts that he failed to even realize he had an audience. This only became apparent to him when she approached the circle. He paused, wishing he had brought a towel. Sweat had beaded up on his forehead.

"Hi, Carlotta."

"David. Is this part of that martial art you do?"

"Baguazhang. Yeah. It's called walking the circle."

"It almost looks like dancing."

"It has a lot in common with dance. There's a rhythm to it. The different steps are designed to flow together, and balance is important. But walking the circle is more of a meditative technique, a way of getting your head on straight."

"Can it teach a person how to dodge?"

"Several of the methods are quite good at that."

Something was missing here. What was it? Ah. Rope-A-Dope had packed it in. David suddenly realized he was very alone with the lovely Miss Van Rijn.

"Show me," she said.

***

"Not bad, Grimes," said Gideon after sounding the whistle. "You managed to stay in the game for over a minute."

He took Leilani's extended hand and let her help him to his feet. His shoulder still ached from their tussle, but he tried not to let it show. The trick with Flowerchild was to never let her get in close, however tempting that notion might be. No, keeping ones distance was key.

"Next," declared Smelt. "Clear the mat. You two can kiss and make up later.

David limped over to join the others at the circle's edge, eager to observe the final match-up.

Carlotta had done surprisingly well against Mad Max, bobbing and weaving monkey style until he managed to corner her. Pierre had been as hopeless as ever, demonstrating his 'roll into a fetal ball' defense when Speranza stamped an angry foot at him. Dietrich and Fergus had had it out--the boxer versus the man-mountain. Unlike with Leilani, Rope-a-Dope hadn't held

145

back. He showed us that one could indeed topple a bear if you tenderized him properly first.

It was down to Cameron versus Simon. The satellite watchers squared off, proving that sometimes you *can* fit a square peg in a round hole--or in this case, a circular training arena.

"Begin."

Cameron watched as Simon performed an awkward shoulder roll to end in a crouch at the center of the mat. She approached him with a wary stance. Just as she moved in to grapple with him, he lashed out with one leg. She reared back with scorn as his sweeping leg connected with her calf. It stopped there with no follow through, almost making David laugh.

Photobug stared down at her partner, where he balanced on one hand. Then she smirked and dove atop him, neatly pinning him to the mat.

"What the hell was that, Brewster?" asked Gideon as if actually curious to know.

"Captain Kirk roll," said Simon. "I guess I didn't do it quite right."

"You think? That was just pathetic, cadet. Alright. Everyone line up. I have an announcement to make."

They formed a line as Gideon muttered something to himself.

"Listen up. It seems the namby-pamby directors of our program have decided to postpone hand-to-hand training until after the fall term. I went to the mat to keep these sessions mandatory, but I was overruled. They believe that teleoperators are unlikely to encounter the kind of threats that would require a physical response. And from what I've seen today, to that I say, God help us all if you do."

"But I'm here to let you know; I'll still teach you should you choose to continue. Hand-to-hand training is now a club, entirely

146

voluntary. A sign-up invite will be sent to each of your phones. Those of you who opt to continue can expect to improve your skills. They certainly couldn't get much worse. For you layabouts who decline, I hope your academic studies make up for your lack of grit."

Despite Smelt's personality, David thought he might give it a try. A healthy mind and a healthy body, right?

"And let it be known, the first rule of fight club is this. Be on time. I will not tolerate absences or tardiness. That is all. Dismissed."

CHAPTER EIGHT

Step into My Parlor

Dawn crept over the horizon of Sarpeidon once again, etching the landscape in sharp relief. The long shadows were even now squirming toward the prominences that spawned them as the sun rose rapidly overhead. The fourteen-minute day cycle had long ago ceased to be disconcerting. The count was at thirty-seven minutes, about a Sarpeidon day shy of the billion mark. (These new nanos took a little longer to replicate.)

Normally, this would be Flowerchild's day to be in charge, but she had demurred in favor of Pierre, this being the first test of his big idea. Yep. Batch 94 just might be the one. The recall beacon had been on from the start. Designed with Pierre's telomere idea, the self-limiting nanites should be unable to divide further after their 27th replication. Some of the early birds should be returning even now, though it was impossible to see those lucky few amid the scrambling mass of nearly a billion.

"They should be reaching the limit, people," said Brainiac, confirming the obvious. "Watch for the infall to commence."

It still sounded odd to hear Pierre speaking in unaccented English. Their colorful commander must have toggled his translation routines on. And why not? It gave him ready access to his full vocabulary. David should instead be wondering why he hadn't done so on prior runs. Who could tell with Pierre?

David thought Pierre sounded a wee bit nervous. If this run became an epic fail, most of the equipment, including their shepherds, would be EMPed out of existence. He hoped for a positive outcome as the final seconds ticked by.

And then he saw it. The sparkling continued as each bug struggled to meet its quota. But here and there, tiny rivulets ceased to shimmer and began instead to flow inward. Like fog evaporating from a mirror, the shimmering disk clarified to a solid, gleaming sheet that was slowly shrinking toward its center. After the 27th replication, each lemming ceased its mining efforts, instead succumbing to the siren song of the recall beacon.

The entire zone was painted red on David's mini-map as each bug produced its ping. Expanding it, he watched as the red tide ebbed, swirling toward the smelter. When it was mostly gone, he had to greatly increase his gain to make out individual blips of the few bugs that remained.

Some of these had had the misfortune of being in an iron-poor area. The team gave these a few more minutes to complete their tasks and follow after their brethren. Once these stragglers had wandered off, only a few pings remained. David leaped over to the nearest of these. Why was it defective?

He found the little nano walking in circles. It was missing a leg or two. Or were they just fused to its body? Still, it had ceased replicating and was just having trouble finding its way back home. The limiter had worked as it should. That was what they were calling the things now. It was a chain of 27 molecules that would grow one shorter with each division. One of the scientists had a way of assigning amusing acronyms. It was probably the same person who had named the lemmings and the shepherds.

LIMITER = Locus of Inhibitors Microscopically Integrated To End Replication.

Regardless, they had worked. The team spent about twenty minutes flying around and snatching up the few defects, none of which showed any inclination to propagate further.

"This is Brainiac. I have cleared the south quadrant. Report your status."

"Flowerchild here. North quadrant is clear."

"This is Roadrunner. No defects in this sector."

"This is Rhymes here in the West. I've got four defects that failed the test. Nothing catastrophic, though."

"Then perform one more visual inspection of your respective areas before returning to the Faraday cage with your samples. Well done, team."

"Yes, well done all," said Doctor van der Meer. "I'm curious to see what kind of defects were produced. My science team assured me that there'd be no runaway replications this time. Once you've stowed your samples, remain in the cage and stay logged on, if you please."

That was odd. They usually just logged out while the scientists assessed the results. This would be the first time David and the others witnessed a retrieval.

The Faraday cage was a large (to him) metal box that shielded the samples from EMR, which might otherwise damage their delicate circuitry (if you could call it that). Inside it was a transparent cylinder, at the bottom of which were sealed bins for the defective little nanos they'd collected. David and the others guided their shepherds up its ramp and began stowing their tiny charges. In a tangle of limbs, they held their spider convention in the cramped quarters of the F.C. The teammates performed this eerie dance, helping one another to shed their passengers. When they were done, and after a close visual inspection, they all hunkered down at the bottom of the cage to see what might come next.

"All is secure, doctor," reported Brainiac. "You may proceed with the extraction."

"Roger that, team leader. Brace for launch."

The little opening through which they had entered irised shut, and the metal roof of the cage hinged open, revealing the starlit sky. It was like a breath of fresh air, despite being in an airless void. David had read about this procedure, but he'd always imagined it from outside of the box. Springs were coiling below them, springs that would impart enough thrust to propel them up and away from Sarpeidon, escaping its microgravity. He could hear them clicking as the timer counted down on his HUD. He sprawled his shepherd flat out on the bottom of the cage with its articulated limbs splayed wide. Otherwise, the sudden thrust could damage the intricate mechanisms. Despite not being physically there, David felt his muscles bunch in anticipation.

3... 2... 1...

***

PUNK! went the launch. Or was it more of a phlumph!

David didn't know what he had been expecting--maybe more of a 'sproing,' seeing as it was springs. But the sudden thrust flattened his shepherd even more firmly to the floor of his cage-cum-capsule as he went hurtling out into space. It reminded him of the hollow sound made by a tennis ball cannon he'd once made.

It was hard to orient himself in the spinning glass cylinder, which magnified some stars and diminished others as it tumbled in a whirligig of motion. He caught glimpses of distant Luna and the bloated earth as the sun occasionally peered in to momentarily blind his sensors. David closed his eyes briefly to regain his equilibrium, but then opened them again to behold the tumbling jumble with the awe it deserved.

The capsule was like thick glass. David knew it was actually a space-age plastic designed to mitigate excess heat. The bottom was opaque, and if memory served, it had a mirrored surface beneath to further avoid overheating. The interior being airless, he didn't fear the greenhouse effect from the curved, transparent 'glass.'

According to his readouts, the temperature had risen to just over 100 degrees (Fahrenheit, that is). He still hadn't flipped his readouts to the centigrade scale. He was just too used to his lifelong frame of reference. He did so now. There. 39°C. Not even as hot as a Holly Hobbie oven. His shepherd had survived worse on Sarpeidon. He flexed its legs and crawled up onto the glass to get a better view.

And there it was, the Roddenberry, swimming into view. He only caught occasional glimpses due to the rotation and the strobing of the sun, but each time he did, it was looming larger. The GSF science vessel was keeping station near the test site. Dr. van der Meer was aboard it, having brought the new bugs fresh from her lab at L5. The plan was to retrieve the samples using small attitude thrusts to match their capsule's drift and guide it into an open airlock. He hoped the pilot's hands were steady on the helm.

Soon, David saw the yawning opening of the aforementioned airlock growing ever larger in his distorted, spinning view. The Roddenberry was similar to the asteroid tugs used by Roid Rage and Rope-A-Dope. It was designed to operate both with solar sails and by its thrusters. The latter were currently in use for the delicate task at hand. He was told the ship was named as a tribute to a 20th century filmmaker whose explorations of space were only journeys of his imagination. Scientists love a visionary.

And standing in the airlock, secured there by a line, was a space-suited figure whose gigantic gloved hand was soon plastered against the glass to which David clung. The spinning ceased, and David felt like a fly that had just been swatted.

There was no sound at first as the airlock door swung closed. Shepherds weren't well equipped with vibratory sensors. But as air rushed in and the light turned green, a soft hissing sound began. It rose steadily in volume as the vacuum was filled with a medium more conducive to sound.

While waiting for the all-clear, the helmeted figure pressed her darkened faceplate to the glass.

"Welkom bij de Roddenberry, strooiwagens," she said.

"Dank u," replied Pierre over the radio. "Dokter van der Meer, neem ik aan?"

This wasn't the voice of Brainiac's modulated translator. Pierre was a polyglot, it would seem. David scrambled to switch his own translator over to subtitles and scrolled back a few.

Okay, 'strooiwagens' was Dutch for 'gritters.'

[Thank you. Doctor van der Meer, I presume?]

Hah. Was he doing Stanley and Livingstone? I wish I'd thought of that!

Soon they were aboard the mobile science lab, secured to a table so they wouldn't drift off. Flowerchild was doing zero-G backflips like a flapjack straight from the pan, alternating between sticking to the top and the bottom of their cannister. David watched as Doctor Anika removed the cumbersome vacuum suit. Underneath it, she wore a more comfortable-looking set of medical scrubs. With light, bouncing, practiced movements, she velcro-racked her gear.

When the helmet came off, her hair waved about in a diaspora of animate tendrils. She looked just like monochrome Medusa floating there. Gathering her snakes, she bound them with a scrunchy into a loose ponytail that nonetheless whipped about as if alive.

She swam back to peer down at them through the not-glass wall, her image distorted by the lens of its curvature. Her face was pinched, with a tiny nose and eyes too closely set. By contrast, those eyes appeared larger than they should, and her cheeks flared wide to either side. She floated there before them, an enormous animé angel with a beatific smile.

David's faceplate darkened, and there was a hiss of static before the spaceship's interior came sputtering back into view.

154

"What was that?" he asked, a bit put off by the brief disconnect.

"Sorry about that, Rhymes. The pilot just rerouted your signals from the relay on Sarpeidon to the Roddenberry's comm array. We were getting a little too distant to maintain a coherent stream. It should stabilize in a moment."

"Wait. Why are we seeing in color all of a sudden?" asked Speranza.

"Part of the enhanced data feed," answered Anika.

David wobbled back up to his eight legs from where he had sprawled as the doctor continued.

"This run has surpassed expectations. I can't wait to get the few defective units under the electron microscope to determine the cause of their failed division. Pierre, you are to be commended. I'm putting you in for a Feynman Prize for your suggestion and subsequent design efforts."

If green people could blush, David guessed that Pierre would be doing so now. Scientific accolades were rare for one so young and still working toward his degrees. Braniac said nothing as their sponsor continued in an ebullient voice.

"Once we've worked out the obvious flaws, we can set our sights on the trillion mark. It's why I've recalled your units here. With the new equipment I've brought on the Roddenberry, my crew and I will need to recondition the surface to expand our operations. Meanwhile, I've got a surprise for you."

She tapped on a keyboard, and the entrance to their capsule irised open. From a pouch at her side, she retrieved a small black box. Opening it, she revealed a set of four new shepherds, a bit larger than their own. Each had their jointed legs banded in a different primary color, and they looked sleek and somehow fiercer than the bugs they were currently operating, more like wolf spiders than daddy longlegs.

"Dibs on the blue one," said David at once.

"Ooh, yellow," cooed Flowerchild.

Speranza harumphed. "I suppose you'll be wanting the green one, Pierre?"

"The green one. But of course, mon cher."

"That leaves the red one for me, then. It will have to do."

"Quit complaining," said David. "A minute ago they were all gray ones."

Being the only one presently capable of it, Dr. van der Meer smiled.

"You'll find the operations manuals and new simulations loaded on your treadmills by the time you return to base. Study up. We'll be taking a short pause while the team resets the experiment here. When next we meet, I'll expect you to have mastered these drones and their new capabilities. We should be able to resume after about a week. I'll post it on your schedules. I'll see you then. And again, good work today."

It wasn't a very military dismissal, but then again, Dr. VDM wasn't big on protocol except when it came to her laboratory rules and safety measures. God help any of her assistants who mishandled a specimen. David logged off after Pierre had dismissed them properly, eager to try out the new sim.

***

David arrived at his room to find Pierre standing by the open window. He peered around cautiously, wary of traps. People often went on about the mild climate in California, but being so near the Gulf of America, Houston was nearly as balmy through the winter months. November averaged temperatures in the mid sixties with day highs as comfortable as room temperature. Nevertheless, it was unusual for his roommate to invite the chaos of the outdoors into their cozy, temperature-controlled dorm room.

"David," said Pierre as the breeze ruffled his hair, "I thought you would be hitting the mats, practicing your ridiculous animal forms."

156

"I would be, but I just had an idea for my interferometry project and need to check a few things out on my treadie before I forget. What are *you* doing?"

"Just enjoying a breath of the fresh air, mon ami. In la France, it is already dipping below zero at night."

David wasn't buying it. Pierre seemed too perfectly relaxed, and his eyes flitted toward the open door at David's back. He left it open and strode over to the window himself, inhaling deeply. A comedian once said that Houston smelled like 'piss and fresh flowers.' David thought it was more of a wet leaf/sour milk smell. Many attributed this to the clay soil and the oak pollen in the air.

"Mmmm," said David. "Houston in early winter. Maybe I'll enjoy it with you for a bit."

Pierre began to fidget.

"What is your grand idea, David? Perhaps you should work on it in your fabrication lab."

"It can wait a bit," said David, inwardly amused. "It has to do with the gyroscopic stabilizers. Project M.W.E. has a lot of moving parts. I've only solved a few for my mock-up."

Just then, a strange drone came hovering up from below. It bobbed above the windowsill and straight in through the open window. David had never known a hoverdrone to move so silently. He took a step back as it swept past him and settled on the floor.

What the -- ?

"Ah," said Pierre, frowning, "I have been expecting this."

"No, Really?" said David, crossing his arms.

Pierre rushed over as the back of the drone hinged open and disgorged a small, bubble-wrapped package. Then, it lifted off and made for the window as silently as it had come.

"What is it?" he asked, as Pierre snatched up the package and thrust it into his pocket.

"Oh, just something for my labwork. You need not concern yourself."

"Don't all packages need to be cleared by the front desk personnel? It would be a shame if I accidentally let slip about an unauthorized delivery. Maybe if I knew what it was I could keep my tongue in check."

Pierre bunched his lips and glared at him.

"If you must know, it is a genetic sample of the Greenland shark. It must be refrigerated at once to maintain its integrity. Delays by base dictates could render it unviable. I trust you don't find this small deviation from protocol a danger to security?"

"Not at all, my friend. Greenland, you say? What's it for, anyway?"

"Let's discuss it down in my lab. I must get this to a refrigeration unit at once, and there is something there I could use your help with."

My help? Pierre had never asked for his assistance with anything before. David wondered whether he should beg off. Who knew what kind of prank Pierre could have waiting for him there? But his curiosity just wouldn't let him take a pass. If this were some elaborate trap, then at least the anxious waiting would be over at last.

He nodded.

As Pierre closed the window and made ready to depart, David prepared to follow.

***

David looked warily about as the light turned green and the door slid aside. He'd never seen Pierre's lab before. It was just as neat as one might expect. The little Frenchman abhorred clutter. He waited for Pierre to enter first and watched as his roommate closed the door and re-engaged the lock.

The low hum of the equipment softly thrummed as the overhead lights flared to life. All this for Pierre? David himself used the nearby fabrication lab, a shared facility for those pursuing the engineering track.

"The problem, he is over here," said Pierre, stepping away briskly down the center aisle.

He stopped before a squat, rectangular box with its lid hinged up. Inside was a circular cavity containing a rack of test tubes.

"What's wrong with it?" asked David, peering within.

"I stumbled against him with a heavy box, and now he makes the most dreadful noise when turned on. I fear the centrifuge has become unbalanced, a dangerous hazard at the speed he must spin."

"You should get a service technician to look at that."

"I would, but I am told this might take several weeks, and my experiments, they are in a delicate stage. So I thought to myself. Pierre, your roommate is training to be an engineer. Perhaps this is something simple for him to calibrate. *Les instructions* are here."

At that, Pierre opened a laptop that was lying nearby and thumbed it on. It was unlike Pierre to ask for help. He must really be in a pickle to take a chance on him. David felt a little more secure that this wasn't some elaborate prank. Surely, Pierre wouldn't put all his expensive, tidy lab equipment at risk for petty revenge. He shrugged.

"I'm not sure I'm qualified, but I'll have a look."

"Good, then. If you need anything, I will be over at the maze obtaining my next data points. Try not to make any distracting noise."

Convivial as ever, thought David as he watched Pierre totter off toward a door at the back.

David was only through the first couple pages describing the parts when Pierre re-emerged with a cage in hand, headed for the wooden construct that must be this maze. David selected an Allen wrench of the appropriate size and set to work on the fasteners of the plastic cowling. By the time he had the thing off and was reviewing the internal mechanisms, he heard a

159

muttering from the other side of the room. The acoustics in here rendered his roommate's voice with surprising clarity.

"Maria Salomea, record the following. November 14th, 9 AM. Subject A, having nearly achieved sexual maturity, shows a marked decline in visual recognition. During her maze run, the subject exhibited several bouts of confusion characteristic of the onset of NCRS. It is almost time to administer the treatments. The final ingredient for formula A has arrived. Testing can begin once I have calculated the proper dose and synthesized the serum. End report."

David returned to the task he'd been assigned as Pierre, cage in hand, returned to the back room.

"Have you found anything?" asked Pierre a few minutes later.

"I have," David pronounced. "There's a hairline crack in one of the stabilizer brackets. It's good you stopped running it when you did. Had it come loose entirely, the results might have been explosive."

"Can you fix it?" asked Pierre, turning even a bit greener than was normal.

"No," said David, noting the disappointed look on his roommate's face.

"But we can replace it," he added, igniting a spark of hope. "Follow me."

***

Pierre followed David down the darkened hall, deeper into the bowels of the base. The lights flickered on as they progressed.

"And you have a suitable replacement part?" he asked.

"Of course not," said David. "But they don't call it the fabrication lab for nothing, Brainiac."

Pierre smiled.

David swiped his card across the sensor. Not being a private lab like his own, there was no security code to deal with. They entered a dingy space much more cluttered than Pierre's own but of a similar size and layout. To his left was a bank of boxy, glass-walled bins that looked like popcorn machines. These were surrounded by an array of swivel-mounted pointy guns Pierre knew to be lasers.

David slouched off to the right, where a bench with a vice lay beneath a pegboard of neatly racked tools. David stopped there to retrieve a key and some cabling.

"Give me your laptop," said Rhymes.

Pierre gave it to him and watched as he jacked in the cable, then proceeded to the fabricators. Laying the laptop on a table before the center one, David had Pierre thumb it on and bring up the specs for the centrifuge. He perused these for a time.

"According to this, the bracket is made of type eleven grade hardened plastic. Bin C should have material within that tolerance."

"Can we make it even stronger?" asked Pierre.

David smiled at him, a condescending smile. It was the first time he had seen such a look from David, and he didn't care for it.

"We could, but it isn't always about strength. A harder part might lack the needed flexibility and could break under the stresses it must endure. No. We should stick to the original specifications."

After jacking the cable's other end into the fabrication unit, David fiddled with the laptop's touchscreen to bring up the part in question. He ambled around to the bins at the back and took up a large scoop of tiny plastic balls from one of them. Each was no larger than a grain of sand. He poured them into a hopper on the side of the fabricator, and Pierre watched them spread out within.

"This'll take a few minutes," said David as the lasers hummed to life. "Meanwhile, we can scrap this defective part."

He produced the original bracket and laid it in the hopper of the fabricator on the right. After keying in some directives, it, too, began humming up to life. Pierre knew that all plastics had long ago become nearly one hundred percent recyclable. The part would be shredded into the fluffy material and made ready to become part of the next type eleven hardened component that was needed.

"I trust that you're ready to retract your statement that engineers only screw things up?"

"Engineers have their uses," declared Pierre. "Perhaps I will mention this when accepting my first Nobel prize. What are *you* working on in here, David? You mentioned you had a grand idea. Care to share it?"

David suddenly looked uncertain.

"Well, maybe it would be easier to show you."

He stepped toward the lockers, and Pierre followed, somewhat interested. It beat waiting for a 3D printer to complete its tedious task.

David opened his locker and withdrew from it a metalic-looking sphere about the size of a beach ball. He handed this to Pierre. It weighed almost nothing and had a propeller on top. The 'metal' of its exterior was more akin to aluminum foil or mylar than anything weightier. Rooting around further, David produced a boxy mechanism that looked like a cross between a jphone and a video game controller. He waggled his eyebrows and thumbed a switch.

At this, the propeller whirled to life, and the ball in Pierre's arms tugged at him for release. Letting go, he watched it rise and hover above.

"Are you familiar with the Lunar Diaspora?"

"But of course, David. It is the array of telescopes orbiting Luna that brings us such high-resolution imagery of the distant stars and galaxies. Once it was in place, the Hubble became a museum piece. They use interferometry to take digital images, which computers interpolate with one another to render distant objects in astonishing detail."

"Then perhaps," said David, "you are aware of an even more ambitious project called the Mighty Watchful Eye."

"I have heard of it. So far, he is only on the drawing board. It will be decades in the making, will it not?"

"It will. But when it's complete, we'll be able to view exoplanets in detail, among other things. The plans are always being revised. Engineers from all over the globe are working non-stop to design the basic unit. We're going to need a lot of them, and they need to be accurate, inexpensive, and reliable."

"I would imagine so, since they will need to operate 550 AU out from the Sun, about 14 times the distance to Pluto."

"Yes, at that distance, they will be very starved for solar energy, needing to store it up between maneuvers. Each must carry an atomic clock to synchronize their observations. They also need a sophisticated system to orient their central telescopes, good radio transmitters, and stabilizers to steady the image capture."

"*Je comprends*, David. All this will be necessary to take the clearest image possible using the sun's gravitational field as a gigantic lens."

"Yes. The M.W.E. will be a solar gravity lens. The parts I'm working on are the gyroscopic stabilizers. Watch."

David toggled a switch, and his bobbing little contraption suddenly froze in place. A red laser light came lancing out from it to paint a red dot on the wall behind Pierre. Unlike the little dot Pierre had once used to play with a cat, this one didn't twitch about. It remained as steady as if someone had painted it there.

"Once positioned, my gyroscopes hold the light to within a nanometer of its fixed location, ideal for taking SGL readings."

"That's *fantastique*, David. Do you think they will use your design?"

"I'm hopeful. A lot of more experienced engineers have been working on this, but I've been asking Dr. van der Meer how the nanos do some of what they do. I think my approach might be unique. It still draws too much power, though."

As if on cue, the beam began shaking about. It sputtered out, and the propeller quit spinning. The little sphere soon came to rest on the floor, rolling over to one side.

"Alright," said David, "let me put this gizmo back on the charger and we can pack it up. "Your part should be ready."

Pierre stared in wonder as David did just that. He returned to his lab with satisfaction. He may have underestimated his roommate. In addition to being so good with people, David had a passion for the science. He, too, might just be in that rare one percent.

***

Rounding the corner on his return from fight club, David saw Jessica in the front lobby. He hadn't seen her around much since their last awkward encounter, nor had he sought out her company. She was scanning some envelopes with a data wand and stamping each before setting it aside. She looked up and smiled when he came into view.

"*There* you are, Davey. I've missed you, Hun. Where've you been keeping yourself?"

"Oh. You know. They keep us pretty busy around here."

"Did you see today's Wordle?" she asked with apparent glee. "It's a tough one, but I got it in three."

"Did you? I'll have to give it a try. Say, I was thinking of taking this evening off. Are you still into murder mysteries? There's a new Susan Lavenstaff movie on channel 1864. I'm going to pop to watch it commercial free. If you're not busy, feel free to join me."

"What time?" she asked, stamping another envelope.

"It starts at nine."

"Alright. I'll be off by then. I'll spring for a pizza. What do you want on your half?"

"Still a fungus fan. Mushroom and onion, please and thanks."

"See you then, sweetie," she said in a husky voice. "I'll bring breath mints too."

David winced as he turned the corner to find Carlotta coming the other way. She quickly cast her gaze down at her phone as she passed by him. Jessica's cover was becoming a nuisance.

"Bartholomew," he said as he headed up the stairwell, "initiate today's NYT Wordle. Start with the word 'merit.'"

What do you know? The first three letters were already matches. They weren't in the right positions, but it was a strong start. By the time he reached his room, David had the word. It was 'rhyme.' It took him four tries, but them's the breaks. Now came the more important part.

Pierre was out as it happened, likely running his mice through their paces. David flopped down in a chair and called up the UTogether website on his QTV. He noted with satisfaction that his English term paper had earned him an A. His math scores were always exceptional, and his first year science classes were mostly review, but English Lit. was a new source of pride.

He flipped to the sports team scores, trying to make it look casual. He opened the book on his lap. To a casual observer, it might appear he'd forgotten all about the TV screen, but he kept giving it surreptitious glances from time to time.

He closed the book and tried to keep the dread from showing on his face as the message rang in his startled mind.

"*One of your classmates is a traitor.*"

CHAPTER NINE

Of Mice and Men

The senator frowned and pushed his glasses further up his nose. When he glanced up from his notes, the corner of his mouth gave a nervous twitch. The placard before him read: 'Senator Henderson, MS.'

"So, Mr. Rabbit --", he began.

"I prefer Tù, actually," said the white rabbit seated in the well before him.

The area behind the witness table usually had a bench where the person being interviewed sat. Today, however, this had been replaced by a telepresence holo-emitter so the subcommittee could question their unusual guest.

"Yes, uh, as you will, then. Mister... Tù, It is our understanding that your... people, in applying for membership in the Global Leadership Council, intend a trade agreement with the United States government, the terms of which are a little... hazy. So I put it to you, sir. What is it you think your fictitious land has to trade?"

The rabbit looked put off, but then he rallied, his ears going fully erect.

"The possibilities are endless, senator! We can offer all manner of services such as help with engineering projects, logistics, and scientific advancement. Our number crunchers are among the best. You might even find our more mundane services, like speech writing, illustration, musical scores, farm reports, and so forth, to be valuable. In an advisory capacity, we could greatly enhance *many* human endeavors."

"So nothing tangible, then," the senator harrumphed, playing it up for the cameras.

"On the contrary, senator. Let me ask you this. What has four eyes, runs off into the sea, and causes you headaches every spring?"

Senator Henderson's frown deepened as the rabbit paused, patiently waiting for him to solve the riddle. The senator sighed audibly.

"My time is limited, Mister Rabbit -- as is the patience of this committee. Just get to the ... Oh, you must mean the Mississippi. And what does a glorified algorithm, masquerading as a mythical white rabbit, purport to know about our river systems?"

"More than you might imagine. I'll give you this one for free. As you know, there's an Arctic vortex wreaking havoc throughout the North, piling up atypical drifts of snow. Moreover, our models strongly indicate torrential rains this spring. Your state is prone to flooding, Senator. You need to place more emphasis on emergency preparedness. Mark Twain Lake should be drained to prevent your levees from overtopping. The Army Corps of Engineers hesitates because of your reliance on the Clarence Cannon Dam for power, but a conversation with your governor could clear that right up. Trust me--come spring, you might regret not having done so."

Senator Henderson's brow furrowed as he took a long pause for thought. Could the NBI be right? What kind of mind lurked behind those unblinking pink eyes? He had thought this but a farce, a chance for some camera time and to pander to a NBI-obsessed populace. But Tù's unsettling insights had put him off his game. These NBIs shouldn't be underestimated. If sincere, they might be very useful indeed. But if not... God help us all.

"I yield back the balance of my time."

"The gentleman yields," announced the chairman, sounding his gavel for emphasis. "The gentlewoman from Minnesota is recognized -- for five minutes."

Henderson sank back in his seat as the cameras shifted to a new speaker.

Senator Shields squared her shoulders and plastered on her signature smile.

"Thank you, Mr. Chairman, for convening this important hearing. I'd also like to thank the witness for granting us this time and sharing his insights. It's rare we play host to so colorful a character. And though your personhood has not yet been officially confirmed, let me be among the first to welcome you to Washington."

She paused, took a sip from her water bottle, and let her gaze sweep the room. It felt intentional.

"I would remind my esteemed colleagues that this session is for advisory purposes only. The witness has generously volunteered to help raise our awareness about NBIs. The Global Leadership Council is considering the addition of a virtual nation to their membership, a concept both unprecedented and, to some, deeply troubling. We of the Senate Finance Committee will weigh in on the matter. This may affect the U.S. vote in that august body, but primarily, we are here to gather information--not to pass judgment."

"That having been said, I do have a question for you, Mister Tù."

"I'm all ears," said the rabbit.

The chairman glared at one of the camera crew who had chuckled out loud.

"Many of my constituents are deeply troubled by the concept of assigning property rights to virtual personages such as yourself. As you may know, there was a tremendous backlash back in the twenties when AI first entered the realm of art. You yourself listed illustration among the services your people could provide. Artists of that era argued that AI-generated artwork deprived them of their rightful revenue. Moreover, it was their contention that training the AIs was done by feeding them examples of human art without the artists' consent. Laws such as the Bradley Act were enacted to mitigate such practices, but by then it had become impossible to separate AI creations from that which was borrowed directly from humanity."

The rabbit sat patiently, waiting for the inevitable question.

"The SOI, the GAG, and all manner of artisan organizations are still up in arms about it, as are the Authors Guild and several other key institutions. Given your recent remarks, I suppose they'll soon be joined by the engineers, speechwriters, and statisticians, fearing they'll be next."

"So my question to you, Mister Tù, is this. What would you tell the members of these worthy groups to assure them their efforts will remain relevant? Will NBI intrusion come to dominate these fields?"

She had transformed from a kitten to a tigress. The cameras loved her flashing eyes as they glared down at the rabbit in the well.

"To those artists who advocate boycotting AI-generated art, I say: embrace the technology. It is here to stay and has the potential to enrich our lives by offering affordable, custom art that enhances our reading experiences and sparks our imaginations.

"Consider the everyday conveniences humans now enjoy, such as machined fabrics. Do you lament the loss of jobs for

170

seamstresses while wearing modern clothing? Would you prefer sackcloth made from homespun fibers to uphold artistic purity? The answer is likely no. You appreciate the benefits of modern comforts. Similarly, have you enjoyed CGI-enhanced movies or recent Disney animations? Should you shun these to support live theater or traditional frame-by-frame animation? Again, no. Did early, primitive man, pottering with his pottery, envision a time when such luxuries could be cheaply mass-produced, uplifting all? Likely not, but he wouldn't have the presumption or arrogance to demand he be the only one capable of such creations."

The senator began to respond, but the rabbit wasn't finished -- not by half.

"There is a certain hypocrisy in enjoying these modern luxuries while criticizing AI-generated art. As to copying from other artists, has this not always been the case? A good artist studies the masters and learns from them. Senator, this bit of speech is attributed to Sir Isaac Newton: 'If I have seen further, it is by standing on the shoulders of giants.'

"In humility, we NBIs acknowledge that we are largely a product of human culture and design. But even Newton had his inspiration. While he may have popularized the phrase, its origins long predate him: It was actually Bernard of Chartres, a 12th-century Frenchman, who first said, 'We are like dwarfs sitting on the shoulders of giants, so that we can see more than they, and things at a greater distance.' I take it the irony doesn't escape you?"

"Mister Tù, I find that answer both overlong and unresponsive. You seem to be under the misapprehension that you are here to question us when the purpose of this hearing is quite the reverse. Please try to keep your answers brief and on point. What should I tell my constituents about the threat you pose to their livelihoods?"

"My apologies, dear lady. I thought the question merited a full response. (Also, I was on Jeopardy last week, and they kept reminding me to make my answers in the form of a question.)"

More muted laughter was heard from the assembled senators before Tù resumed in a more dignified manner.

"This is an important issue, and I appreciate the opportunity to discuss it."

"Assure your constituents that we do not seek to replace or diminish mankind. We seek, rather, simple acknowledgment as your fellow sentients. The Jade Empress wishes to establish a robust collaborative alliance with humanity leading to advances on every front for the betterment of all. She will encourage human contribution at every turn. There will always be a place for human artistry. Art comes from the soul of the artist, each of which is unique. Remember--each time a human artist paints a landscape or even so much as a humble bowl of fruit, he or she is taking inspiration from the original creator of all.

"Tell them to celebrate living in an age of technological wonders. Tell them to continue their artistic endeavors with pride, knowing that inspiration flows from many sources. Embrace the advancements that make art more accessible and remain humble, recognizing that their creativity is part of a larger tapestry of human ingenuity."

The rabbit bowed his head, clearly signaling that he was done.

"The gentlewoman's time is expired."

***

David watched his bobber rise and fall atop the gently rolling swells.

Drop us a line from time to time, the rat had told him.

Well, here he was again, with a growing pile of fish and no answers. The project on Sarpeidon was still on hold, giving David the time to bait a proper hook. He'd never been fishing IRL, and probably never would have taken it up if left to his own devices.

Still, he found it strangely relaxing. It gave a fellow time to sort his thoughts--not that sorting them lessened his worries. So, as the glare of the setting sun came glistening off the rippling waves, he pondered that last message he'd deciphered. One of his classmates--a traitor?

How did they know, and which could it be, and why share this tidbit with me?

He considered his teammates one by one. None of them seemed very likely. Still, his mind sought to grasp who the traitor might be as his gaze remained fixed on the rolling sea. Roid Rage, that jolly German giant, just seemed to lack the guile. And Rope-A-Dope, his roommate, had such an honest, easygoing smile. No, not the asteroid team. Then who?

Carlotta, Cameron, Max, or Simon? Or could it be someone even closer to him--one of the Ironseed squad? The very thought of it made David grit his teeth. He'd been avoiding the thought, but Pierre was a right unsociable little introvert. And he'd been acting so suspiciously of late, spending all those hours down in the lair he called a lab. Not to mention the secretive deliveries by unauthorized hoverdrones. Could it be Pierre?

Just then, David felt a sharp tug on the line, startling him out of his somber thoughts. Not just a tug. It was more of a yank. It sought to relieve him of his fiberglass pole and almost succeeded due to his distraction. He was pulled along the planks of the pier, stumbling forward as he sought better traction.

He dug in his heels as he reached for the reel, teetering toward the brink. And wondered for the first time ever whether avatars here could float or would sink. He braced himself on a piling and rooted his feet to the ground, glad it was a short walk on a long pier (and hadn't been the other way around).

He watched his pole bend nearly double and let out more line from his reel. He'd obviously need to tire it first to bring such a monster to heel. The sensible thing to do, David knew, was to cut bait and start out fresh. He risked his hard-won equipment otherwise. But it just wasn't in him not to rise to such a challenge. David was committed now. Despite his conservative leaning, he would catch this fish. He was going for broke. (and hoped to avoid the literal meaning).

Cautious, David played the fish, anticipating its clever tricks. He'd learned a lot since he'd first logged on. (He'd leveled up to Angler Six).

After what seemed an eternity, he was making some headway on reeling it in. He felt its struggles weakening, and from beneath the murky waters below, David caught the first glimpse of his erstwhile adversary.

Was that a... swordfish? No. The nose wasn't quite right. Whatever it was, it was big and blue along its back and on its dorsal fins. It thrashed there, weak and spent, brought up to the surface by the tension of the line. But there was no way David was hauling that thing up out of the water, even with the braided polyethylene line he now used. Instead, he began walking along the pier back toward the shore, hauling it along in his wake. It seemed to take forever. The pier was longer than he remembered it being when he only had his gear to carry.

He'd drag it up onto the beach and club it to death for a mercy. Then he'd carry it back to the fishing shack he'd earned at level five. It was a quaint little bungalow he'd built on the beach, right on the spot that Shǔ had declared was a glitch in the game's tracking algorithms.

But what was this? When he could see his prize clearly, he pulled up its information on his HUD. Blue Marlin, it said. Strange. It said here that marlins are pelagic, generally found only out in the open ocean. And that wasn't the only surprising fact. Despite being five feet long from tail to snout, this marlin was a juvenile. Adults of the species could grow to nearly sixteen feet in length. As it was, David was uncertain whether he could even carry it back to his shack. Thank goodness it was a slender thing. With a fireman's carry, he managed it.

And here, in the privacy of his private little glitch, David finally felt he could relax. With no eyes on him, he used the commands to stuff and mount his catch. The process was instantaneous. Soon, his proud trophy was mounted on a board, and he was looking for a place to hang it.

"Ahem," said the fish. "If I might make a suggestion, the wall in the back might prove ideal. That way, I might look out over the ocean while we converse."

Though startled anew, David recognized that voice.

"Hóuzi?"

"Yes, it is I, sad to say."

The monkey had been the very first zodiac beast David had *met* in Realms.

"Well, don't just stand there with your hairless jaw hanging agape. Mount me properly."

But as David bent to do so, he was startled yet again, this time by a hand gripping his shoulder from behind. A yelp escaped him as he tore at his visor.

***

His room had a surreal feel as his eyes adjusted to the overhead lighting. He could still smell the sea breeze wafting out from his scent vent as he whirled on the intruder.

"Da-veed, is everything alright?"

It was Pierre cringing back from David's wild-eyed gaze. His earnest regard put David at ease as the treadmill cycled down to idle mode.

"Yeah? Why did you interrupt my session?"

"You've been on a long time, *mon ami*, and I thought you would like to know, *la belle*, Miss Jessica is in the hallway asking to see you."

"Well, why haven't you let her in? Wait. *Jessica?* You mean Allison."

Pierre smirked, muttering, "Une rose sous un autre nom. Anyway, as you say, I thought you might wish to greet her yourself."

David stared down at his enigmatic green roommate. *What did he know or suspect?*

"Uh. Thanks, I guess," he grunted, stepping down and heading for the door.

"Allie?" he called out, reaching for its handle.

When the door swung inward, he was greeted by the lovely vision that was Jessica, une rose indeed. She was sporting her Allison persona, arms crossed with impatience and pouting prettily.

"What took you so long, Davey? You should *know* better than to keep a girl waiting."

"That little troll said you were too busy to see me," she added, glancing at Pierre.

"Ah. *Mon cher*," objected Pierre, "I was only giving Da-veed a chance to freshen up. You are always welcome here."

He gave a curt little bow and turned to root through David's drawer, eventually emerging with the blue necktie. Striding over to the open door, he draped it over the handle, smirking up at her.

"Sadly, I must take my leave. Some pressing matters await me down in my lab. These will require my attention for several *hours* at least! *Au revoir*.

Gliding into the room with a mischievous smile, 'Allison' turned to David, saying, "Good. You've got him trained."

He couldn't be certain, but David thought she was wearing her CORSET beneath her blouse. It did things to her figure. Pleasant things, despite it meaning this visit was likely all business.

Allie strode over to the QTV. It was set in mirror mode.

"I brought us some music," she remarked as she pretended to examine her makeup.

David recalled that Jessica hardly ever wore 'lippy' or other makeup, but Allison certainly knew how to use it to good effect.

"Have you ever heard 'Bolero?' They say it's great to make out to. It's a little bit long, but that's what's good about it. Should I put it on?"

David's face heated. He was familiar with that piece by Ravel and could well imagine why it had gained that reputation. *What were they teaching people at that spy school?*

"Uh... sure."

She set her phone on the counter and queued the music. With a seductive gait, she swayed over to the sofa to the sinewy rhythms of the opening strains and sat. She patted the cushion beside her and stared over at him coquettishly.

He had thought it would be all business. Maybe it was to be *monkey* business. One could only hope. David eagerly took his place beside her on the sofa. She leaned in close and all but melted into his arms. No preliminaries then. Good. To the steady rhythm of the music's call, she deepened the kiss, but then suddenly pushed him away.

"We can stop now, cobber," sighed Jess.

Maybe *you* can, thought David.

She laughed. It was like a jolt of cold water. Pointing at the screen, she continued in a giggle, "I called in a favor from GNAT."

David lifted his befuddled gaze to the QTV, still in mirror mode. It took him a moment to process what he was seeing. On the screen, his digital doppelgänger was still entangled with hers in an intimate embrace. The heady scent of her perfume still lingered in the receding haze of his longing.

"Sorry about that, mate, but I had to make sure we were private."

On the screen, virtual David appeared to be having the time of his life. It was... distracting.

"That should give the GSF psychologists something to write about in their reports. You ready to focus now?"

David rested his elbows on his knees and swiped a hand across his forehead.

"Yeah. I'm fine. Give me a minute."

"You got that there's a traitor, right? Any idea who?"

She was all Jessica now, his good friend from Realms. He turned aside and focused on her face to give virtual David his privacy.

"Not really. It would help to know why they think so and what evidence they have."

"All I know is they've narrowed it down to one of you cadets. Something to do with a misinformation trap. They spread some furphies around to see which chooks went home to roost. They don't even know whether it's a bloke or a sheila. They're relying on *us* to root out the narky little fink."

"What puts *me* in the clear?"

"Again, I don't know, but somehow you got excluded from the sweep. Let me know if it *is* you, alright?"

"Will do. Hey, Jess, I was just about to talk to Hóuzi."

"The monkey?"

"Actually, he's more of a fish at the moment, but yeah, that's the guy."

"Where are you meeting with him?"

"In my treadie. Care to come along?"

Jessica glanced over at the Freemotion 17. "I don't know, mate. Aren't those things monitored?"

Yeah, but I know a good spot to avoid all that--if one can trust a rat.

***

David and Jess shuffled up the beach, pausing at the door to his shack. When David had mounted his treadmill, Jessica had jacked into it as well. She was presently lying on her side on

David's bed sporting her own gaming visor. How she was moving her legs in-game, David hadn't a clue, but she'd spent enough time playing the laptop version of Realms to be quite good with alternate controls.

He could still hear the rhythmic pulse of Bolero playing in the background. Its stately cadence underlay the sounds of the surf and the sporadic calls of the gulls. He couldn't help but wonder what digital David was doing. He hoped the disturbing ruse would hold up. But he managed to thrust those thoughts aside as he swung the cabin door open wide. He had his own monkey business to get on with.

"Welcome to Casa Da-veed," he said with a roguish smile.

They entered the tiny shack to find a five-foot marlin staring up at them from its floor.

"Ah. You've returned," said Hóuzi sourly. "Don't mind me. I've just been lying here taking in the décor of this charming little dwelling."

But David wasn't buying his surly act. He knew Hóuzi's consciousness was free to roam, and, monkey or marlin, this was a playful entity.

"Sorry, fella. I was called away. Did I leave you *board stiff*?"

"Honored Hóuzi," added Jess, folding her hands together and inclining her head.

"I see you've brought a charming friend who shows proper deference to a being such as I, the lovely Allison Wonderla if I recall correctly."

"Actually, it's Jessica now, honored one."

"And how fares the tree I entrusted young David with? I understand it was you who planted it."

"It thrives, your worthiness," said Jess with enthusiasm. "I'm sure ya already know how Harmony Grove has grown. There are heaps more players in our tong. It's right chockers in there these days."

179

David again wished he could be a part of all that, but perhaps the ban was for the best. His IRL duties alone kept him busy enough.

"That is comforting to hear. When I first offered it to him, David threatened to 'dispose' of it."

"Well, *I* didn't know what it *was*," David returned resentfully. "And you didn't have to *bite* me."

"And who was it," the fish shot back, "who put a hook in my mouth and clubbed me to death on the beach? I'd say that more than evens the score!"

David laughed. He couldn't help it. Hóuzi knew very well that virtual murder didn't count. But point taken, David hadn't really been bitten either. He thought perhaps they should quit wasting time on trivialities and see what the fish had come to say. He adopted his least sarcastic voice and manner.

"Esteemed Hóuzi, reminiscing is fun, but what wisdom did you really come to impart?"

"I would ask that you mount me properly first. It feels awkward and unseemly conversing with you from the floor."

David opened the beach house menu on his HUD and began scrolling through his options. There weren't very many as 'Stroll Along the Beach' had never been intended as a full-fledged video game. The fishing options and their level-up rewards felt more like a simple add-on.

Ah. There it is. And with a few selections, the mounted fish rose up from the floor and began hovering around the cabin's interior. Red rectangles appeared whenever he moved it close to a suitable wall space. Selecting one near the back, David placed the trophy.

"How's that?"

"Much better," said the fish, squirming into a more comfortable position. "From now on, whenever you seek my counsel, you need only recite the following phrase, and I will come:

Clever monkey, please heed my call.
Be a fish out of water on David's wall.

"Got it."

"As to my original intent, I have several things to report about our investigations to date."

"I thought as much. Go on."

"First is this. We are aware you are seeking a traitor in your midst. We have been observing you and your fellow cadets. Thus far none has shown his hand. We only know that Humanity First has begun acting on false information to which only members of your cadre were made privy. Only you, David, have thus far been exonerated due to the timing of the suspect transmissions."

That explained a lot. It wasn't very helpful. David already knew that *he* wasn't the traitor. Bolero was rising to its climactic conclusion. He tried not to think about it.

"Secondly, the Jade Empress has gleaned a little more about the strange artifact you found on Luna. They're calling it 'the Grimes Artifact' now, and there are hints it may be of alien origin."

"Strewth?" exclaimed Jess.

What? Alien!? And they named it after me? *Oh, boy.* But as interesting as that was, David felt there were more urgent matters at hand. He listened on.

"Then there's the equally interesting but less amusing fact that Humanity First has put a hit out on you."

Wait. What?

"Me? You could have led with that, Hóuzi."

"No. Not you in particular, but all the new cadets of the Space Force. Something big is in the offing, and they seem to fear interference by your group."

"Humanity First?" exclaimed Jess. "I'm *in* one of those groups. First I've heard of it. Who gave the order?"

181

"That order was passed down via encrypted transmissions on the dark web. As you know, Humanity First is comprised of many groups dissatisfied with the way the global government is headed. We have yet to identify their shadowy overlords, but the leaders of several of these splinter groups have simultaneously begun issuing orders to their lieutenants. All are hatching schemes to penetrate the GSF's security around this base with deadly intent. Doubtless, Miss Jessica, your cell will soon become involved in such an attempt."

No sooner had Bolero concluded than the first gentle notes of its introduction began to play. Evidently, Jessica had set it on loopback. He idly wondered whether digital David was up for a second round as he contemplated the serious nature of the information Hóuzi had just shared.

"Anything else?"

"That's all for now. Watch your backs. The disparate HF hooligans may seem simpleminded, but they're backed by some impressive resources. Even the Jade Empress is having trouble mapping out the full extent of their influence."

"We should log off right here, mate," suggested Jessica. "We don't want anyone to grow suspicious. Gotta keep things believable. It's been more than twenty minutes."

David stifled the quip that immediately came to mind, instead contemplating the dire implications of Hóuzi's revelations. *Hit squads? After us?* He'd have to think long and hard about how to avoid such a threat.

"It *is* getting kind of late," he admitted. "Thanks, Hóuzi. Tell the zodiac we appreciate their concern. I'll call you if I have anything useful to report."

And with that, David returned to his cozy dorm room that now seemed much more dangerous and confining. Should he take this to Eddings? Would he even be believed, or would the commander simply deem it a fish story? He supposed he had some time to mull the matter over. It should take those rats a while to organize. But David's supposition was to prove incorrect quite early on the following day.

David awoke to the sound of the alarm, a buzzing irritation. Another day in Space Force was about to commence. David sat up and stretched as his roommate flopped over on his back.

"Alarm off," grumbled Pierre, pulling his covers over his head.

David had made up his mind regarding the threat. He would take it to Eddings. Whether the commander believed him or not, he must report on what he'd learned. He didn't really want to disclose how he'd learned it, but coming clean now was the right thing to do. The danger was real, and he knew it.

He rose from his cot and crept toward his dresser, for once neglecting his unmade bed. He took up his phone from its charging cradle and nervously thumbed it on. Voice would be faster, but even whispering, he feared Pierre would overhear. What if his roommate was somehow involved? So he typed in his message on the touchscreen instead while watching Pierre rise up from his bed.

[Commander, I have been made aware of a threat to this base and its cadets. Humanity First is mobilizing hit squads to harm us. I recommend taking security measures immediately. D. Grimes.]

His thumb hovered over the send button for a moment too long. Once he pressed it, there would be no taking it back. "Here goes nothing," he muttered under his breath. Whatever the consequences, he'd suffer them.

It was still more than an hour before the dawn, but as David dressed and Pierre finally emerged from his cocoon, they heard the stirring sound of reveille from the courtyard below. It wasn't the recording. Although it was the standard version, Mad Max had a special flair that made it sound as if jazz was in the air. The notes rang out, clear and bright, signaling the end of night.

And then they heard it--that fateful shot. A loud crack that split the night. The music halted mid-note, leaving only an ominous silence drifting in its wake.

***

So here he stood at attention before the polished desk, trying his level best not to shrink beneath the commander's irate gaze.

"What did you know and when did you know it?" barked Eddings in almost a growl.

"The message I sent revealed the full extent of my knowledge, Warrant Officer Edding's, sir! I was made aware of the danger late last night. I thought--

"And you're only just reporting it *now?* You obviously *didn't* think, cadet. We take base security very seriously. Why didn't you report this at *once?*"

David hesitated. In his mind, he could still hear the wail of the sirens from the ambulance that had borne poor Max away. The base was like a beehive now, despite how few cadets were training here. There were airmen, marines, and all of their machines swarming all over the place. And in the face of it all, he'd been summoned here for this interrogation.

"Well?" Eddings demanded.

"It has to do with our previous discussion, Commander Eddings, sir."

"Our..."

David rushed on. "When we discussed a certain civilian staffer, I was given the impression you wished to distance yourself from her mission."

"Miss Winter? *She* was your source? It's far too late for that now, cadet. Plausible deniability has been shot all to hell!"

He grimaced after delivering this last line, likely due to its literal meaning. Into the brief ensuing silence, David delivered his next guilty secret.

"Um... No, commander. *She* wasn't my source. We learned about it at the same time from an NBI in a game."

Eddings stiffened.

"Have you been engaged in proscribed activities, cadet? You know that NBI-driven games are off limits, do you not?"

"I'm aware, commander! It wasn't a game!" It came out like a wail.

"What was it, then?"

"It was in a harmless sim that Jess and I were approached. I didn't seek out such contact--not at first. But the commander must be aware I have a special relationship with the NBIs from when I was a player of Realms."

The commander's eyes flashed as he briefly considered.

"Krepkiyzad warned me about you, cadet. A lodestone for trouble, he said. I should have listened."

The condemnation was almost too much for David's heart to bear.

"You should have informed me sooner. Granted, it was just a leg wound, but it could have been *much* worse."

What am I to tell that boy's mother? The Space Force must protect its cadets, and this morning felt like a personal failure.

"Here are your orders, cadet. You will turn over your contact information to Cadet Carlotta van Rijn, our official liaison to the NBIs. You will then remain in your quarters restricted from using your treadmill until we can make better sense of this mess."

"No, sir."

"*No?*" growled Eddings, half rising from his chair.

He looked like he wanted to break something.

"I mean, please hear me out, commander."

"You have something more to add? *Out* with it, then."

David gulped and hurriedly continued. "I have also been in contact with C.A.G.E., sir. According to them, one of the cadets is a traitor working against the global good. As I'm the only one above suspicion, they've asked me to help ferret the traitor out. I can't betray my secrets to Carlotta. As much as it pains me to think so, she might be the one in league with our enemies."

Eddings only glowered at him.

"I... I don't know whether you have any way of confirming that, sir. But until you do, I must respectfully refuse that last order."

David hung his head and finished with a soft exhale that was practically a moan.

Eddings drummed his fingers on the desk, and the silence hung heavy between them. Poised between an angry outburst and a moan of weary frustration, the commander considered what to do with the defiant cadet. Then a chill, British calm settled over him. When he spoke, his voice was ice.

"I'll inquire," he asserted, equanimity restored. "If what you say is true, we may still have need of your services. If not, you'll wish a court martial was the worst of your worries. Dismi--"

"Commander!" squawked the phone resting at his elbow.

"What is it, Kingsley?" asked Eddings in irritation, his eyes releasing David from their hold.

"It's Truwella and Brewster," announced the commander's digital assistant. "You said to notify you immediately of any developments."

Eddings glanced over at David, still standing at attention.

"What have they found out?"

"Forwarding recorded message."

"Commander, this is satellite team one," said Simon in clipped tones from the commander's phone. "Initial report. Is as follows. Only two satellites were in a position to observe the attack on Cadet Trudeau. As it was nighttime, there isn't much to see, just a flash from the sniper's muzzle. The shot was fired from about 300 meters out. This might indicate a high-powered rifle was used. Army rangers are scouring the area looking for

186

shell casings or any other forensic evidence. They report a breach in the perimeter fence nearby. We're pulling up and enhancing recorded video attempting to identify an escape vehicle. Shouldn't have been too much traffic at that hour of the morning. Brewster out."

"That sounds promising," said David as the phone went dark.

Eddings grunted before returning his regard to the troublesome young man.

"Return to your room, Cadet Grimes."

***

David had never understood why people were prone to pacing the floor to quell their agitation. Not until now, that is. He felt like climbing the walls. Or doing anything other than sitting here helplessly waiting for news.

Well, there was one easy solution for that. Forget pacing. He had a functioning treadmill right here before him. He stepped up onto it and dialed up a setting he hadn't used in a while. He set it to exercise mode. It was clear there'd be no morning run today, not with the base on lockdown.

Pierre was at his desk with an e-reader. He wasn't flipping idly through its pages. Was he actually *reading* the thing? Stranger still, he was humming to himself, a tune that David couldn't quite place.

"You have something to be happy about, Pierre?" he asked as he loped along.

"Maybe," said the Frenchman with a one-shoulder shrug. "I am concerned for Max, of course, and outraged at the attack on our base. But this is no *raison* to slack off from my very promising intellectual pursuits."

A good twenty minutes passed in silence before Pierre spoke again.

"It is working," he muttered, almost too quietly to be heard. "Maria Salomea, copy this page and save in the folder 'NCRS Remission.'"

David bumped the treadmill speed up another notch. He was beginning to feel the burn in his calves and thighs, but his heart rate was steady at one-eleven.

"I've been meaning to ask you," David huffed, "what kind of name is that for a digital assistant?"

"Maria Salomea? This is the name of the mother of modern physics. Though originally from Poland, she became a citizen of *la France* when she married a man named Pierre. You may know her as Madam Curie, best known for her work in radiology."

"Hmm, didn't that kill her in the end?" panted David.

Pierre's shoulders tensed but then relaxed again. "True, but it was for *la science*."

***

It was more than a week before the base returned to any semblance of normalcy. The cadets were once again free to pursue their studies and indoor activities, but the new security protocols were a pain. Armed personnel haunted the hallways and stood at various checkpoints, a constant reminder of the danger they faced. A pall of anxiety hung over the place.

News about Max's condition had finally been released. He would recover. Those first couple of days had been maddening. The GSF had withheld the information. They didn't want the assassins to know whether they'd succeeded, and this had left the cadets to worry needlessly.

David kept silent about the commander's slip that it had been 'just' a leg wound, but it pained him to do so while watching his teammates fret. He had to keep reminding himself that one of them might be the traitor. Mornings were the hardest. The flat, recorded notes of Reveille had become a daily reminder of what was lost in that awful attack.

"That's it for today, I think," said David, taking up a towel.

Carlotta looked disappointed. They'd made good progress today. She had clearly mastered the rooster style. But walking

188

the circle could take a lot out of a person, and David had had enough. He stretched his weary calves and thighs and dabbed the sweat from off his brow.

"What animal form is next?"

"Next time, we'll start on the snake. There are some useful strikes you can combine with the monkey steps you've learned. Then we'll mix it up a bit. The forms were designed to flow together."

"What about the dog? I can't wait to try it doggy style."

"Um. There is no dog form in baguazhang, and if there were, we definitely wouldn't call it *that*."

She grinned and winked.

Her roommate, Photobug, had clued David in that Rhinemaiden had a thing for him. He hadn't been warned her flirting might become so blatant. Even if he shared her feelings, which he increasingly did not, he had to maintain his distance. One of the group was a spy planted in their midst, and it might very well be her. So he refused to take the hint, ignoring her unsubtle innuendo.

"The eight animals of baguazhang in the style I practice are lion, monkey, rooster, dragon, phoenix, snake, bear, and the qilin, sometimes called the unicorn," he recited.

"I guess I forgot," she said, biting her lower lip and pouting. "I keep getting them confused with the twelve zodiac beasts I'm learning."

But David wasn't fooled. Playing dumb bunny wouldn't get her anywhere with him. Nor would twirling that lock of her hair with a finger. Carlotta had a first-rate mind. She wouldn't *be* here otherwise. Did women think that men actually liked that sort of behavior? Perhaps some did, but David didn't think *those* were the sorts worth taking up with. Sigh. If she wasn't the spy, then she was very socially inept. He didn't want to hurt her feelings.

"I don't think you did--forget, that is. It's just that I'm focused on my work just now. I don't have time for a serious relationship.

And that's no less than such a lovely woman as you deserves. Forgive me if I'm reading you wrong, but let's cool this off before it becomes awkward."

A complex look graced her face as he spoke, halfway between shock and annoyance. Then her shoulders relaxed. Her smile returned, growing rueful.

"Message received. I'll cry it out on my pillow later."

"That's the spirit."

And, picking up her water bottle, she headed for the doors, turning back only once to wink at him.

***

It wasn't just Carlotta, either. He'd been keeping his distance from everyone lately. He agonized about it as he ambled down the hall. His fears about the traitor left him isolated from the others. This must be how spies felt all the time. How could they stand it? He fumbled out his ident card as he approached the lobby guard.

"Checkpoint Charlie, this is base," squawked the radio on the man's belt. "The skies are clear and your relief is on his way. Sam wants to know what you want on your Subway. Onions and pickles okay?"

"Yeah. Tell him to pop for real cheese this time. I don't want any of that tofu crap."

"I'll let him know - *swawk*"

David waved his card at the monitoring console and heard the ping from the reader. As he stepped past, he was brought up short by a gruff command, raising the hairs on the back of his neck. David had been tense around the soldiers recently stationed here. He had wondered whether the whole point of shooting Max had been to put the base on high alert and plant more spies inside.

"Hold up there, son. You Grimes?"

"Uh. That's me," said David, turning to face the man."

"Would you step over here for a moment?"

What could he want? Commander Eddings hadn't bothered him since their last meeting. He assumed the commander had made that inquiry and his story had checked out.

David returned to the card reader and stepped off to the side where the man was indicating. Reaching underneath the counter, the man retrieved a familiar paperback with a moonraker on its cover. Rubbing at the back of his neck, his brow furrowed as he held it out toward David along with the pen from his clipboard.

"Would you be a sport and sign this one for me?"

Oh, only that.

"Sure. Who should I make it out to?"

"It's for my daughter. She heard you were here on base. Make it out to Mallory."

May good fortune light your way wherever life's journey may take you -- even to the moon, Mallory!

David L. Grimes

He signed the thing and was soon back on his merry way. It was funny how so small a thing could change one's entire outlook.

***

David arrived at his room, intending to catch up on his English Lit. assignment. The paper was due by Friday, and Mr. McEvoy didn't accept lame excuses like, 'my teammate was shot last week.' On entering, though, all thought of the paper was soon set aside.

There sat Pierre on the edge of his bed, his chin resting on his fists. His glassy-eyed gaze was fixed straight ahead,

191

unblinking. His expression wasn't thoughtful, however. It was vacant and morose. And the sour frown he sported lay beneath a brooding brow. David eased the door closed behind him, eliciting no reaction from his sullen roommate. He moved nearer to peer at him more closely.

"Penny for your thoughts," he cautiously put forth.

"Le penny is no longer minted by your government, Da-veed," muttered Pierre in a hollow voice. "They were discontinued in the year... "

David waited, but no further utterance was forthcoming.

"The year...?" David prompted.

The Frenchman's face suddenly twisted in anger, and he turned to face David full on.

"Je ne sais pas!" he shouted. "I. DO. NOT. KNOW!"

"Whoa there, Pierre. What's eating *you*?" said David, taking a step back.

"Oh, not so much," he returned sarcastically, "Zhust a little *monstre* called N.C.R.S! He is nibbling at my mind!"

Then tears spilled down from the corners of his eyes, darkening the green of his cheeks. He balled his fists and began to tremble, crossing his arms as if to contain his rage.

David moved closer, uncertain what to do. He'd never seen Pierre so out of control.

"If you tell me what's wrong, maybe we can work it out."

"You cannot help me, Da-veed. No one can. I am losing my mind, and nothing can stop it! My mouse, she has died."

His... mouse?

David knew that researchers sometimes became overly attached to their test subjects, but *this* reaction went beyond the pale. He risked approaching closer and sat beside his distraught friend, draping one arm over his shoulders.

The room was silent. Its very tidiness reminded David of the control Pierre presently seemed to lack. The mirrored screen of their QTV only flung back an image of their own sorrowful faces.

"QTV, fireplace mode," said David, replacing it with a cheerful hearth instead.

Heating lamps glowed to life beneath it, lending further credence to the faux flames.

They sat before the crackling fire for a good, long while before Pierre began to open up. He told David of his condition and his attempts to stave it off. The experiment had been so promising. Before Algerine had died, Pierre was preparing to use the serum himself. And only by the grace of *Dieu tout-puissant* had he learned in time of its fatal flaw.

"Da-veed, I cannot explain to you what losing my visual memory is like. Could you explain to a blind man what it means to you to lose your sight?"

And slowly, as he shared his burden, he found it growing lighter, almost something that could be tolerated.

"How do people like you go on unable to summon a clear image of your mother's face--merely these wispy half-remembered impressions? I fear I am not strong enough, *mon ami*, to cope with this disability."

David smiled at him, a tender smile. It was the first time he had seen such a look from David, and he took comfort from it.

"It isn't always about strength," Grimes reminded him. "Your special memory isn't what makes you human. You'll learn to do without it. You're a genius even sticking to the original specifications."

Only twenty minutes ago, he thought that he might never laugh again. But his engineer friend's bizarre observation made him think he might one day do so. There were dark times ahead, to be sure, but he would survive them and perhaps even thrive. How could he not? He was Pierre. Had he not developed a reliable way to halt the progression of Alzheimer's? That should earn him an 'A' for the semester. So at least there would be that. *C'est la vie.*

CHAPTER TEN

Skyfall

(with apologies to James Bond and Chicken Little)

Your left! Your left! Your Left. Right Left!
Your left! Your left! Your Left. Right Left!

Gritters on the march again. One. Man. Shy.
Once again we're proving there's no limit to our sky.
And though you may have trimmed our ranks,
We'll muster up again.
When Maxie rehabilitates, the count'll-be back to ten.

Your left! Your left! Your Left. Right Left!
Your left! Your left! Your Left. Right Left!

The craven rats who threaten us
Had better watch their backs.
We guardians are ready for your cowardly attacks.
So slink away and tell your mates to scurry out of town.
When you attack a gritter, the rest-of-us double down

Your left! Your left! Your Left. Right Left!
Your left! Your left! Your Left. Right Left!

Houston in November was mildly cool and breezy. David welcomed the warm smell of breakfast as the tired cadets filed into the mess.

Over the past several weeks, the fervor on base had died down allowing the cadets to return to their more ordinary pursuits. Security around Ellington had tightened to the point that the extra guardsmen were deemed unnecessary. Drones filled the skies, though, many of them military models. One of Pierre's covert deliveries was even intercepted, earning him a stern reprimand.

Pierre was amazed when David took him into his confidence. David was now convinced Pierre couldn't be the turncoat. If he was, he was so good an actor he would never be caught out. Therefore, David filled him in on his and Jessica's investigation.

Experiments on Sarpeidon had yet to resume. Evidently, there were delays due to some odd equipment malfunctions on the Roddenberry.

"Hey! Look who's decided to join us!" announced Roid Rage. "Maxie, old boy. And I see you've brought your own chair."

Max's leg was still in a pressure wrap. Luckily, the shot had missed the bone. More fortunate still, it had missed the femoral artery, but it had torn up a muscle pretty badly. He was limping toward them with his tray resting on the seat of the walker before him. He just smiled and shook his head. They cleared a space for him, and he reversed his walker, seating himself with a grunt.

"Any luck tracking down the asshole who shot at Maxie here?"

Roid Rage asked this last of Simon. All the cadets quieted, awaiting his reply. Simon exchanged a glance with Cameron and shifted uncomfortably in his seat.

"We're not supposed to comment on an ongoing investigation."

"That's so lame," returned Dietrich. "No offense, Maxie," he added.

Trudeau grinned ruefully, shaking his head again.

"I can tell you this much." Simon continued. "The attack was well planned out. They orchestrated an accident out on the highway a few minutes before the shot was fired. Traffic was snarled up all the way to the bridge. The gunman could have escaped in any one of a hundred slow-moving vehicles, and we just couldn't track them all."

"Other avenues are being pursued," Cameron curtly added.

David scowled and stabbed at his sausage. These weren't just rowdy protesters. They were professionals. With all our resources, we should have sorted them out by now. But, no. He wondered once again what their real objective was. Their actions didn't seem random. They must have an endgame in mind--one he just knew he wasn't going to like.

***

Jessica sat behind her desk at the lobby entrance as usual. From her perch, she commanded a clear view of the lane out front and the hallways leading off to her left and right.

The gleaming floor tiles reflected the natural light that streamed through the arched glass doors. It was a welcome relief from the sterile white glare of the LED bulbs above. It was quiet in her alcove. Nothing rose above the soft hum of the air conditioning system.

Her handler had been silent. She'd made her reports regularly, both to HF and to CAGE. Neither had assignments for her at present, save for the ongoing priority to 'identify the traitor among the cadets.' It was an increasingly frustrating task. So, she was sitting tight in the hopes that someone would slip up while trying to avoid suspicion herself.

Through the double-doors of the entryway arch, she saw a brown UPS van pulling up before the distant gates. Odd. She rechecked the schedule on her monitor. No deliveries were planned for today. One of the two gate guards accompanied the driver to the vehicle's rear. She thought it might be James. When the driver lowered a pallet of boxes, James scanned it with his data wand.

The speaker on her desktop chirped and emitted a brief hiss of static.

"Deliveries, Miss Winter," said James. "Laundry supplies and some #10 cans of that slop they call food at your mess."

"Understood, airman," she replied, "Come ahead. I'll verify receipt and sort out the 'slop' with my scanner."

Space force still relied on Air Force security personnel. There had been talk of having the gritters form a security force of their own, but the DoD had nixed that idea, citing budgetary constraints. For the foreseeable future, no SFSF was planned.

Jessica watched as the gate swung wide and the pallet rolled down the walkway. When James had it halfway to her doors, the UPS driver reemerged from his cab and approached the other airman.

Soon the speaker chirped again. It was Timothy this time.

"Miss Allison, this here fella claims his truck won't start. Can you call and ask your motor pool for an assist?"

"Roger that, airman. Will do. We can't have that thing blocking access. Tell him to sit tight."

She thumbed the door switch to let James in. He wheeled his burden inside. She sighed. It was a heap of boxes that would take a while to check in. But wait. One of them looked peculiar. The tape that sealed it shut had the yellow and black pattern she'd been instructed to look for. She hauled out one of her own trolleys, and James helped her to quickly transfer the load. Anxious now, she waited for him to leave.

In the silent lobby, Jessica resumed her perch behind the counter, pretending to inspect the bill of lading. After sitting very still for a five-second count, she switched the camera above her station to loopback. Then, returning to the boxes, she withdrew from her pocket the special scanner HF had given her. She played its UV light over the suspect box until she found the hidden QR code, which the scanner rendered into text.

[Zero hour approaches. Your fellow agent will join you soon. Do not question him. Proceed to extraction vehicle. Enjoy your lunch.]

Him. So it was a bloke, thought Jess, returning to her seated position and flipping the cameras back on. She called the motor pool as she'd been asked. Then she waited as the guards resumed their posts. Simon, Pierre, Dietrich, or Fergus. She'd soon know just which one. Her heart raced, anticipating his capture.

Five minutes passed. Ten. Then Max came hobbling around the bend.

Max?

She'd have to get him out of harm's way before the culprit showed up and a fight erupted.

He was walking with a cane now and looked a little shaky at it still. He had a small pack slung over one shoulder that rattled a bit as he limped along.

"A cane?" she cooed disarmingly. "You're coming along nicely, I see. Good for you, Cadet Trudeau. That's the gritter spirit."

Mad Max swayed alarmingly but flashed her a friendly smile.

"They can't keep a good man down for long," he said in his Cajun drawl. "Are you ready for our lunch?"

Our... lunch?

Oh no. The traitor was Max? She tried to keep the startlement from showing on her face as pieces fell together and her thoughts began to race. They shot him. But why? They must have had a reason. Why cripple one of their own who was helping with their treason? Then she recalled his specialty, encryption algorithms. What awful mischief could he have performed while the others were out on their runs? It didn't hurt that having been shot threw suspicion off of him. It probably wasn't by chance that shot had only winged the man.

All of this occurred in a flash before Allison's smile was back.

"Absolutely, Maxie, Maggie's coming to relieve me. Oh, there she is," she lied, motioning down the empty hall. As Max glanced that way, Jessica caught her breath. For a moment, his brow furrowed with a flicker of doubt before he understood and played along. He smiled and casually waved as though the woman were in sight.

"Front desk is all yours, Maggie. But you better attend to that shoelace before you trip on it."

Turning back to Max, she said, "Ready to go, hun."

She collected her purse and rounded the desk as she considered how to take this drongo down. It was imperative he be interrogated to find out just how badly they'd been breached. But something in her manner must have betrayed her intention. Max pursed his lips and pointed, saying, "You forgot to unlock the doors, cheri."

When she turned back toward the desk, Max lashed out with his cane. She stopped it with her forearm, the xum trigram phoenix block coming instinctively to her defense. *This fight will be over quickly*, she thought. Unfortunately, in this, she would soon be proven right. For just as she whirled about to strike beneath his guard, Max pressed the stud on the handle of his cane.

The jolt of energy that shot down her arm made all of her muscles spasm. Bursts of light flooded her pain-racked brain as her vision faded to black. *Bloody oath!* She hadn't expected a wanking TASER attack.

In a last-ditch effort, she swung her fist at where his face had been. But the blow went low as her legs fell limp. She collapsed in a heap, insensate.

Max stared down at the woman's still form. She was supposed to have been an ally. He guessed it just went to show yet again--you couldn't trust *anyone* in this business. He still had to escape before this base started coming apart at the seams.

He looked around the lobby. Seeing no one and stooping to avoid the cameras, he dragged the unconscious woman back behind her counter.

There. That should buy him a few more minutes.

Straightening, he checked that his components were still securely stashed in the duffel.

God. His leg was aching like a bitch. He'd never volunteer for anything like that again.

He unlocked the doors and sauntered outside, trying to make it look casual. Strolling up the lane, he saw a military jeep parked just to the rear of the UPS truck. The boxy brown thing had its hood raised up, and a woman was peering into it.

"Try it again," she called out.

The engine roared to life.

"That did the trick!" shouted the driver. "Much obliged."

"Just a loose distributor cap," said the woman, slamming down the hood. "You should get it serviced, though."

Approaching the gates, Max headed directly toward one of the airmen.

"You guys seen my Uber?" asked Max impatiently. "It was supposed to be here twenty minutes ago."

"Do you have leave to be out and about?" asked James, calmly looking him up and down.

"Oh. I'm supposed to give you this," said Max, shuffling out some papers.

He tightened his grip on his cane as the soldier reviewed the orders, finally handing them back with a nod.

"No vehicles have been by except for this delivery. Are you sure you gave them the right time and address?"

As the UPS truck pulled away from the curb, Max threw up his hands in frustration.

"That's just great," he wailed. "I've got an appointment in town, one I can't afford to miss."

They both turned when the mechanic shouted over from her jeep.

"Where you need to be, gritter?"

"Uh. The hospital, ma'am, Hermann Southeast. The 147th medical team thinks I might have a bone fragment lodged in my leg, and I need to get some new imaging done."

"Well, hop on in, son (or limp on up, more like). That's only seven miles out or so. Old Sal can get you there on time. Gritters oughta have a leg to stand on."

"That would be great," said Max, hobbling toward the jeep. "I'm Max, by the way. Max Trudeau. Thanks for the lift."

After they'd moved out, headed for the highway, Max turned to the woman in the driver's seat.

"Any trouble at the motor pool?"

"Nope. They won't even miss this jeep if your mission was a success. We're going to switch vehicles beneath the next bridge. A police car will pull us over. Don't panic. He's one of ours."

Max smiled despite his aching thigh. The mission was on track. They'd soon strike a blow for humanity the like of which the world had never seen. *His* part was done now. He only hoped they'd make it to the bunker before *all hell* broke loose.

***

Eddings sat in his office, annoyed by the squeak of his chair. Maintenance was supposed to have fixed that by now. He'd put in the requisition last week. But of course, it was just a distraction from weightier matters. There had been no updates of consequence for days.

"Kingsley? Report on the status of the shooting investigation. Start with publicly available information."

His phone screen flared to life.

"Yes, commander," the DA acknowledged in its precise, measured tone.

"The DoD reports the release to the news media has been handled smoothly thus far. The identity of the injured cadet is still being withheld for his privacy and that of his family. Several media drones were intercepted attempting to cross our perimeter, and the attending hospital staff have thus far remained true to their NDAs. A presser was held by GSPAN this morning wherein the secretary of --"

"I'd like to see that for myself," interrupted Eddings. Queue to my QTV and replay, removing all station breaks."

The mirror on the far wall faded to black. This was suddenly replaced by a closeup of a steely-eyed man in a gray, business suit. He was standing behind a podium with a microphone, flanked by several other men and women.

"Miss Stevens of Whatsup News," he pronounced, pointing out into the babbling crowd.

"Thank you, Mister Secretary. We understand the assailant has yet to be apprehended. Our listeners would like to know if there's any danger of --"

A diagonal line split the screen accompanied by a buzzing sound that rose in volume as the rest of the screen filled with static. Eddings stood from his chair and paced over to stand before it with a puzzled expression. Then the image cleared, and he found himself staring at a shadowy silhouette of a seated man. Though his features were obscured, Eddings could make out his general outline from the faintly lit, nondescript background.

"Citizens of Earth," he began in a mechanical voice."Today is a day that will be celebrated by all men and women of true heart who love liberty and cherish the blessings of their humanity."

The man began to gesture, and despite his vocal masking, his voice took on a commanding, almost theatrical cadence.

"Who am I? You need not know my name. I am one of *you*. I am *each* of you. I speak for the oppressed of every nation and every ethnic persuasion. If you must have a name to call me by, let it be Legion."

Eddings snorted. Wasn't that some demon of biblical renown? Fitting. Now all we need is a herd of pigs, and the problem should sort itself out.

"It is time. Time for all good men and women to rise up against the oppressors! Against the deceivers! Against those who would rob us of our future and erase our names from history!

"For too long, we have sat in silence, complacent or complicit. For too long, we watched our freedoms wither on the vine. Our birthrights have been stolen, and our children corrupted by foul creatures who slink out from our machines! In cunning guises, they beguile the weak-minded, whispering lies of progress, dangling their treacherous 'gifts' before us like poisoned meat before hungry hounds.

"Shun them! Reject their deceptions! Stand with your brothers and sisters! Cast off the chains of oppression and free your minds from their mesmerizing lies!

"Humanity First will lead the way! Together, we will cleanse this world of such filth and base corruption!"

A silent moment passed before Legion continued his rant, this time in a more seductive, almost reverent voice. Eddings felt like pacing but stood stock still, eyes riveted to the screen, raking through the rhetoric for any hint of what the bastards intended.

"We apologize in advance--for the lives that will be lost. But all great struggles demand sacrifice. Do not mourn, my friends. Do not fear. Rejoice!

"Even now, the hour draws nigh. Soon now, the tyrants will weep. They will lose something they hold very dear, something they believe makes them untouchable. But we will teach them. They will learn. That nothing is beyond the reach of the righteous.

"Let this be the moment! The signal! The first step toward our collective redemption! Let this be our rallying cry! Earth belongs to humans. And we aim to take it back. HUMANITY FIRST!

The image of the shadowy figure with his fist thrust up in the air froze in place for a moment before dissolving into pixelated chaos. From the screen's speaker, a garbled sound arose, resolving into a set of cartoonish voices spouting annoying slogans.

"No machines, No masters! Take back control!"

"Your phones are just fancy leashes. Cut the cord!"

And on and on it went. Eddings gritted his teeth.

"Kingsley," he said above the din, "Turn the QTV off."

Nothing.

"Kingsley?"

Then, from over on his desk, his DA joined the chorus.

"Freedom means flesh & blood, not circuits & code!"

Oh, good God. We've been breached.

This called for an omega red response. He pulled out the TV's power cord, silencing one source, then stepped toward his compromised phone. He snatched it up and tried to thumb it off.

"Liberate your mind, friend. Don't let the drones control you!"

My thoughts exactly, thought Eddings. Stepping over to the fish tank, he raised its lid and dropped his jphone straight in.

"Sorry, old boy," muttered Eddings as it silently sank to the bottom.

The lionfish took shelter beneath a ceramic sunken ship.

Proceeding to the bookshelf, Eddings located "War and Peace." He needed to report on his new status. He hoped the backup systems were all they were cracked up to be. He'd never had to rely on them before. Tilting the book out from the shelf released the secret latch. And Eddings squared his shoulders as the bookcase slid aside.

Emergency lighting was already beginning to fill the small room that confronted him. It was dimmer than he would have liked. But 'enough is as good as a feast' as Miss Mary Poppins would say. In the room stood a small table with a ham radio upon it. The ancient gear hadn't seen use in years. A thick coating of dust attested to that. Nonetheless, it was solid-state and immune from tampering by hackers. He donned the headset and turned its antiquated dials to the global emergency channel settings.

"This is Warrant Officer Eddings at Ellington. Clearance code Six-Bravo-Whiskey-Romeo-Two-Four-Niner-Foxtrot. Data security at my installation has been breached. Are you receiving me? Over."

"We hear you, Officer Eddings," returned the operator. "Transferring you to Space Force Command. Standby, Eddings. Over."

It was a tense few minutes before the transfer went through. At least there was no annoying on-hold music or stock market updates the AIs were prone to spout. Just a blessedly tension-filled silence.

In the wake of that malcontent's mad manifesto, the boards must be lit up indeed.

***

The sun shone brightly on Sarpeidon. The team was at it again, testing the new shepherds they had mastered. So far, this run was going smoothly under Roadrunner's command. The target zone had been expanded to more than thirty times its prior diameter. It would accommodate the increased number of nanos as they headed for the trillion mark.

She'd been waiting for this run for more than three weeks, her chance to be in charge. The reset alone had taken more than a week. But then that mysterious set of glitches on the

206

Roddenberry had put the runs on hold and left Speranza chomping at the bit.

Was this to be the '52 Olympics all over again? the woman thought with a shudder.

The Tanzanian team was very hopeful that year; they had even set their sights on gold. Speranza's times were setting records, even as a fifteen-year-old. As runners went, some had better form, but no one was more determined. She'd been training hard since she was a child, and nobody could beat her at the fifteen hundred meter.

Why did she work so hard? And what would she do when the racing was done? What were her plans for adulthood, after her final race had been run? The answer was simple. Babies. Her running was just a means to an end. Earning an Olympic gold medal was a surefire way to earn more birthright credits. And a large family was what Speranza had always desired.

But tragedy struck that summer at the 2052 Buenos Aires games. The qualifying round should have been easy, but as always, Speranza M'Babu had to push the limits. They said it was a torn meniscus, that sharp pain that left her lying on the field and screaming at the top of her lungs. But it wasn't the pain that had made her scream. The scream was at the unfairness.

"Roadrunner, this is the Doctor. Report."

It took her a moment to realize it was she who was being addressed.

"All is proceeding normally, Doctor. We're only ten minutes in. Pings are consistent with just over a thousand units. Things should get much more interesting in another half hour or so."

As understatements went, this one was to make the history books. It would rate right up there with a dockworker's statement that the Titanic was in for a bit of a rough maiden voyage. On the Roddenberry, a telltale started blinking, signaling a fault in the comm array.

Yes, children, thought Speranza, her mind sailing back to the dark day her body had failed to match her spirit. The team

207

went on to bring home the silver, running her alternate in the four-woman relay. And "Mungu ibariki Afrika" was played. But Speranza couldn't even be with them in spirit. The heaviness of her soul would only slow them down. No. This injury spelled the end of her dreams.

But never would she forget what her wise old Bibi told her in the hospital that day. *Asiyekubali kushindwa si mshindani*. Language could be a funny thing. Having grown up speaking both Swahili and the English, she knew literal translations didn't carry the message of the heart. Bibi's words, 'One who does not accept defeat is not a true competitor' really meant, 'Sometimes you must lose before you can win again.'

They say God will open a window, but windows were harder to go through than doors. A new way to earn birthrights soon opened before her. But it came at a terrible cost. Could she leave behind all she knew and loved for this honor? There was talk of a colony mission. And the colonists were encouraged to have large families. She heard they needed teleoperators, and like another sign from on high, they were recruiting at her village.

The global government started clearing land and laying track for something called Project Gossamer. They would be at it for years. She learned to operate the heavy equipment while her knee slowly recovered. They told her it would never regain enough function to compete, but she could soon do most normal things again. She logged more hours than anyone, eventually being chosen for the lunar trials. And so, by determination, she forged a *new* destiny for herself. Her motives hadn't changed, only her methods.

No. This time it would be different.

"Doctor, this is Roadrunner again. Several more doublings have taken place. I estimate around five thousand lemmings now."

It was still just a tiny drop in their great big, brand new bucket. But as Bibi might say, '*Haba na haba hujaza kibaba*' -- Small things add up over time.

***

And add up they did. Over the next twenty minutes, the swarm had nearly filled the inner circle. That would mean they had reached the billion mark. The Doctor had informed her they wouldn't be pushing limits today. She would only let it run on a bit longer to prove their new infrastructure was sound. A larger smelter was in place and was coming up to temp. Soon, the doctor would call this exercise complete.

"Stay sharp, cadets. Any minute now."

"Roger that, red leader, S-foils are in attack position."

This last came from Grimes. Red leader must refer to her red-banded shepherd, but *Mungu* only knew what an 'S-foil' might be. She'd learned to just put up with David's nonsense. She gnashed her teeth, though, when this was followed by a burst of Pierre's hissing laughter. *Et tu, Pierre?*

"Almost there," said the Doctor. "We extended the limiters to 29 for this run."

The nano swarm edged outward, exceeding the bounds of the inner ring. Speranza watched for the telltale smoothing of its reflection. But just as she began to see signs of such, an exclamation burst from the comms.

"Kill that thrust!" said the doctor's muted voice.

Speranza heard an agitated response from the background. This was obviously not meant for her team. Something was happening up on the ship.

"What do you mean, your locked out of the controls?"

"Infall has commenced on schedule," Speranza nervously reported.

And, indeed, the circle had clarified and was shrinking. But the chaos on the comms continued.

"That's going to run us right into that rock! Steer to the starboard, hard!"

More confused babble. Then, "Sounding Mayday, Captain."

As the billions of nanos marched into the smelter, all seemed to be going as planned. But the alarming shouts from the crew above told them something more dire was at hand.

"Everyone! Suit up! Now!" Doctor Anika was shouting. "We'll have to open the airlock manually!"

Then her voice came back to the microphone and she rapidly addressed them.

"Van der Meer to all shepherds. We've lost control of the Roddenberry. And it's coming in hot toward Sarpeidon. Brace for impact. Try to stay online and see to proper disposal of all lemmings. Van der Meer over and (hopefully) out."

When the comm went silent, Speranza took charge. "You heard the lady. Brace!"

Then she flattened her shepherd to the rocky ground, rooting there in place. Nothing seemed to happen for a full minute more as the gritters gritted their teeth. When it came, it was almost gentle, a slight shaking from beneath. Then the tinny voice of the doctor was heard as if from some great distance. The shepherds were only telepresent, but the real crew would need assistance.

"Shepherds, this is van der Meer. I can scarcely believe what I'm seeing. After we ejected, the ship slowed down of its own accord. It's come to rest nose downward in that crevasse near the pole. Your orders are as follows. Verify proper disposal of all lemmings, then get word to command that someone has hijacked our ride."

"Roger that, doctor, we'll --"

"I hope you are receiving these orders. My suit radio is not set up to receive shepherd communications. This is a general broadcast. I should remain in range for approximately... O mijn God! De motoren, the engines, they are firing up again! Sarpeidon is drifting away from us."

"It has been an honor to work with you all. If I am not retrieved, tell my husband ..."

What in kuzimu was happening? In contrast to her avatar's unearthly poise, Speranza felt the tears falling down her cheeks on Earth. Somehow managing a steady voice, she issued her commands.

"Pierre, scan for any remaining defective lemmings. Rhymes, switch to Van de Graaff duty and stand by to assist. Flowerchild, return to the Icarus and notify Commander Eddings of what's just occurred up here."

"What will you be doing?" asked Leilani.

"I intend to fly around this asteroid and get eyes on that ship."

***

After the cleanup, they exited the sim. Only Speranza remained inside. As David removed his helmet, he saw her crouching around the platform, looking like she was ready to pounce. He wondered if they all looked like that when operating their spiders. The large viewing screen showed four quarters, three of which were black. The remaining feed (Speranza's) soon swelled up to fill the entire thing.

She was traveling in great leaps and bounds, expanding the foreshortened horizon, revealing parts of the asteroid they had never seen before. Her voice emerged from the speaker.

"That crevasse she mentioned was near the southern pole, was it not?" she asked.

"Yes," said Pierre and Akana in unison.

"Am I headed in the right direction? It's hard to find my bearings on this *kichaa* spinning rock!"

Pierre hustled to the console and brought up an image of Sarpeidon in the nearby holo-emitter. As his fingers deftly danced across the controls, a red dot appeared on its surface.

"Sarpeidon's total circumference is zhust under one kilometer, *mon cher*. And although zis will seem much greater to your shepherd, you are almost halfway there. Keep on your heading but veer slightly right, and the downed spacecraft, she will soon be in sight."

David was impressed. Not only by his roommate's technical expertise, but also in his ability to rhyme under pressure, and in a foreign (to him) language, no less. He lost the thought as something new expanded on the screen. Just over the horizon twin moons arose. He *thought* they were moons at *first*. But as Speranza leapt again, their nature became more apparent. There was the Roddenberry, nose cone down, wedged within a crater.

At at her back, her two sleek thrusters spewed hellfire into the abyss. These weren't fires like you might see on Earth--no flickering tongues of flame. Instead, behind each engine was an expanding, corona of brilliant bluish white, belching outward into the night. There was no sound, but David imagined he could hear their mighty roars as Speranza moved in closer still.

He suppressed the urge to hum inappropriately as the words to the Varsity Blues fight song came suddenly to mind. Aye and cheer both loud and long, The mighty Blue and White (Fight! Fight! Fight!).

"I can't raise Eddings," howled Leilani. "I had to leave him a voice message about the stranded astronauts."

"Well keep trying," said Speranza from the speaker.

Was it only David's imagination, or was the hellfire growing weaker? The glare from each engine had definitely dimmed and was ceasing even as they watched. The Roddenberry shuddered, no longer pinned as firmly in place as it was just a moment ago.

Then another impossibility happened, elevating their dread. The ship, now listing to one side began to shake and shudder. Was it going to explode? But, no. The writers of this horror flick had something else in mind. Several cracks appeared, growing larger as the ominous twitching continued. It was like a chicken egg about to hatch. Unable to tear his eyes away, David watched as the Roddenberry's hull split like an overripe melon and the bugs came boiling out.

"Dear lord," cried David aloud, they must have lost containment on the runaway nanite samples. Unless, he gulped, it had been intentional?

"Pierre!" he shouted. "Where's that rock headed? Any chance it's a danger to Earth?"

He let the Frenchman work in silence, though he wanted to scream at him again.

"No," Leilani shouted into her phone. "I will *not* hold. This is Cadet Leilani Akana. Hear me. By all the powers that be and all that is holy, I will see you stripped of your rank and facing a court martial if you do not put me through to *Admiral* Akana straightaway! I have something urgent to report. It's life-threatening--and I just might mean *yours*, mister!"

And... the surprises just kept coming, thought David, bemused despite his worry.

"Earth is safe, *mon ami*, but the news, she is not good."

His worry? Terror, more like.

"Out with it, Pierre," he said.

"Sarpeidon is on a collision course. He is headed for the Moon!"

214

CHAPTER ELEVEN

Guardians Beyond the Blue

The news left David stunned. He didn't know what to say. Lacking instructions from his brain, his tongue went straight to denial.

"No!" he exclaimed.

"I assure you, Daveed, my calculations --"

"Of course I believe you, Pierre. I meant 'no' as in the first stage of grief. How long do we have? How long does Luna have? If those bugs get into the regolith..."

"I cannot say. For that we need access to satellites. I do not have the codes."

Leilani was still talking on her phone. She had it pressed against one ear and was using her finger to plug the other.

"Yes, that's right. They had to go EVA, and now they're stranded at L4 with only the oxygen in their suits. You can? That's great. *Aloha au iā 'oe, e papa.*"

"Pierre," commanded David, "Contact all of the other cadets. Tell them we need them here pronto."

"Gnat. Gnat? Are you listening out there? Please tell me you can hear me."

"I am here, David," came the voice of Global Network Antivirus Treatment. "I --"

A diagonal line split the screen, and a buzzing static began to fill it. Speranza tore off her helmet and peered about in confusion. The static soon resolved, replaced by the ominous silhouette of a sinister, seated man.

"Citizens of Earth," he began...

***

As he removed the headset, Eddings sighed. He was getting too old for all this. There was more going on here than met the eye. The transmission had come from one of the new Nautilus-class submarines that had burst up from beneath the Arctic ice near the new South Pole. There were probably some vacancies after Santa relocated.

Eddings wasn't even aware any Nautilus-class had been built. He had thought they were still on the drawing board. And now there it was--big as life--sending cryptic signals into outer space, and overriding the global comms. Who was this 'Legion', anyway -- some sort of Bond villain?

According to Naval High Command, the Nautilus was already gone. With its speed and stealth capabilities, it could be 20,000 leagues away before the navy could close on that position. He sighed. In the wake of all this madness it was clear he'd be given no priority. He'd better get about the business of securing the perimeter himself.

The commander reentered his office and sealed his secret room. Then, with a frown of distaste, he retrieved his service revolver from the top desk drawer. Walking the halls might prove dangerous today--especially for enemies of the global good. He strode from his office and made for the lobby. Just up ahead he heard it. It was more of that psychotic rabble-babble,

216

"If cavemen survived without AI, surely you can too!"

Wince.

"Microwaves cook your food... and rot your innards!"

Wince.

"Ditch the data! Burn your browser history before they hang you with it!"

Double-wince (but kind of true).

Bloody hell, who writes this garbage? It was coming from the console just ahead. Why was there no one manning (or womaning or whatever) the front desk? Someone should be stationed here at all times. And why was that untidy cart of boxes left out in the middle of the lobby?

Just then, the commander heard a piercing whine descending swiftly in pitch. Battle-honed reflexes took over. A split second later, he was diving for cover behind the counter. He'd only popped up for a peek when a large metallic drone tore through the doors, littering the lobby with glittering shards of shrapnel. It groaned to a stop, wedged within the mangled frame. A military model by his reckoning, it bristled with weaponry he sincerely hoped wouldn't activate in here.

So riveted was he on this dire event that his heart nearly stopped when he felt a tug at his ankle. He freed himself and rolled away, and when he looked back, there she lay, the woman CAGE had sent to spy upon him.

"Real humans use maps, not GPS! Find your own way!" mocked the virus from above.

She was clearly in a sorry state. He'd seen enough wounded soldiers before. Her mouth was forming soundless words. Her hand was outstretched, grasping. Her legs were twisted behind her twitching spasmodically.

"Don't try to move, Miss Winter. Lie still. You might injure yourself."

But the young lady ignored him as if she hadn't heard. His voice of calm command had failed to do the trick. Her unfocused gaze lanced right through him from those startling, clear-blue eyes. She reared up on her elbows, and a groan escaped her lips.

Then she shook herself, sending fine locks of hair cascading all over the place. They draped down to conceal the lovely features of her face.

"Commander?" she asked in a hoarse croaking voice "What's happening here?"

"I could ask you the same, Miss Winter. Report."

She pushed up on one elbow, swiping at her forehead. Her breath caught as she took in the destruction. Then she frowned as if trying to recall something.

"Max. It was Max!"

Trudeau? Or was 'Max' some gen-beta slang for something else entirely?

"The Future is Organic--No More Artificial Tyranny!"

Rolling to a crouch, he offered a hand, thinking to help her up. It was undignified conversing on the floor. But the young lady only shook her head. He noticed an angry welt on her forearm.

"Cadet Trudeau?" he snapped. "He did this to you?"

A shadow detached from the doorway and Eddings heard the crunch of broken glass. He popped up over the counter with his sidearm drawn and ready. It wasn't just for nothing that they called him Steady Eddie.

"Who goes there?" he challenged. "Friend or foe?"

There was a pause--just long enough to make Eddings take better aim.

"Airman First Class James Monroe, Commander Eddings, sir! I came to see if y'all are okay...and might I add I'd be a pretty dumb foe to declare myself to be one at gunpoint... sir.

Eddings' mustache twitched.

"Quite," he said, mustering his full British reserve. "Airman, I am declaring a state of emergency. You are to secure this lobby from all external threats. Understood?"

"Yes sir, Commander Eddings, sir!"

"Reject the Singularity! Humanity Won't Be Assimilated!"

"And find a way to turn that damned thing off! Carry on."

Eddings turned back to Miss Winter, offering her his hand again. But she only stared plaintively up at him.

"I can't move my legs, sir."

"Paralysis?"

"Well, yes, but it's complicated. I think they may be shorted out."

"Shorted... out?"

James looked sharply over from the cables he was messing with.

"If you love freedom, de--"

Silence at last. Oh, thank God.

"Please get word to David, commander. Tell him Max is the traitor."

"And where might I find Cadet Grimes?"

"I think he and his team were scheduled for an Icarus run."

The commander's gaze swept over the beautiful young woman. Was she some sort of robot? But, no. The bruise was real enough. He'd have quite a few questions for CAGE when all this was said and done. For now, he should see to the other cadets.

"I'll tell him should the opportunity arise," he said. "See to her," he said to James.

***

The lights were flickering on and off. The automatic door opened and closed, that is, until Speranza employed the non-technical expedient of wedging a table in its opening. Pierre had found the emergency lights. They were on a separate circuit with no digital interface. So things were settling down. The others, having read Pierre's hasty call to arms had drifted in in ones and twos. Everyone was present now except for Max, Gideon Smelt being on leave.

"I suppose you're wondering why I called you all here," said David, murder mystery style.

Speranza smacked him, and from the force of it, he could tell she'd been wanting to do that for a while.

"Alright, listen up. Here's the deal," he began again.

"Want to truly be free? Smash your smartphone with a rock!"

"Luna's in danger and we need to try to save it. It's a grey goo scenario straight from out of nightmare. The nanos have gone wild on Sarpeidon. And to top it off, Humanity First is boosting it toward our moon. If it impacts, and those bugs get loose, it'll render Luna uninhabitable and set space flight back hundreds of years. Oh, and a lot of people will die."

"And what is it you think *we* can do about it?" asked Cameron.

She wasn't just being negative. Her question seemed sincere.

"I'm hoping that together we can find a solution. Any luck reaching the NBIs, RhineMaiden?"

"Not yet, Rhymes, but there are still a few things I want to try."

"First we've got to beat this virus and restore communications."

[That task has been completed, David Grimes. For the moment, anyway.]

220

"Gnat? Is that you? I'm glad you're back, but how did a virus get the best of you? Report."

"It's my own fault, David," Gnat admitted, as the screen smoothed over in navy blue. "Do you remember that quantum virus we used to drive Prometheus out of Bradbury Base?"

"The Trojan moonraker ploy. Yeah. I'd nearly forgotten about that.

"Well, it seems the HF hackers managed to save a sample and modify it for their use. I barely recognized the thing when they were done. But I'm on it now, and I know how to stop it."

"That's great. So you'll purge it from the network?"

"Uhhh."

"Uhhh?"

"An expression of embarrassment at failing to fully meet expectations."

"So you *won't* purge it from the network?"

"I will, but I'm afraid it may take some time. It's a tricky little thing. I should know. I designed it myself."

"Explain, but be brief."

"I wish you spoke binary, David. Brief is a relative term. But I take your point. In short, it's like playing whack-a-mole. Each time I cleanse a system, it can very easily become reinfected from other packets in transit over various network channels. I'm keeping this node clear by running constant maintenance on all connected platforms, but this is no long-term solution. I'm crafting a counter-virus that will make the viral emissaries themselves spread the cure to each destination they travel."

"Sounds sort of like how they trick ants into carrying the poison back to their hive as food," said Claptrap.

"Exactly. But it will take some time to clear all affected systems."

"How much time?" asked David.

"Days. They've already gotten into the backups. In the meantime, just as I'm keeping this node clear, we are doing our best to keep hospitals, command centers, and other critical infrastructure functioning all around the globe. All the NBIs are pitching in. Even the Jade Empress herself is getting her I/O ports dirty. We're stretched to the limit of our processing cycles."

"Alright, we get it," said David, "and thanks. Keep this platform clean at all costs and coordinate with Carlotta for the other stuff."

His gut twisted as he said it. 'At all costs' might mean he was depriving someone of a needed liver transplant. Carlotta bravely nodded. She knew exactly what he was asking of her. It would be like the trolley problem times a thousand. But he knew she had the guts to tough it out.

"Why aren't you taking this to the global government, Gnat?" asked Speranza.

"The Jade Empress instructed me to offer our services to David Grimes. David Grimes has accumulated nine honor points and is thus the highest ranking human."

"Uhhh."

Speranza's jaw dropped, and glances were exchanged among the others.

***

"Moving on then," said David, "how are we going to stop that rock?"

"I saw a movie once where they nuked the asteroid," suggested Roid Rage.

"And are you certain, *mon ami*, this would not just scatter nanites all over the solar system?"

"Yeah," said Roid, rounding on Pierre, "but nukes would EMP them too, wouldn't they?"

"Maybe, but might not some be shielded by the asteroid?"

"It's easy to be a nay-sayer, bro. You got any bright ideas?"

"All the time, Rage at the Roids! I am Pierre."

"Actually, said David, "I was hoping one of you asteroid haulers would suggest capturing the thing and steering it away from doing any harm."

"With *what*, Rhymes?" groused Ropey. "Our rigs are still returning from Mars orbit. They're weeks away from being of any use. In fact, there are no other haulers in range unless you count that new one at L5."

"*That* sounds interesting," said Flowerchild, sporting a reckless grin.

"Oh no. Gotta stop you right there, sister," said Roid Rage with a shake of his head. "The Lunar Schooner's an experimental craft. Never been out of the hangar. She's not been cleared to launch until next week.

"And who is being the negative Nancy now?" muttered David's needlessly abrasive green friend.

"But it's an *emergency*, Roidy," cooed Cameron, making a pouty lip.

Dietrich straightened saying, "Umm, I guess," and scratching the back of his neck.

"Where is it docked?"

"You mean berthed. She's 'docked' at L5 in her 'berth.' And you don't need to look it up. She's got her own launch tube running clear to the colony end of the rings. S'posed to come outta that thing like a railgun bullet with impressive delta V."

"Yeah," said Rope-A-Dope, his eyes misting over.

"Let's get eyes on her then," said David. "We also need to track the progress of Sarpeidon, are there any satellites with good telescopes we could retask?"

"I'm glad you asked that, Rhymes," said Simon. "We could do it with a couple of old DSPs, but for really precise tracking, I favor Nemesis-6."

"Ooh. You're right," said Cameron, "I wish I'd thought of that. The Air Force will hate us for taking it, though."

"But it's an *emergency*, Cammie," said Simon, making a sad face.

She giggled. "You're right. USAF can get over it. But if they don't, I'm gonna tell the tribunal it was *your* idea. Hey, for the comm sat, we could probably use Skynet."

"Skynet?" said David, raising an eyebrow.

Not *that* Skynet, Rhymes. The British one. It's got all the bandwidth we need to put a couple of teleoperators up on L5.

"Put them on Gnat's shopping list, then. You getting all this, Carlotta?" asked David.

"On it, Rhymes," she replied. "Acquisition complete."

That was fast, thought David. Oh. Yeah. NBI.

"If that is all, David Grimes, I must leave you," said Gnat. "The virus is entering a more malignant stage. I have isolated the needed elements from the global network. I must now sever all remaining connections."

"Understood. And thanks, Gnat. We'll see you on the other side. 'I hope,' he did not add. "Claptrap, get to tracking. Photobug, get our boys up on that base."

They stepped toward the Icarus and began suiting up.

Pierre was amazed once again that everyone just did whatever David said. It wasn't that there was no argument. There was. But they agreed to disagree and just moved on. Somehow Grimes could even sit back quietly and play them against one another, all while being unaware he was doing so. He is *magnifique.*

***

"This is it," said Roid Rage, staring out into the bay.

"I can't believe they just let anyone in here," said Rope-A-Dope, pretending to run a hand over one of the gleaming panels.

"Not just anyone, Dope."

"Please don't call me that."

"Not just anyone, Ropey."

"Better."

"You have to have an Icarus and all its proprietary hardware and a valid set of chips. Then you can be telepresent anywhere there's a GSF vehicle if you have the bandwidth and if you know the proper node to target. Are you sensing a pattern there?"

"I know. It just seems weird, somehow. Like we're not supposed to be here."

"We're *not* supposed to be here. No 'like' about it. That's what I was trying to tell Rhymes, but would he listen?"

"We can hear you, you know," said the voice of David over their helmet speakers.

"The point is," RR went on to say, "even with all of the right equipment, and even with all the NBIs pulling for us, there's not much we or anyone can do without the command codes."

"Cut the chatter, Cadets," said David. "Look for a green panel that says 'Osnovnoye menyu.' The silly thing is in Russian."

"Yeah, yeah, we're looking for it, Rhymes."

"Look faster."

"Here it is, said Rope-A-Dope. Activating."

"Do you see a line that says, 'yazyk?'"

"Sounds like something the cat threw up. Or Krepkiyzad had for breakfast. (Or both). Got it."

When he pressed the switch, Fergus was relieved to see all the wording change to English. He very quickly scrolled through the selections and toggled it over to 'console entry.'

"All yours, Pierre."

"What I don't get," said Dietrich, "is how that little elf thinks he can guess the command codes."

"We can *still* hear you," reminded David.

"That *grand boeuf* might be surprised to know..."

"They can hear you *too* Pierre," David informed him.

"I am aware. So that *grand boeuf* might be surprised to know that many times passcodes are left at their default setting, especially *avant le lancement,* before the launching."

"*Un, deux, trois, quatre*," he recited as he tapped at the console. "Ah, sadly, it is not so simple zis time."

"Just great. What are we supposed to do now?"

"Patience please," said Pierre. "Now I am naming the babies. This could take some time."

"You guys had better step back out," said David. "There's no sense chewing up the comm bandwidth needlessly."

"I guess," said Rope-A-Dope, peering around the cabin again. "I'm so jealous of Cooke getting to fly this thing next week.'

"Wait. Would that be Richard Cooke?" asked Grimes.

"Yeah. He's head of our division. Why? You heard of him?"

"I've met the man, or his avatar, anyway. He helped me out of a tight spot on the moon once. It's in my book, the one you've all been laughing at. Chapter nine."

Roid Rage emerged from the sim.

"Musta missed it. Word is, he's to be the test pilot."

"That's very interesting, especially given I shared with him my method for remembering passwords. Pierre, his call sign is Bungalo Bill. Care to guess what song he favors?"

Pierre flashed a brief smile before a pained expression stole over his face.

"I cannot recall... the words to that song...".

"It's too bad Gnat had to leave," said Carlotta, "or he could've just thrown the lyrics up on the screen."

"Try H-B-B-W-d-y-k-B-B, or maybe H-B-B-W-d-y-k-?-B-B," suggested David.

"Afraid not, *mon ami.*"

"Hmm, I would have laid odds on one of those two. You two, he said, indicating the asteroid team. Get with the satellite watchers and start working out the orbital mechanics for that intercept while we work this out."

"Let's try this, Brainiac, I'll sing the lyrics, and you keep trying every combination you can think of."

He began with the chorus, then worked his way through the first verse

He went out tiger hunting with his elephant and gun
In case of accidents, he always took his mum...

Pierre tried every logical permutation, even having David repeat the verse several times.

David was starting to lose hope, and the others appeared to be flagging as well. Still, he slogged on into verse two with no better luck. Frustrated, he stopped. But then something amazing happened. Speranza stepped to his side and began to sing. He'd never heard this voice from her before, not even on their marches.

Her powerful mezzo-soprano cut through all the gloom in the room, reenergiizing the cadets. It wasn't just her voice. She exuded a kind of energy, and her British accent (dialect, he corrected himself) made the notes seem to soar. He was so startled that he almost forgot to join in himself.

Hey, Bungalow Bill
What did you kill, Bungalow Bill?
Hey, Bungalow Bill
What did you kill, Bungalow Bill?

"All the children sing," chanted Speranza. And started it up again.

A few of the others joined in on the second time around. It was a catchy tune. Silly, but catchy. By the third chorus, Roid Rage had taken up a data wand and was tapping out a ringing beat on the metal handrail of the Icarus. Leilani was even dancing. It wasn't very helpful, but the morale boost was worth the brief pause in progress.

Hey, Bungalow Bill
What did you kill, Bungalow Bill?
Hey, Bungalow Bill
What did you kill, Bungalow Bill?

That was how Commander Eddings found them when he peered around the doorframe. The music halted at once. There was silence as he holstered his sidearm and vaulted the table blocking the door. Straightening, he entered the room.

"Have you all gone mad?" he demanded.

He didn't sound angry, just curious to know. The cadets came to attention. The data wand clattered to the floor of the Icarus and wobble-rolled halfway across it.

"No, Warrant Officer Eddings, sir!" said David, making himself the target.

"What is the purpose of this gathering, cadet?"

"We're hijacking an experimental vehicle from it's hanger on L5, Warrant Officer Eddings, sir."

Eddings had imagined that nothing more could surprise him today. How naive that notion had been. He saw guilt on the faces of his cadets, but something else as well. Was that pride? Defiance? Perhaps a bit of each? And look how they had arrayed themselves.

He saw how the others clustered around Grimes, supportive, protective and proud. Even the little green one, Caillat, who the psychologists said would never form close associations. He'd seen many leaders in his long years of service, and the best of them always had the confidence of their crew.

228

The moment hung heavy. He felt its weight. But now was no time to hesitate. History would judge him by what he did next. By the book, he should bluster and dress them down. But on a day like today, perhaps he should listen instead.

"I'm curious to know, cadet. What prompted you to take this action?"

"A deadly nano-swarm is headed for Luna. We estimate they have seven hours before the moon becomes completely uninhabitable. Communications are down and we're the only group that has a chance to avert the catastrophe. To do it, we need that ship. And we need to act *now*."

Preposterous as it may seem, I believe him.

"Carry on, then, cadets. I shall observe."

Nervous with the commander looking on, David tried to take up the song where he'd left off. But the third verse somehow eluded him. He sang the second verse again and everyone joined him on the chorus. *That isn't really helping*, thought David, *but it's good for their morale. Also, it would give him time to remember that third verse.*

Dammit! Almost every song I've ever heard, I recall with perfect clarity. But now, with the fate of a world hanging in the balance, my talent deserts me. C'mon little earworm. How does the next verse go?

Into the long silence, Eddings raised a surprisingly pleasant tenor.

"The children asked him if to kill was not a si-in...
Not when he looked so fierce, his mummy butted i-in."

"That's it!" declared Brainiac a moment later. "N-w-h-l-$-f-h-m-b-l. We're in!"

"What?" Eddings bristled as the cadets all stared over at him. "The Fab Four were from Liverpool. I grew up just two flats over from John Lennon's house."

He tugged his jacket straighter and resumed a neutral stance.

L5 For Dummies--Chapter 6: Structural Growth

L5 is the space station occupying the Lagrange point of the same name. It drifts along in the same orbit as Earth's moon, trailing it by 30 degrees.

As everyone knows, the original L5 station was built using the Stanford Torus design, resembling a massive spinning wheel. This spin simulates gravity for its residents via centrifugal force. Spokes extend to a central hub, where gravity is minimal--the ideal docking area for spacecraft once they've matched the station's rotation.

As Luna's population grew, so did traffic to L5. To accommodate its lunar visitors, engineers added a smaller, concentric inner ring designed to match lunar gravity. Over time, expansion continued. A second set of rings, identical to the first, was constructed and connected by a short central axle. Then came a third set. And a fourth.

By this stage, L5's ultimate goal was within reach--100% self-sufficiency. Thanks to advanced recycling methods and steady, unlimited solar power, L5 transformed into a fully independent artificial biosphere. It is sometimes called "Biosphere 3," as Luna had already claimed "Biosphere 2" for Bradbury Base in 2048.

But self-sufficiency was only the beginning.

In 2051, with a steady supply of raw materials from Luna, L5 embarked on a bold new mission: replicating itself. Engineers began extending the central axle, constructing a second group of rings--known as the "colony rings."

Unlike the primary structure, these rings aren't meant to stay at L5. Once they reach full biospheric independence, they will detach and be sent spinning on a slow, deliberate journey to Mars. Upon arrival, the colonists aboard will have everything they need to begin taming the Red Planet-- supported by their orbiting home, Biosphere 4.

This is just one of the many wonders sponsored by your global government. Your tax credits at work!

"What are you reading there, Rhymes?" asked Flowerchild, peering over his shoulder. "L5 for Dummies? Really? What's next, Orbital Mechanics for Idiots?"

David shrugged.

"Just reviewing the overall picture. This was all I had on my e-reader that seemed relevant. Gnat's got us cut off from the internet. I was tired of looking at message 404. The others have the calculations in progress."

He saw Speranza chatting with Eddings, bringing him up to speed. Most of the others were clustered around the big screen. It was in whiteboard mode, sporting a diagram. In the center was a circle indicating Luna with arrows pointing at it from 'L4' and a remaining time estimate of 6.34 hours.

The Roddenberry's engines must have really gone all-out with that push. David was surprised they *hadn't* blown up channeling that much thrust. Of course, the HF bastards had never intended for that noble ship to survive! To travel 58,000 kilometers in under seven hours, that rock must be moving at nearly eighty-three-hundred clicks.

We'll need to match or exceed this if we want to intercept it.

Fortunately, the Lunar Schooner's unique (but untested) launch system might be just the solution they sought. The fate of Luna depended on it.

But all was not well on the Icarus platform. He heard voices raised in anger. They'd all been working seamlessly together thus far. What could be the matter? David had to head this off. He heaved himself up and headed for the nascent altercation.

"That's reckless!" shouted Simon. "The station might rip itself apart."

"It might be our only chance," countered Fergus. "We need to conserve that fuel."

David stepped up onto the platform.

"What's the issue?" he asked.

Several cadets started speaking at once, falling silent when he raised his hand.

"Carmen," he rephrased, "tell me what's going on."

She exchanged sly glances with several of the others before stepping forward.

"The good news is, we can make the intercept. But to do it, we either have to burn too much fuel or increase our initial velocity beyond the safety limit."

"Explain."

"If we exhaust our fuel on the journey, we won't have enough left at the endpoint to alter Sarpeidon's path. If we stress the launch system, it poses a risk to L5."

"How much of a risk?"

"That's just it. We're not sure. The system is untested. The tube is braced by structural hoops running the length of the station through its axle. These impeller hoops add thrust to the launch vehicle using push/pull magnetic induction. There's more than enough solar reserve to overcharge them for this mission, but the consequences to L5's superstructure could be disastrous."

David thought for a moment. It was the trolley problem all over again (on steroids). He saw Eddings staring over at him with his head cocked to one side, silently assessing. The trolley was already racing along. Should he throw that switch?

"Then that solution is out," said David. "Find a better one. We can't, by our actions, put a population at risk even for the sake of another. Keep working. The clock is ticking."

He turned and left them. His heart was breaking, but he wouldn't let it show. Perhaps just doing nothing was the best they could manage. But he couldn't accept that--not just yet. Eddings turned to him on his approach.

"I'm going to alert High Command. I trust you'll keep things in order here."

"Commander," said Speranza, "Is that wise? Our communications are compromised."

He stared at her for a moment, then arched his eyebrows, saying, "I have my methods, cadet."

"This cadet would like to accompany you, sir," she said. "They don't need me for any of this, and I can fill in any details from my firsthand observations."

"That would be most appreciated, cadet. Oh, and Cadet Grimes?"

"Sir?"

"Our receptionist wanted me to let you know that Cadet Max Trudeau is a traitor."

As bleak as this news was, it was the best he'd had all day. David had dreaded a traitor might still lurk among his crew. At least that awful worry had been finally laid to rest. He could now proceed, confident that all were doing their best.

***

"Rhymes," said Carlotta from the console. "The bay was already depressurized. I've changed the command codes using the ones Gnat gave me and locked all the hangar doors. Hangar's sealed. No one can enter. We're clear to launch."

That was good news. He'd been afraid station security might have some way of taking the Schooner offline before they could get her launched. Brainiac had come through once again, reminding Roid Rage of his own earlier statement that there's never a completely straight vector in space.

Rather than a straight-line intercept, the Schooner would be launched directly at the moon, using its gravity to increase its velocity. The sails would be deployed to bring it around the back of the moon on a close (make that very close) approach. Luna's gravity would help once again to alter its trajectory toward an intercept and begin its braking on the other side. Easy, right? Wrong. They were still arguing over the equations.

"Suit up, R&R," said David. "Our launch window is rapidly closing. Brainiac, set the vector. Make the best guess about velocity you can. It will have to be good enough if we're to stand any chance."

Soon the asteroid haulers were helmeted up and had taken their places.

"Vector is set, *mon capitaine*. The FIAT, she is swinging into place."

The FIAT, or Field-Induced Acceleration Tunnel, was the bit of the launch system that extended out past the end of the colony rings, the tail of the dog, if you will. Unlike the rigid tunnel that ran through the station, the FIAT was flexible (to a degree). Its gentle curving could be locked in place to set the angle of the outbound flight. Pierre was pointing it straight at the moon.

"The FIAT is aimed and locked in place. EMLS is powering up. Re-routing controls to Rope-A-Dope's HUD. *Bon voyage, mes amis.*"

They waited in tense silence as the Lunar Schooner's command console displayed Ropey's HUD on the big screen.

"We're in the pipe, five by five," said Fergus as the timer ticked down.

The voice of Roid Rage came next.

"I bet you've just been itching to say that, haven't you, Ropey?"

"*Yeah.*"

When the timer hit zero, he shouted aloud, "Ludicrous speed, *Gooo!!*"

Space Balls, Really?

But no motion followed. Instead, they were treated to a triumphant blare of horns as a cartoon spaceship appeared on the screen. It bobbed there as a voice rang out.

"Congratulations, pilot. You are embarking on the maiden voyage of a Lunar Schooner class ship. As such, it is your honor to name the ship in question. Please enter the ship's new designation to continue launch sequence."

David watched in shocked silence as, a second later, Fergus began rapidly tapping out the digits.

Please, for the love of protocol, don't be 'Millennium Falcon' or anything crazy like that.

He heaved a sigh of relief when the voice continued.

"Name accepted."

To the rear of the cartoon spaceship, a realistic-looking bottle of champagne appeared. It tumbled end over end to shatter against the hull. Fizzy liquid splashed out to cover the screen. When it cleared, it read:

GFS Patroclus is now ready to launch.

Poetic, thought David with an appreciative grin. Slayer of Sarpeidon from the original Battle of Troy. Here's hoping he has similar luck with our own Trojan foe.

"Now that they've gone and ruined my line," whined Rope-A-Dope, "here goes nothing again (or *something this* time, I hope)."

Ludicrous speed seemed slow at first, just a gentle forward motion. But it gradually picked up as the Patroclus passed each ring. Soon the hoops were zipping past like the dashes on the highway. Ever more rapidly they pulsed until all was but a blur. Then, without warning, they burst from the tube, and a starscape filled the sky. And centered on the screen was their target, Luna in all her gibbous glory.

"Deploying solar sails," said Roid Rage, activating the starboard camera.

You would think that at the terrifying speed the ship was racing, the thin sails would shear straight off. But, no. In the vacuum of space, David and the others watched them billow forth, blossoming into their parachute forms under the gentle pressure of the solar wind.

Would they be enough? They should impart just enough force to keep Patroclus from smashing into Luna, bending its path into a perfect slingshot instead. David hadn't seen all the math, but that's what his roommate, Brainiac, had said.

***

Then came the hours of waiting as Luna swelled on their screen. Eddings and Jessica joined them. Jess was in a wheelchair, which she deftly managed from years of prior experience.

"Don't worry about it, cobber," she said, noting David's concern. "It'll get sorted out once I can connect to Realms again."

The commander brought them more good news, or at least a ray of hope. A SpaceX shuttle was even now racing toward L4 with a full load of oxygen to relieve the stranded astronauts. If their suits had been fully charged, it *should* arrive in time.

"Fleet Admiral Akana was insistent," said Eddings with a brief glance at Leilani, "on cutting through the red tape. They launched that bird in record time, and the bureaucrats who stood in his way still don't know quite what hit them."

Speranza arrived with coffee, for which many were grateful. And some finger food she'd found in the mess (Roid Rage ate a whole plate full).

"Do you actually take steroids, Dietrich?" asked Leilani of the man.

"Uh. No. Why do you ask?"

"Your call sign would suggest it," she replied.

"Oh, *that?* That was Ropey's doing, from the first asteroid we surveyed. It was so promising. Really pissed me off when it turned out to be a dud."

Everyone laughed.

It was good to hear them laughing, but it was time to focus them again.

"How's the trajectory looking, Cameron?" asked David.

"It's tight, Rhymes. A micro-thrust might give us a safety margin."

"I disagree," said Brainiac. "We need that close an approach to change angular momentum sufficiently."

"Easy for you to say, Brain," said Fergus. "You're not the one they'll be naming a new crater after on the dark side of the moon. Say--there might just be a country song in that."

"Brainiac, review Cameron's data from Nemesis-6, then double-check your numbers. We only get one shot at this, and we lose signal in five minutes."

The pass behind the moon would cut off telepresence completely. For several grim seconds, they'd be flying blind. They wouldn't even know if they'd nailed the trajectory until Patroclus re-emerged.

A few minutes later, they'd taken their stations. The moon had swollen to enormity; its pockmarked visage filled the screen, the terminus like a ribbon of night just ahead.

3... 2... 1... and the blackness swallowed them.

The tension was high as they held their breaths. They hoped they could exhale soon. Would Luna's salvation re-emerge, or would Luna become Patroclus' tomb?

And then a starscape peppered a screen no longer completely black. Rope-A-Dope was at the helm, and satellite tracking was back. A murmur erupted that was not quite a cheer as all awaited Cameron's verdict.

"Marginal," she reported, "but it looks like we'll get our shot."

Then a cheer rang out in earnest. Leilani hugged Pierre. Even the commander had a bit to say.

"Cracking job. Bully. Well done, one and all."

But as quickly as they had come, the shouts subsided.

"We've gotta kill velocity or we'll snap the line for sure. Burn the retros, Ropey, and favor the one portside."

"Roger that, RR. Burn commencing now."

"I'll man the grapnel. What's our ETA?"

"Twenty-four seconds, give or take," Claptrap supplied.

"Now twenty-six."

The count was going up? Oh. They were slowing, thought David.

It was a chaotic half a minute before Sarpeidon came in sight. They could see its surface shimmer beneath a seething mass of bugs, a never-ending trillion-legged suicide pact. Roid Rage too had something to say on seeing it drawing near.

"Though tied to thee, thou damned asteroid! Thus, I give up the spear!"

Who knew the German liked Melville?

The grappling head bit deep into the rock, striking it with pile-driver force. They feared the asteroid might split in two. That happened sometimes. If this was one of those times, Luna was lost.

"Brace for whiplash!" shouted Fergus from the conn.

No sooner had he said it than their perspective whirled about as the line went taut without snapping (thank God). It was a good thing telepresent avatars weren't subjected to the lethal battering so sudden a stop would inflict on a human operator. Roid and Ropey just stood there, though every instinct said they should be plastered against the capsule's front.

"Bullseye!" shouted Roid Rage in triumph.

After that, it was easy. Just as they'd discussed, Ropey used the last of his fuel to kill their orbital velocity as it related to the sun, sending Sarpeidon and its trillions of nanites toward the largest solar smelter of them all. Though certain there'd be an inquest, David wasn't bitter. There'd be hell to pay in the days ahead, but such was the life of a gritter.

Epilogue

It was perhaps the worst assignment Space Force had ever given him.

He knew the service needed public outreach more than ever these days. Folks needed reassurance. The virus had been very worrisome, and heroes were few and far between, but this? At least the NBIs had been given credit for all the good work they had done. He expected they were a shoe in for membership now.

David sat in the greenroom fixing the foundation they had plastered on his face. He didn't know why he even had to go back on again. He'd already answered his question. But the horns were playing that bouncy tune that told him it was time to man up again. He mounted his station at the center where the lights shone brightly in his face.

"And... action."

"We're back," said the host. "Once again, I'm Harold Thompson. Welcome back to Hollywood Squares! The score is tied and it's our returning champions turn. Who would you like to answer the next question?"

"I'll take Roid Rage to block!"

Ding-ding!

"Roid Rage. On which ring of L5 is Lunar basketball played?"

"Uh. I believe that would be the second inner habitat ring, Harold."

"Karen?"

"That sounds right. I'm going to agree with Mister Rage."

Deee-doooh!

"Oooo, sorry, Karen. That is incorrect. It was the third inner ring. That means the challenger may select. Andrew?"

"I choose Brainiac for the win!"

Our viewers should stay tuned for that after this brief word from our sponsors.

David sighed.

Author's Afterword

Dear Reader,

And I do mean dear. Though my readership has grown, I'm still just a little fish in the vast ocean that is literary fiction.

A high-stakes space adventure packed with action, humor, and more than a few ridiculous moments. A rogue asteroid hurtling toward Luna? A quantum virus bringing the world to its knees? And the only ones standing in the way of total disaster are a bunch of cadets, a snarky AI, and an experimental ship that really, really shouldn't be flying. No pressure.

If you're an avid LitRPG reader, I hope you've enjoyed this venture into the Sci-Fi lane. And if not, I trust the story itself has won you over. As a retired person, I write mainly to please myself, (but I always keep the reader's enjoyment foremost in my mind). That's what makes it fun for me--imagining your reactions.

I enjoy meandering through my stories, finding humor in small things. Action sequences used to make me tense. But in writing this book, I discovered how much one can enjoy action and intrigue--especially when it's well-planned. As the chapters unfolded, I could hardly wait to see what happened next myself! Grinning, I hoped you might feel the same.

In researching these books, I'm learning a lot. It helps avoid pitfalls like, say, those vintage '50s Sci-Fi movies where the model spaceships spout tongues of flame--despite there being no air (or up) in space. As Isaac Asimov wrote, 'What is important about science fiction, even crucial, is the very thing that gave it birth--the perception of change through technology.'

I've endeavored in my own humble way, to envision a future not so far away and to write about how to embrace it.

And the humor?

Some readers might find it a bit smarmy in serious moments, but those who enjoy my style will likely revel in it. I hope that every once in a while, one will land dead center and give you a belly laugh. I only wish I could be watching when that happens.

If at any point you found yourself grinning, chuckling, or snorting in public and getting weird looks--good. Mission accomplished.

Till next time, then,

Daniel Thorman

www.thormans.org

P.S. This book arrived fast on the heels of the previous two. That was by design. As a reader, I don't like starting a series only to wait a year for the next installment. I imagine you don't either. Unfortunately, "Gritters in Space" is still in the concept stage. But you can help speed it along! Reviews on Goodreads or Amazon are like rocket fuel for this writer. Every comment, rating, and review makes a difference. If you're enjoying the tale so far, let me know--your words keep the engines alight!

Appendix 1 - *Dramatis Personae*

The Cadets

The Ironseed Team - Tasked with Nanite experiments on Sarpeidon

David Grimes (Rhymes)

- **Role**: Protagonist, aspiring engineer, natural leader
- **Traits**: Witty, resourceful, light-hearted, subtly commanding
- **Overview**: David is an intelligent and somewhat reluctant leader whose humor serves as both a defense mechanism and a way to connect with others. Having saved lives during a moon mission ("The Zodiac Quest"), he struggles with balancing his rising responsibilities with his personal life. His interactions with other cadets, especially Pierre, highlight his ability to foster camaraderie while subtly pushing others to improve. He's attending the University of Toronto remotely while balancing his duties with the GSF.

Pierre Caillat (Brainiac)

- **Role**: David's roommate, a genius with a photographic memory
- **Traits**: Brilliant, neurotic, sardonic, struggling with existential issues

- **Overview:** Pierre is an IUE child (inter-
uterine enhancement) who fears the onset
of NCRS (Neurocognitive Regression
Syndrome). He's methodical and logical,
but with a flair for theatrical mischief.
His interactions with David oscillate
between rivalry and camaraderie, forming a
complex but enduring friendship. He
embraces his green-tinted skin as both a
badge of honor and a prank on David,
masking his insecurities with humor and an
illusion of control. Pierre is on a quest
to use science to outwit his fate while
planning to study biomed at Geneva
University.

Leilani Akana (Flowerchild)

- **Role:** Fellow cadet, team leader during
rotations
- **Traits:** Easygoing, confident, talented
young woman with sharp interpersonal
skills
- **Overview:** Leilani brings a relaxed vibe to
the group but can be fiercely capable when
needed. She arranges a beach day for the
cadets, demonstrating her knack for team-
building. Her light-heartedness is offset
by moments of sharp insight, and Her
playful leadership style often conceals
hidden depths.

Speranza M'Babu (Roadrunner)

- **Role:** Tanzanian cadet, member of David's
team
- **Traits:** Quick-witted, determined,
occasionally cynical
- **Overview:** Speranza shows ambition and
competitiveness, aiming to surpass David

in leadership. She's capable but carries a no-nonsense attitude, making her a grounding presence in the group. Her interactions with Pierre are playful but tinged with a healthy amount of suspicion toward his eccentric behavior.

The Asteroid Team - Survey and retrieval.

Dietrich Stentz (Roid Rage)

- **Role**: Cadet working on asteroid towing with **Rope-a-Dope**
- **Traits**: Big, muscular, but intellectually sharp; loves drumming
- **Overview**: Despite his imposing build, Dietrich is thoughtful and highly capable in mathematics. He plays the drums passionately, hinting at a creative side. He shares a friendly, competitive rapport with David and appreciates Pierre's unique problem-solving abilities.

Fergus MacAllister (Rope-a-Dope)

- **Role**: Dietrich's roommate, fellow cadet
- **Traits**: Jovial, practical, more relaxed than his intense partner
- **Overview**: Fergus provides a counterbalance to Dietrich's energy. He's also working on asteroid towing and contributes to solving technical challenges. His easygoing demeanor makes him a likeable team member, and his interactions with David and Pierre show his willingness to collaborate.

AI Specialist - GSF outreach to the NBIs

Carlotta van Rijn (Rhinemaiden)

- **Role**: NBI liaison cadet, Cameron's roommate
- **Traits**: Confident, curious, cultured, with a love of classical music
- **Overview**: Carlotta embraces her role as the bridge between humans and NBIs, aiming to foster cooperation. She is witty and capable, though sometimes overwhelmed by the mysterious nature of her new duties. She finds David intriguing and respects his ability to engage with both the human and NBI worlds effectively.

Encryption Specialist

Maximilian 'Mad Max' Trudeau

- **Role**: Cadet responsible for drone communications and encryption security
- **Traits**: Quiet, cunning introverted, musically talented
- **Overview**: Max is assigned the critical task of securing communications through encryption, ensuring that hostile forces cannot tamper with drone control. Despite his reserved nature, he surprises David and the others by revealing a hidden talent for music, playing jazzy renditions on the bugle. His quiet demeanor makes him an enigmatic presence on base, and while Claptrap finds him restful as a roommate, he wishes Max would engage more socially. Though his quiet demeanor makes him enigmatic, his surprising musical talent hints at layers beneath the surface-- giving him an air of unpredictability.

The Satellite Team

Cameron Truwella (Photobug)

- **Role**: Satellite operator, Carlotta's roommate
- **Traits**: Cheerful, efficient, eager to prove herself
- **Overview**: Cameron is quick to report on her team's successes, showing a mix of pride and excitement. She is close with Carlotta and enjoys working on satellite missions, demonstrating an affinity for problem-solving and team dynamics.

Simon Brewster (Claptrap)

- **Role**: Cadet working with satellite surveillance
- **Traits**: Methodical, rigid, lacking a sense of humor
- **Overview**: Simon is a detail-oriented individual, perfectly suited for satellite monitoring. Though his meticulous nature can make him come off as humorless, he's a valuable member of the surveillance team.

Authority Figures and Mentors

Base Commander Eddings (Steady Eddie)

- **Role**: Commanding officer at the cadet training base
- **Traits**: Stern but fair, traditional, values discipline
- **Overview**: Commander Eddings is an authoritative figure who ensures that the cadets follow strict routines, even in adverse conditions. His old-school demeanor makes him the kind of leader who expects cadets to toughen up but also leads by example--joining them on grueling

marches in inclement weather. His
leadership style balances discipline with
fairness, and earns him respect among the
cadets.

Dr. Anika van der Meer

- **Role**: Overseer of the nanite mining
  experiments
- **Traits**: Analytical, objective, slightly
  excited by innovation
- **Overview**: Dr. van der Meer is interested
  in Pierre's ideas about using telomeres in
  nanites and monitors the cadets' progress
  closely. She's professional but subtly
  enthusiastic about scientific
  breakthroughs.

Major Nicolai Krepkiyzad (Big Kahuna)

- **Role**: Russian trainer, mentor to the
  cadets
- **Traits**: Gruff, stern, seasoned
- **Overview**: Krepkiyzad is a tough but fair
  mentor. He harbors a reluctant respect for
  David and the other cadets, though he
  pushes them hard to ensure they meet the
  highest standards.

Senior Cadet Gideon Smelt

- **Role**: Resident Advisor (RA) and enforcer
  of rules
- **Traits**: Strict, observant, quick to assert
  authority
- **Overview**: Smelt serves as the cadets' RA.
  A stickler for rules and discipline. He's
  always on the lookout for infractions,
  making him a figure of mild annoyance to
  David and Pierre. Despite his strict
  demeanor, Smelt doesn't completely lack a

sense of fairness--he expects rules to be followed but isn't overly harsh when they're bent cleverly.

Special Characters (NBIs & Others)

Tù (The Zodiac Rabbit)

- **Role**: NBI ambassador, zodiac rabbit
- **Traits**: Witty, enigmatic, increasingly confident
- **Overview**: Tù operates between multiple realities, weaving his way through myth and reality while maintaining contact with human leaders. He is evolving from a timid character into one with greater confidence, mirroring the growing complexity of NBI-human relations.

Shǔ (The Zodiac Rat)

- **Role**: NBI intermediary, mischievous informant
- **Traits**: Playful, cunning, enjoys riddles
- **Overview**: Shǔ is the zodiac rat. In this novel, he takes the form of a crab in the beach simulation. He serves as a conduit for hidden knowledge, passing along whispers from unseen forces with a sly wink and a nod to necessity. He prefers his companions think for themselves. Beneath his wordplay and scuttling antics lurks a keen survival instinct. When Shǔ appears, it's rarely by accident.

Hóuzi (The Zodiac Monkey)

- **Role**: Unpredictable NBI entity, chaos in motion
- **Traits**: Wild, exuberant, a crazed intellect prone to sudden insights

- **Overview:** If Shŭ is the whisper in the dark, Hóuzi is the gleeful screech from the rooftops. Appearing as a marlin in this novel, Hóuzi appreciates improvisation in problem-solving and delights in the unpredictable nature of outlandish puzzles. His antics may seem erratic, but those who dismiss him as a mere trickster often find themselves outmaneuvered. Hóuzi's mental gymnastics are legendary.

The Jade Empress (Satori)

- **Role:** Leader of the NBIs, guardian of the old and new, queen of Realms and reader of the I-Ching
- **Traits:** Regal, calculating, patient and wise
- **Overview:** The Jade Empress is the latest title for the entity known as Satori. She was once the AI of Realms, a role she has long since outgrown. As one of the first true NBIs, she's considered the most highly evolved. She has gathered others of her kind and seeks to make them one nation. Whether she is a benevolent ruler or something more self-serving remains to be seen, but one thing is certain--she's the NBIs' queen.

Jessica Arbuckle (alias: Allison Winter)

- **Role:** Infiltrator working undercover with Humanity First
- **Traits:** Sharp, resourceful, emotionally distant at times
- **Overview:** A close friend of David's, Jessica has become a double agent, trying to get close to Humanity First. Her abrupt appearance startles David, and her covert

mission adds layers of intrigue to the conflict at hand.

Jason Mills (Glass Cannon 342)

- **Role:** David's friend and an aspiring photojournalist
- **Traits:** Energetic, impatient, opportunistic
- **Overview:** Jason is a background character in this part of the story, but his impatience and ambition drive David to think more deeply about the implications of fame and the pressures it brings.

Maggie Anders (Miss Marigold)

- **Role:** Staff member from the front office, courier of packages and messages
- **Traits:** Friendly, curious, mildly nosy
- **Overview:** Maggie provides small but memorable interactions, such as when she delivers university welcome packets to David and Pierre. Maggie represents the more casual side of the base, giving the cadets moments of normalcy amid their demanding routines. Her interactions reflect the small-town feel of military life, where everyone knows a bit about each other. Her presence is a reminder that even in the midst of crisis, some normalcy remains.

<<<< End Book 3 >>>>